T0199104

Darkness Returns

Books by Alexandra Ivy

WHAT ARE YOU AFRAID OF?
YOU WILL SUFFER

And don't miss these *Guardians of Eternity* novellas
TAKEN BY DARKNESS in YOURS FOR ETERNITY
DARKNESS ETERNAL in SUPERNATURAL
WHERE DARKNESS LIVES in THE REAL WEREWIVES OF
VAMPIRE COUNTY
LEVET (eBook only)
A VERY LEVET CHRISTMAS (eBook only)

And don't miss these *Sentinel* novellas
OUT OF CONTROL
ON THE HUNT

Published by Kensington Publishing Corporation

Darkness Returns

Alexandra Ivy

LYRICAL PRESS
Kensington Publishing Corp.
www.kensingtonbooks.com

LYRICAL PRESS BOOKS are published by

Kensington Publishing Corp.
119 West 40th Street
New York, NY 10018

All Kensington titles, imprints, and distributed lines are available at special quantity discounts for bulk purchases for sales promotion, premiums, fund-raising, educational, or institutional use.

Special book excerpts or customized printings can also be created to fit specific needs. For details, write or phone the office of the Kensington Sales Manager: Kensington Publishing Corp., 119 West 40th Street, New York, NY 10018. Attn: Sales Department. Phone: 1-800-221-2647.

Lyrical Press and Lyrical Press logo Reg. U.S. Pat. & TM Off.

First Electronic Edition: April 2019
ISBN-13: 978-1-5161-0842-8 (eBook)
ISBN-10: 1-5161-0842-6 (eBook)

First Print Edition: April 2019
ISBN-13: 978-1-5161-0845-9
ISBN-10: 1-5161-0845-0

Printed in the United States of America

Chapter 1

The sweeping mansion on the edge of Chicago was the perfect setting for an old-time movie star. Built behind a high fence and surrounded by a manicured lawn with a profusion of gardens, it possessed a faded, ageless beauty. Inside, it had an abundance of marble, fluted columns, and gilt that encroached into every nook and cranny. Including the toilets.

But there was no aging human drifting through the thirty-odd rooms. Instead, the place was filled with demons. Vampires, a pureblooded Were, fairies, and a few imps. Oh, and the Anasso, the King of the Vampires.

The current Anasso, Styx, was a six-foot-six male with the stark Aztec features of his ancestors. His dark hair was pulled into a braid that was threaded with turquoise medallions and hung down his back. His massive frame was covered in leather. And he rammed through the house like a bull in a china cabinet.

Not that anyone was stupid enough to laugh when he busted a fragile knickknack. Or when one of the antique chairs collapsed beneath his weight.

Everyone knew he'd chosen the elegant estate at the urging of his mate, Darcy. He would move heaven and earth to please his female. Plus, there was the healthy fear that he would happily lop off the head of anyone who insulted him with his badass sword, which was usually strapped across his back.

Currently, Styx was in his private study, a room he'd managed to strip of most of the froufrou nonsense, although there was no getting rid of the gilt. It infected the place like a plague. At least it had nice, sturdy furniture, along with shelves filled with rare books, manuscripts, and scrolls.

He was standing behind his desk when the door was pushed open and a male vampire strolled in.

Unlike Styx, Viper's long hair was the silver of moonlight, and he preferred satin to leather. In fact, he dressed like a Regency dandy, with a frilly white shirt and a long velvet coat. Still, anyone foolish enough to think he was anything less than lethal rarely lived long enough to regret their mistake.

"You rang?" the male drawled as he strolled toward the center of the study.

Styx and Viper had been through hell together. Quite literally. In the past few years, they'd battled the Dark Lord, evil witches, and dragons. Which was why he was confident his friend wasn't going to be happy with what he had to tell him.

"I wanted to let you know that I will be out of town for a few days," Styx said.

"Not another honeymoon?" Viper arched a brow. "You do know that eventually they're just called vacations?" He tilted his head, pretending to consider his words. "Unless there's an orgy involved."

"I have to go to Vegas."

"Ah." Viper smiled. In the light from the chandelier, his fangs glistened as white as snow. "Then there *is* an orgy involved."

Styx rolled his eyes. He could only wish he was taking his mate to Vegas. Regardless of what his friend might think, there could never be too many honeymoons.

"This is no vacation. I've requested a meeting with the Rebels."

Viper looked momentarily disappointed, as if he'd been hoping for the orgy scenario. Then his expression brightened.

"Wait, are you going to kill them? I'll go home and get my sword."

Styx held up a hand. The Rebels were a clan of vampires, led by Tarak, who'd led an insurrection against the previous Anasso after he'd taken command of the warring clans and consolidated them beneath his rule. At least, that's the story he'd always been told after Tarak had disappeared. And the one he'd chosen to believe.

Since he'd taken on the duty as king, he'd ignored the Rebels. As long as they minded their business and didn't cause trouble, they could do what the hell they wanted. Until last night.

Then everything changed.

"No, I'm taking Levet to them."

Levet was a three-foot gargoyle who'd been a pain in the ass since Viper's mate, Shay, had rescued him from a slave auction. The creature was intrusive, maddening, and his magic was dangerously unpredictable.

Styx would have him stuffed and mounted on his wall if Darcy and the other females hadn't been so attached to the ridiculous pest. And there were a few occasions when the gargoyle's rare talents actually came in handy.

"Ah. An even more devious plot," his companion drawled. The only one who loathed Levet more than Styx was Viper. "You intend to torture them with that aggravating pest until they kill themselves. Very clever, oh wise and ancient master."

"Did you just call me ancient?"

Viper shrugged. "Prehistoric?"

Styx narrowed his gaze, the lights in the mansion flickering. All vampires had individual talents. Styx's was a blast of energy that could cripple his opponent. Unfortunately, his power tended to interfere with modern technology when he was annoyed. "Careful."

Viper grinned, gloriously unrepentant. "Tell me why you're taking a gargoyle to Vegas."

Styx folded his arms over his wide chest. "You remember I told you I was cleaning out the caves?"

"No, but to be fair, I rarely listen when you're talking."

Styx made a sound of disgust. "Why do I bother to pretend I'm the Anasso? No one ever pays attention to me."

"Someone has to be king," Viper informed him with a shrug. "Tell me about your cave."

There was more flickering of the lights and a small shudder beneath their feet, but Styx managed to maintain command of his temper. Nothing less than a miracle.

"My Ravens have been using it as temporary housing, but I completed the barracks beneath the estate," he said. The caves were several miles away and had been his home for decades before Darcy had insisted that his role as king demanded a more elegant setting. He hated to tell her that he far preferred the dark, dank, and sometimes moldy caverns. At least there he didn't have to worry about breaking something. And he certainly hadn't had to worry about unwanted guests dropping by. "With no one to guard the entrance, I needed to do something with my previous master's belongings."

Viper's pale features hardened with a sudden burst of fury. The original Anasso had kidnapped Viper's mate and intended to use her blood to extend his own life.

Needless to say, the two males hadn't been BFFs.

"Burn them," the younger vampire snapped. "Or better yet, let me burn them."

"That's what I intend to do with the majority of the stuff," Styx said. In truth, his first impulse had been to pile everything in the middle of the largest cavern and toss a match on top. Unfortunately, he had taken time to sort through the boxes, trunks, and hidden stashes. Now it was too late to solve his problems with a bonfire. "There are a few sensitive items I need to deal with personally."

"Sensitive?"

"We both know that my master could be ruthless even before he started going mad," Styx said.

"He was a jerk."

Styx's lips twitched. His own relationship with the Anasso had been complicated. He'd admired the vampire's determination to force the savage vampires out of the Dark Ages and to unite them in a common cause of survival. But his methods had been…questionable.

"As eloquent as always, Viper," he said dryly.

Viper waved a slender hand. "It's a gift."

"Anyway, I found this hidden beneath his bed." Styx leaned forward to grab the thick scroll off his desk. It was made of papyrus and rolled around a heavy bronze rod. It smelled of age and blood.

"What's that?" Viper demanded.

"It's a pact with a coven of witches."

"Witches?" Viper took a step backward, eyeing the scroll with horror. Magic was the one thing all vampires feared. They had no ability to sense it, which meant they had no way to protect themselves. "No vampire would willingly deal with witches."

"It gets worse."

"What?"

Styx felt something in the middle of his chest. A strange pressure. Darcy would no doubt tell him it was guilt, but he refused to accept such a stupid hypothesis. He was a predator. A king. A badass warrior with a badass sword that lopped off heads.

Still, that pressure was annoying.

"My master came to me and swore that Tarak had turned traitor and tried to kill him to claim the throne for himself. He said he'd been forced to exile Tarak and that he wanted me to stand at his side when he proclaimed Tarak's clansmen as Rebels."

"Did you?" Viper demanded.

"Yes. I stood proudly beside the king as he made the proclamation that the Rebels were being driven from our territory." The words were clipped. He hated admitting he was wrong. And he had been epically wrong.

He should never have dismissed Chiron, who'd been Tarak's most loyal servant. The young male had come to him and pleaded for his help after Tarak had disappeared. The younger male refused to believe his master had been a traitor. "I wouldn't listen to the accusation that the king had captured Tarak."

"Shit." Viper widened his dark eyes. It was one thing to kill a chief in battle. In the olden days, it had happened with depressing frequency. But it was considered a cowardly human trick to take a fellow vampire as a hostage. And especially when that vampire was a member of one's own clan. "It was true?"

"Unfortunately."

"What happened to him after he was captured?"

The pressure in the center of his chest became more pronounced. As if a very large troll was sitting on him. The damned thing weighed a ton.

"As far as I know, he's still imprisoned."

Viper grimaced, then, as if struck by a sudden thought, he took a step forward.

"You're not thinking about letting him out, are you?"

Styx shrugged. "What choice do I have?"

"Let me think." Viper mockingly tapped a finger to his chin. "You could release the powerful clan chief who has had several centuries to consider the most creative ways to kill us for holding him prisoner. Or leave him safely locked away." More tapping on his chin. "Hmm. Tough decision."

Viper had a point. If Tarak was released, he most certainly would track them down to seek his revenge. That was the least of Styx's concerns. He was far more worried about the possibility that the vampire would come out of his prison completely insane. Tarak could rampage halfway across the world, slaughtering the innocent, before they managed to stop him.

Styx had spent the previous night contemplating the various risks before he'd made his decision. He wasn't a vampire who liked to rush into things. Calm. Logical. Persistent. Those were the traits he used as a leader.

"I have to do what's right," he said.

Viper snorted. "What's right is keeping my head attached to my neck."

"I didn't ask you here to debate the issue. I just wanted to let you know I would be gone."

Viper paused. Was he considering the odds of convincing Styx to forget Tarak was locked in some mystical prison? Probably. But the younger vampire wasn't stupid. He knew once Styx made up his mind, there was no changing it.

Why beat his head against a brick wall?

"What exactly are you going to do in Vegas?" he instead asked.

Styx held up the scroll. "I'm going to give this to Chiron."

"Chiron," Viper repeated. "I don't recognize the name."

Styx had lost track of the younger vampire after he'd been banished, although he'd heard rumors that Chiron had snuck back into his forbidden territory and started a casino. It'd taken a few hours of research, and cashing in several favors to various demons, to learn that Chiron had settled in Vegas nearly fifty years ago.

"He owns Dreamscape Resorts."

Viper sent him a shocked glance. "Dreamscape? The chain of casinos and spas spread around the world?"

"I suppose." Styx didn't have any interest in casinos or spas. Viper, on the other hand, owned several nightclubs, and despite the fact that his clubs catered to demons rather than humans, he was constantly scoping out the competition. "As far as I can tell, he's been the public face of the clan. Most of the Rebels disappeared into the shadows over the past centuries."

"Why take the gargoyle if you're just handing over the scroll?" Viper demanded. "It can't be because you enjoy his company."

Styx shuddered. He'd rather spend the next forty-eight hours being flogged by a drunken troll than be forced to travel with Levet.

He glanced toward the scroll in his hands. "This is the original spell that hides the key to the prison. It was given to the previous Anasso to prove the deed was done."

"There's a key?" Viper cast a wary glance toward the scroll. As if it was a ticking time bomb about to explode. Styx didn't blame him. Witches and magic and hidden prisoners were enough to put any vampire on edge. Which was why he was anxious to hand the thing over to Chiron. Let him deal with it. "Where is it?" Viper demanded.

"I don't know for sure. I'm hoping Levet will be able to use his ability to trace the magic. It might lead the Rebels to where the key is hidden."

Viper slowly smiled. "More likely they'll kill the gargoyle before they can ever find the key. No sane demon could endure that aggravating scourge for more than a few hours. At the same time, you'll be celebrated as a hero for making amends for the previous king." Viper offered Styx a mocking bow. "Well played."

Styx ignored his friend's hopeful prediction. His luck wasn't good enough for Chiron to dispose of Levet and give up any attempt to free his master. It was more likely the vampire would free Tarak, who would promptly come to Chicago along with the gargoyle to kill him.

"I should be back before the weekend," he said. He planned to take his jet, which was waiting at a private airfield, to Vegas tonight and fly home before morning, but if he was delayed for some reason, he didn't want Viper rushing to his rescue with the Ravens. He was trying to prevent a war, not start one. Then again, he didn't want to disappear into the Mojave Desert and never be seen again. "If not, come looking for me."

"Got it." Viper stiffened, his nose flaring as the scent of granite filtered through the air. "Call if you need anything. Now I'm bailing before—"

His words were cut off as the door to the study was thrown open and Levet stepped inside.

"I have arrived," the tiny demon announced in a booming voice.

Levet wasn't what most people expected of a gargoyle.

He had the usual grotesque features, the thick gray skin, the reptilian eyes, the horns, and the cloven hoofs. He even had a long tail he polished on a regular basis. But he was barely three-foot tall, and he possessed a pair of delicate fairy wings that shimmered in vibrant reds and blues with veins of gold. Even worse, his magic was as combustible as a harpy's temper, and he had more courage than sense.

It was little wonder he had been voted out of the Gargoyle Guild.

"Too late," Viper muttered.

The stunted gargoyle blew a raspberry toward Viper before he turned his attention to Styx.

"This summons had better be important," he said with a sniff, as if Styx couldn't crush him beneath his size sixteen boot. Levet had a bloated opinion of his own importance. "I was enjoying a lava bath with a lovely fire imp."

Styx forced himself to count to ten. "We're going to Vegas."

"Vegas?" Levet's wings twitched excitement before he abruptly scowled. "This is not a trick, is it? The last time you promised me we were going on a vacation together you locked me in the dungeon."

Styx bared his fangs. "You tried to sell my sword on eBay."

Levet stuck out his bottom lip. "I do not know why your panties are in a kink. It is not like you ever use the rusty thing."

The floor trembled and ice formed in the air as Styx reached over his shoulder to grasp the handle of his massive weapon, which was strapped to his back. With one smooth motion, he had the tip of the blade pressed against Levet's short snout.

"Lucky you," he growled. "I'm taking it to Vegas."

Levet's wings drooped. "I do not feel very lucky."

Chapter 2

Chiron's penthouse office was designed to make a statement. Wealth. Sophistication. Power. The three things that impressed the mortals he dealt with routinely.

The outer reception room had a bank of windows that looked out over the Mojave Desert on one side and the lights of the nearby Vegas Strip on the other. Anyone who entered the room was immediately captivated by the view.

The carpet was silver, the furniture a sleek chrome with black leather. There was one wall covered by shelves that held a priceless collection of pottery from the Persian empire.

Chiron's private space was more suited to a vampire. No windows, dim lighting, and heavy furniture that could withstand the weight of a full-grown orc. It still managed to be an elegant testament to good taste, with a sleek desk and a silver-and-black décor.

It was a perfect setting for Chiron.

Like all vampires, he was blessed with a compelling beauty that was used to lure his prey. But Chiron's was even more dramatic than most.

His glossy black hair was cut short and smoothed from his pale, finely sculpted face that was a breath from beautiful. His nose was long and thin, his cheekbones prominent, his brow wide. His lips could curve into a wickedly charming smile or thin with icy displeasure. His eyes were as dark as ebony and surrounded by thick lashes. They were strikingly attractive, but if one looked close enough, they would discover an ancient pain that smoldered in the darkness.

He was currently wearing a tailored Hugo Boss suit, a crisp white shirt, and a smoke-gray tie. His shoes were Italian leather and his cuff links handcrafted. Seated behind his desk, his slender fingers toyed with the ivory dice that were over four centuries old. They were a reminder that life was a gamble.

And that there was no guarantee of a tomorrow.

He lived each night to the fullest.

"It's a trap," his companion growled.

Chiron glanced toward the corner where his faithful guard was standing at attention.

Ulric was a pureblood Were with golden eyes that glowed with the power of his inner wolf. His skin was the creamy color of cappuccino and he kept his head shaved. He stood over six foot, with the sort of wide, muscled body that was usually acquired by massive doses of steroids. For Ulric, it was all natural. Along with his rabid temper and an eagerness to use violence to solve his problems. He made the perfect personal guard for Chiron.

Chiron had released the Were from the slave pens beneath the Anasso's hidden lair centuries ago. He'd gone there to demand the release of Tarak only to be turned away. At the time he'd released the prisoners, he'd been more intent on punishing the King of the Vampires than performing any act of heroism. It was a childish, petty action; still it was one that had paid off with astonishing dividends.

Although vampires and Weres had a long history of being mortal enemies, Ulric had pledged his life to Chiron. His loyalty and friendship were gifts Chiron never took for granted. They were worth more than the two dozen casinos and resorts Chiron had built from Paris to Monte Carlo to Vegas.

"Perhaps," Chiron agreed. He was still trying to process the visit from the new Anasso.

The male had arrived two hours before, striding into the casino without warning and demanding a meeting with Chiron.

Chiron had met Styx before. The massive vampire had been the top lieutenant to the previous king. He'd also been the one to swear that Tarak had been a traitor who'd been exiled, and that the Anasso would never hold him prisoner.

Now he was claiming he'd been fooled by his former master. And that he not only had proof Tarak had been imprisoned, but he had a scroll that might actually provide the means to free him.

It was enough to make any vampire's head spin.

Ulric took a step forward. "You should have let me kill Styx as soon as he arrived in Vegas."

A bitter smile touched Chiron's lips. Once upon a time he'd been as eager as Ulric to challenge Styx and his master. He'd tried to warn his brothers there was something rotten at the heart of the Anasso. A sickness that had taken centuries to expose. Eventually, he'd managed to convince Tarak the king was a traitor to their cause.

That was when all hell had broken loose.

Figuratively, if not literally.

"We can't fight against the Anasso. We both learned that lesson the hard way," he reminded the Were.

Gold fire flared in Ulric's eyes. "Times change."

Chiron tossed aside the dice and reached for the heavy scroll that was placed in the middle of his desk.

"So it would seem."

Heat flared through the air as Ulric released a low growl. "You can't seriously be thinking about going in search of your master?"

Was he? Chiron's lips twisted. Of course he was. Tarak had been his clan chief. And friend.

And perhaps more importantly, Chiron had been tortured by guilt since the day Tarak had disappeared. He would sacrifice everything he possessed to ease his conscience.

"What would you have me do?" he asked.

Ulric shrugged, his muscles rippling beneath the olive-green Henley he had tucked into his faded jeans. "Stay here and get laid. Or go to Monte Carlo and get laid. Or—"

"I get the point," Chiron interrupted.

"You have a lot of options. None of them involving you risking your life on some wild-goose chase."

Chiron's gaze returned to the scroll in his hand. It was fragile with age and smelled of mold. As if it'd been hidden in a damp location. There was also a fading scent of blood. In the olden days, witches hadn't used ink to write out their spells.

"Why would Styx send me on a wild-goose chase?" he questioned, speaking more to himself than Ulric. "We've managed to coexist for centuries without playing games."

"Maybe Tarak is dead. This could be a trick to lure you away from your guards so they can kill you before you can seek your revenge." Ulric suggested. The Were had a talent for seeing the worst in any situation. "Or challenge the Anasso to become king."

Chiron grimaced. "I have no interest in challenging Styx."

"What about revenge?"

There was a long pause as Chiron considered the question. He didn't think Tarak was dead. Not that he had an actual connection to his master. Unlike many demon species, vampires could only bond with their true mate. But he did have an unusual talent.

He could delve into people's minds. If they were humans, he could pull out their thoughts as easily as plucking a grape from the vine. Demons could be trickier. And vampires were the hardest of all.

Styx had stood close enough for him to get a fuzzy glimpse.

"Not yet," he said. "I believe him."

"You..." Ulric's words trailed away as he gave a vague wave of his hand. "Did your thing?"

Chiron's lips twitched. He'd witnessed Ulric shoving his fist through a goblin's chest and ripping out his heart when the beast had gone on a rampage near their lair, but he was as nervous as a dew fairy whenever Chiron discussed his ability to peer into minds.

"Yeah, I did my thing," he said. "I could sense that he was reluctant to be here. And that he's a vampire of honor. If this is a trap, the Anasso isn't behind it."

Ulric wasn't satisfied. Predictable. "That doesn't make me feel any better."

"I have to know," Chiron said, rising to his feet as he abruptly came to his decision.

He couldn't ignore the chance to release Tarak. Even if there was a risk it was a trap.

He was a gambler at heart.

Ulric heaved a resigned sigh. "I'll pack."

Chiron gave a sharp shake of his head. "Not this time, Ulric. I need you here."

Ulric clenched his hands into tight fists. "Are you out of your mind?"

"Quite likely."

"I'm not letting you leave Vegas without me."

Most vampires would have punished the Were for daring to argue. Chiron, however, understood his guard. The wolf had witnessed his entire pack being sacrificed to the previous Anasso and his perverted hungers. Now Chiron was his family. He couldn't bear another loss.

"You're the only one I trust to take care of my business," Chiron said.

Ulric jutted out his heavy jaw. "I belong at your side."

"I know, amigo." Chiron rounded the desk and walked toward his companion. There was no way he was going to tell the proud warrior he wouldn't risk taking him into an unknown danger. Chiron was the gambler, not Ulric. Besides, Tarak was his master and his duty to rescue. Instead, he placed his hand on the Were's shoulder and used logic. "But until I find the key, there's nothing you can do to help."

"I can watch your back," Ulric muttered.

"I'd rather you watch my bank account."

Ulric's answer was lost in a low growl.

Chiron dropped his hand and took a step back. "I appreciate your concern, amigo, but I'm not helpless. If the gargoyle attempts—" Chiron bit off his words as he realized the tiny demon wasn't standing near the door where Styx had commanded him to wait. "Where'd Levet go?"

"He can't have left the office without tripping the alarm." Ulric tilted back his head, sniffing the air. "He's in the reception room."

Chiron moved quickly through the connecting door, expecting the gargoyle to be admiring the view. It was stunning, even if he did say so himself. Instead, the bizarre creature was plopped on the carpet with a dark bottle clenched between his hands.

Chiron had been mildly amused when Styx had claimed the gargoyle possessed the ability to follow the magic in the scroll to the mysterious key. A convenient talent. But even as the older vampire had assured him the gargoyle was necessary to his search, Chiron had detected some sort of hidden agenda.

As if Styx was eager to get rid of the tiny demon.

Now he understood why.

"Is that my private cognac?" he demanded in disbelief. No one should be able to see through the illusions he paid a fortune to wrap around his private safe in the corner of his office. And even if they could, no one was stupid enough to actually try to steal from him.

No one but this…beast.

The gargoyle gave a flutter of his wings, taking a deep swig straight from the bottle.

"*Oui.* It is not as fine as Viper's, but I suppose it is adequate." The gargoyle gave a shrill squeak when Ulric crossed the floor in three long strides. Grabbing the demon by the horn, Ulric lifted him off his feet. "Hey," Levet protested, kicking his feet. "It is rude to dangle a gargoyle as if he is a sack of pimentos. Release me, you mangy cur."

Pimentos? Chiron frowned. Did he mean potatoes?

"Can I eat him?" Ulric demanded.

"Not until I find the key." Chiron moved to snatch the half-empty bottle out of the gargoyle's hands. "Then you can do what you want with him."

Levet crossed his arms over his small chest. "And I thought Styx was bad."

* * * *

The demon hotel in Florida was well hidden from humans. Not only was it surrounded by wetlands and shrouded beneath a thick canopy of trees, it was protected by a powerful spell that had been placed around the property so long ago, no one remembered who'd put it there.

For those lucky enough to discover the remote hotel, they found themselves in a fairy-tale land, complete with a sweeping, plantation-style home the size of Versailles, and gardens filled with lush flowers that laced the air with an intoxicating perfume.

The owner of the hotel, Lilah, was currently strolling along the paved pathways that led to the back terrace. She was a small female, at least in stature. She stood barely over five foot tall. But she possessed lush curves currently covered by a damp robe. Her golden hair was a mass of untamed curls that fell past her shoulders and contrasted with the honey sheen of her skin. Her eyes hovered between green and gold, depending on her mood.

She'd just finished a swim in her private pool hidden behind a powerful illusion and strictly off-limits to any guests. It was a nightly indulgence that refreshed her in a way she couldn't find anywhere else.

Reaching the stone staircase, she climbed up to the terrace, already prepared to find Inga waiting for her.

Lilah's former nanny stood well over six foot, with the broad shoulders of a human football player. Her hair was reddish and grew in tufts on top of her large, square head, and her features were blunt. Her eyes were blue, but they could turn red when she was annoyed. Her teeth were pointed.

Some might say she wasn't the most pleasant female. She was half ogre, after all, and they weren't known for their charming personalities. But Lilah loved her. In part because Inga had raised Lilah since she was a young child, but mostly because she'd proven to be a loyal servant who remained despite the fact that Lilah was now a grown woman.

Crossing the terrace, Lilah halted in front of the ogress and offered a bright smile.

"Isn't it a lovely evening, Inga?"

As expected, the large female sniffed in disdain. Then she planted her fists on her wide hips, as if preparing for battle. The sight might have been terrifying if the ogress hadn't been wearing one of the muumuu dresses she'd discovered during the hideous fashion trends of the sixties.

No one had the nerve to tell her that it puffed out like a blimp when she was charging up and down the hallways.

Tonight's muumuu was a stunning shade of lime green with huge orange lilies. *Yikes.*

"It's an evening like any other."

Lilah folded her hands together. Inga's mood was even more foul than usual.

"Did you get our new guests settled?" she asked.

The sound of a car approaching had reached Lilah just as she was entering the grotto. She hadn't bothered returning; Inga was capable of handling the hotel without her. Even if she wasn't the most personable hostess.

"I did."

Lilah swallowed a sigh. Inga wasn't going to be satisfied until she'd been allowed to vent her displeasure.

"Is something wrong?"

Inga gave another loud sniff. She sounded like a foghorn. "I don't like the look of them."

"What is it this time?" Lilah tilted her head to the side. "Are they shifty-eyed? Or shady?"

"Both."

"Mmm."

Inga scowled, no doubt sensing Lilah's amusement at her predictable reaction to new guests. As far as the older female was concerned, she would be quite happy if no one ever came to the hotel. She was obsessive in her desire to keep Lilah isolated from the world.

"This time I'm serious," she muttered.

"I suppose they're vampires?" Lilah asked. Inga had a special hatred for the walking undead.

"One of them is."

"That explains your mood," Lilah said wryly. "You are always…"

"What?"

Lilah searched for the proper word. *"Temperamental* when we have vampire guests."

Inga peeled back her lips to reveal her pointy teeth. "I don't trust anything that doesn't have a heartbeat."

Lilah shrugged. Unlike her nanny, she possessed an appreciation for the demons who were willing to offer her money to stay in her home. She needed the income to pay the pack of brownies who came to do basic upkeep and repairs on the ancient house, along with the fairies who tended the gardens. Plus, she had two maids and a cook who depended on her to keep a roof over their heads and food on their table.

"They happen to be our best-paying customers, not to mention the least troublesome," she reminded her companion. "As long as they have plenty of blood, privacy, and a promise to keep out the sunlight, you barely know they're around. Unlike the fairies who stayed here last week and got drunk on nectar and trashed their rooms, including several priceless antiques. Or the Weres who held the mating ceremony in the glades and howled so loud the human police came to see what was happening."

Inga refused to budge. Her rampant prejudice ran too deep. "Vampires are dangerous."

"You've already warned me a thousand times," Lilah pointed out with a small sigh. "Who's the other one?"

Inga blinked in confusion. "Other what?"

"Guest," Lilah clarified. "You said one is a vampire. I'm guessing the other one must be a different species?"

Inga wrinkled her nose, which was perilously close to a snout. "It's a gargoyle."

Lilah jerked, staring at the other female. "Are you joking?" she finally demanded.

"I don't joke."

Well, that was true enough. Inga had many fine qualities, but a sense of humor wasn't one of them.

Lilah glanced toward the vast building. It was large enough to house a hundred demons, but a full-grown gargoyle towered higher than her ceilings, with a ten-foot wingspan.

"I would know if there was a gargoyle here."

"This one is all shrunken," Inga said, holding her hand next to her knee. "Barely this tall, with big fairy wings."

A vampire and a shrunken gargoyle with fairy wings?

Okay. Inga was right. They did seem sketchy.

"Did they pay in advance?" she asked.

"Cash."

"How long are they staying?"

"They paid for two nights."

Lilah glanced toward the wing of the house that had been renovated for vampires. The windows were shuttered and the fireplaces were bricked-over. The leeches were a little touchy about sunlight and open flames.

"Did they say why they chose this hotel?"

"Some nonsense about visiting family."

Lilah wrinkled her nose. "I suppose it's possible. Vampires do create children, although not in the traditional way."

"I haven't met a bloodsucker yet who gives a—" Inga snapped her thick fingers. "About their children."

That was true enough. Vampires rarely stuck around to see if their bite had turned a victim into a fellow vampire. Which was why most of them perished within a few hours of being created.

"It seems doubtful the gargoyle would have family in the swamps," Lilah added, chewing her bottom lip. As far as she knew, the Gargoyle Guild remained in Paris.

"Which means they're here for something nefarious."

"We don't know that." Lilah turned her attention back to her companion. "For now, they're to be treated as welcomed guests."

The older female grunted. "For now."

Chapter 3

Chiron had a clear understanding of why Styx had been so eager to dump Levet in Vegas. The gargoyle was rude, flighty, and he never, ever shut his ugly snout. Within less than an hour in his company, Chiron was considering the pleasure of chopping off his head.

Sadly, things hadn't gotten easier after their cross-country trip to this remote hotel. Standing in a suite that had cost a damned fortune, Chiron wondered for the hundredth time why he hadn't allowed Ulric to eat the aggravating lump of granite when he'd asked.

It was only the hope that Levet could perform the miracle of finding the key that was keeping Chiron from ripping the wings off the bane of his existence and flushing him down the toilet.

Planting his hands on his hips, Chiron glared down at the gargoyle, who was headed toward a minibar that looked distinctly out of place with the antique furnishings.

"Well?" he demanded.

"Well what?" Levet opened the fridge and began pulling out the tiny bottles of alcohol.

Chiron felt his fangs quiver. He wanted to bite something. Really, really hard.

"You brought me here," he snapped. "Where's the key?"

Levet drained the rum. Then the whiskey. He randomly chose another rum before he polished off the tequila. "It is close."

"Close? What's that mean?"

The gargoyle hiccupped, waving his hand in an airy gesture. "Nearby. Approximate. In the general vicinity."

Chiron crossed the Persian carpet in a blur of motion. The temperature dropped to just below freezing as he bent in front of Levet.

"Don't screw with me, gargoyle," he warned.

Levet jumped back. "Do not leap about like that," he yelped; then, regaining command of his composure, the creature offered an offended sniff. "Vampires are very cranky creatures."

"We're here to find the key, not for you to get lubricated on cheap liquor," Chiron snapped.

"Oh, it is not cheap. Did you see the prices on the fridge? This is going to cost you a fortune—" Levet's words were choked off as Chiron wrapped his fingers around his throat and squeezed. "Arg. Okay."

"Where is the key?"

"It is cloaked."

Chiron glared at Levet. Was the gargoyle being deliberately annoying to keep Chiron distracted? Possibly. Hard to believe any creature could be so naturally grating on a vampire's nerves.

"What does that mean?" he demanded.

"I am not entirely certain." Levet wrinkled his snout. "I can sense its presence, but it is impossible to pinpoint its exact location."

The vague answer did nothing to ease Chiron's suspicions. "You managed to bring us to this place."

Levet shrugged. "I could sense it easily until we passed through the barrier. Now it is muted. It must be a trick of the spell."

"Or just a trick," Chiron said, his fingers tightening on the gargoyle's throat.

Levet scowled. "I am not a grape to be squeezed. Release me."

Chiron ignored the command, instead concentrating on using his powers to read the mind of his companion. A physical connection usually made it easier, but with Levet, he could only catch fleeting glimpses. As if his brain was as capricious and unpredictable as Levet himself.

"Ulric warned me this was a trap," he accused. "You lured me to this secluded location—"

"Do not be a drama princess." With a quick movement, Levet jerked backward, escaping Chiron's grip. "There is no trap. It could be that I need to become accustomed to the magic. It is..." He paused, lifting his arm to touch his bruised neck with his claws. "Odd."

Chiron didn't bother to grab the gargoyle again. There was nowhere he could run that Chiron couldn't catch him. "Odd?"

"Unfamiliar." Levet's wings flapped, revealing his frustration. "It is almost fey, but not quite."

Chiron straightened. The gargoyle was genuinely puzzled. That much he could sense.

Not that he fully trusted him.

"I need results, not excuses," he growled.

Without warning, Levet gave a shooing motion with his hand. "Go play somewhere else. I cannot concentrate with you hovering over me," he commanded.

Chiron bared his fangs. One thing was certain: the gargoyle had balls of steel to think he could order around a vampire.

"Fine." He pointed a finger toward the ugly creature. "But if you fail me, gargoyle, it will be the last thing you do."

"Leeches," Levet muttered as Chiron headed toward the door.

Chiron ignored him. The need for a break from the gargoyle's endless chatter far outweighed any urge to punish him for his impertinence.

Stepping into the long corridor, he strolled past the half dozen closed doors. He could sense other guests, but as the annoying gargoyle had said, there was an odd sensation that everything was muffled.

It had to be the spell wrapped around the entire estate.

A shiver snaked down his spine.

He hated magic. And he hated human magic most of all.

With a grimace, he slowed his steps and forced himself to study his surroundings. If he couldn't use his powers to determine the demons who were sharing the vast hotel, or more importantly, if there were any clues to lead him to the key, he had to use his other senses.

Around him, a thick silence filled the air, broken only by the click of his expensive shoes on the marble. He felt a cold chill as he passed one of the doors. A vampire. Maybe more than one. The other rooms felt empty, but that didn't mean whoever was staying there wasn't somewhere else in the hotel.

There was nothing else to be seen beyond the vibrant murals painted on the walls. The artwork depicted the same flowers and shrubbery he'd glimpsed in the gardens when they arrived. As if they were blooming inside.

It looked like the work of the fey. They were the only demons who had the talent to create such delicate perfection.

He headed down the wide stairs and crossed the lobby, which had wooden floors and paneling that was glossy enough to reflect the fairy lights that danced beneath a domed ceiling. There were large pots of plants set in the corners, and the faint scent of salt in the air.

Odd.

Witches used salt when they were casting their spells, but the smell should have faded long ago. Unless there was still a witch at the hotel using magic. He grimaced. He'd rather deal with a horde of trolls than one witch.

Circling the room, he avoided the wide front door. When they'd arrived earlier, the door had chimed with a bell loud enough to wake the dead. He preferred to avoid a repeat performance. Besides, he wanted to inspect the outside of the building. If it had been created by the fey, there should be runes that identified the species. Hopefully, they were a local tribe so he could track them down and question them about any tunnels or secret rooms that were hidden behind illusions.

There had to be a reason the witches would have chosen this spot to leave the key.

He located a hallway that opened directly onto the back terrace and stepped into the night. He grimaced at the fuzzy sensation that wrapped around him and muted his powers. He was beginning to appreciate Levet's annoyance with the spell shrouding the estate.

Chiron paused, allowing his gaze to skim over the verdant landscape that spilled toward the nearby wetlands. Flowers, shrubs, fruit trees, and fireflies offered an explosion of color.

He was addicted to the bright lights and bustle of city life. Was there anything more thrilling than Paris sparkling beneath a midnight sky? Or Vegas, with its shimmering parade of lights? But he had to admit there was something enticing about the serene peace that saturated the Everglades. He could understand why a demon would retreat to this place for an opportunity to forget the world for a few nights. Or weeks.

But he wasn't here for peace.

He was here to find the key that would unlock the prison that held his master.

Walking to the end of the terrace, he turned back to the building and laid his hand against the corner. He could feel the age that pulsed through the warm stones and see the faint runes that had been etched onto the surface. Still, he was puzzled as to who had actually created the structure.

Was the mystery of the place connected to the key? Or just a strange coincidence?

Lost in thought, it wasn't until a soft voice floated through the air that he realized he was no longer alone.

"Can I help you?"

With a hiss, Chiron pivoted on his heel to confront the intruder. How the hell had he allowed someone to sneak up on him? Even with his senses suppressed by the magic, it was an inexcusable lapse.

Prepared to rid himself of his unwelcome companion, Chiron's anger faltered and died as soon as he caught sight of the tiny female.

Bam. It felt like the time he'd been stupid enough to get into a fight with a feral troll. The creature had hit him so hard, he'd actually seen stars. The same stars he was seeing now.

Chiron clenched his hands, his nose flaring as he tried to absorb the lush scent of her.

She was stunningly beautiful. Her hair was a glorious tangle of curls that haloed around her oval face. Her eyes were green gilded with a golden shimmer smoldering with a sensual temptation. Her lips were plush and rosy in the moonlight, her skin the color of melted honey. Her soft, curvy body was revealed to perfection in the robe that clung to her with delicious results.

A natural siren.

His fangs lengthened, a powerful urge to taste her sweetness almost overwhelming.

"Holy hell," he said in low tones. "I didn't know this hotel was blessed with angels."

Her eyes had widened, as if she was equally stunned by the impact of Chiron's presence. Then, they abruptly narrowed as Chiron spoke.

"That's not the worst line I've ever heard, but it's close," she informed him.

Chiron's lips twitched. She was right. It'd been awful. Hard to believe most women found him utterly irresistible. But in his defense, he'd never experienced such an intense reaction. He didn't know if it was natural or caused by the strange magic swirling through the air, but it was undeniable.

"You caught me off guard," he admitted, strolling toward the unknown female and offering an old-fashioned bow. In his mind, good manners never went out of style. Especially when they involved a beautiful woman. "Allow me to introduce myself. I'm Chiron. And I promise my lines are usually much better." He straightened, his gaze taking another slow, lingering survey of her. "But you are breathtaking."

Clearly uneasy at his intense fascination, she took a deliberate step backward.

"If you're hungry, I have each vampire room stocked with blood in the minibar." She waved a hand toward the pathway that led through the garden. "Or there's a town just thirty miles east of here."

Chiron's brows snapped together. He'd assumed she was another guest. Or even the angel he'd claimed her to be. It hadn't occurred to him that she was a member of the staff.

"You work here?"

"Twenty-four/seven." She shrugged. "I'm the owner."

"Owner." The word was torn from his lips. It was worse than he thought.

She blinked, as if sensing his violent surge of emotion. "Is there something wrong?"

Yeah, there was something wrong. This hotel was somehow connected to the key. Which meant she must be connected to the witches.

He moved closer. His powers were muted, but he hoped he could get a glimpse into her thoughts.

"I assumed the ogress was in charge," he forced himself to say.

"Oh. Inga is my manager," she said, her tone defensive. "And she's only half ogre."

Chiron silently cursed. He was behaving as awkwardly as a drunken kobold. No wonder she was eyeing him with sudden suspicion.

If she did know anything about Tarak, or the witches who'd created the spell to trap him, he was doing a damned fine job of ensuring she would never give him any clue to where the key was hidden.

He smiled, careful to keep his fangs hidden. Some demons found them scary. Go figure. "You haven't told me your name."

She hesitated. In the hands of a magic user, a name could be a powerful thing. Then she seemed to recall he was a vampire. His ability to hurt her didn't have anything to do with magic.

"Lilah," she said.

Lilah. The soft word hit his ear like a song. It was perfect for her.

He swallowed another curse, forcing himself to look beyond her dazzling beauty. Not easy when his instincts were fiercely urging him to toss her over his shoulder and carry her to his lair.

Grimly, he concentrated on the features that were lovely, but not as delicate as most fey. And the eyes that were such an unusual color. Why couldn't he sense what species she was? It should be obvious by her scent and the aura that surrounded her.

There was only one thing he could determine for certain: She was much younger than he'd originally assumed. Less than a century.

She hadn't been around when Tarak was taken or the spell created to hide the key.

So did that ease his suspicions? Hmm. Not entirely. He needed more information. A *lot* more.

"Owning such an impressive business is quite an accomplishment at your age."

She remained defensive. Not that she was indifferent to him. But mixed in with her stirrings of lust was a healthy dose of suspicion.

The exact same emotions that were swirling through him.

"I'm older than I look," she muttered.

He didn't have to read minds to know she was lying. "Doubtful."

Perhaps realizing she was giving away more than she wanted, she took another step backward, clearly preparing to retreat.

"I hope you enjoy your stay."

With blinding speed, he was moving to block her path. "Wait."

She came to an abrupt halt, startled by his sudden appearance in front of him.

"Yes?"

"I'd like to know more about this place," he said, sticking as close to the truth as possible. Until he figured out precisely what sort of demon she was, he couldn't be sure whether she could detect lies.

She looked skeptical. "Right."

"Truly." He held up his hands, as if that could convince her of his sincerity. "I'm in the hotel business. I always enjoy learning from my competitors."

His words caught her off guard. "You're in the hotel business?"

"Dreamscape Spas and Resorts." He reached into his back pocket to pull out one of the gold-edged cards he'd had printed for the numerous humans he dealt with on a nightly basis.

She studied the card, a small measure of her tension easing. "I've heard of this place. I thought it was in Paris."

He was ridiculously pleased. As if her approval was somehow special.

Chiron flattened his lips. Where the hell was the polished, sophisticated male who'd been eagerly welcomed into royal households? He'd been replaced by a strange creature Chiron barely recognized.

Thank the gods Ulric wasn't around. He'd never let Chiron live it down.

"I have a couple dozen resorts spread around the world," he said, trying to sound like he wasn't bragging.

She tilted her head to the side. "Don't you cater to humans?"

"I might expand into the demon clientele."

Her mouth parted, her eyes flaring with an unexpected anger. "You're here to steal my customers?"

He chuckled, genuinely amused by her accusation. "There's plenty to go around."

"So says the billionaire with hotels around the world."

He placed his hand in the center of his chest in a pledge of sincerity. "I have no interest in Florida, I swear. There are too many mosquitoes."

Her brief flare of temper faded; then, without warning, her lips twitched at his words.

"You do get the irony, don't you?"

"You mean I don't like bloodsuckers?" He moved close enough to feel the heat of her body seeping through his clothes. *Yum.* "I prefer to be the taker, not the donor."

She trembled, but she didn't step back. "And your prey? What if they prefer not to be the donor?"

"My dinner companions are never prey. And I can assure you, they're always exceedingly eager to provide what I need," he said, reaching out to touch a golden curl. Soft. Like spun silk. A different sort of heat combusted through his body, brushing across each pleasure point. *Delicious.* "Would you like me to demonstrate?"

A captivating awareness darkened her eyes. Then, with a jerky motion, she was brushing away his hand and stepping back.

"Unless you want Inga to demonstrate her ability to rip off heads with her bare hands, you'll keep your fangs to yourself," she warned.

Chiron hid his smile. She could bluff and bluster all she wanted. There was no denying the sizzling attraction between them.

"I would never force myself on an unwilling partner."

Her lips flattened. "You said you wanted to discuss my hotel?"

With an effort, he forced his gaze away from her face and nodded toward the building.

"It is a beautiful place."

"Thank you."

He studied the elegant lines that masked the sturdy construction. "It has the craftsmanship of the fey, but I don't recognize the runes. Who built this?"

"The original owners have been lost to time."

"You don't have records?" he demanded.

Fey were meticulous in preserving the most tedious details of their businesses. He'd always assumed it was to ensure they could track which compulsion spell worked best to lure their customers back to their establishments.

"There was a demon plague when I was a young child that took my parents," she said. The lack of emotion in her voice didn't disguise the lingering wound. He could sense she continued to mourn her parents. "Inga burned their bodies along with most of their belongings. Her eagerness to ensure anything that might have been contaminated with the plague was destroyed meant only the furniture survived."

Chiron frowned. Epidemics were rare among demons, but they were devastating when they occurred. They could take out huge swaths of the local population, and it wasn't surprising the ogress would have chosen fire to try to purge the house of any lingering disease. Still, it was pretty damned convenient that every record that might have revealed the reason this place had been chosen by the witches had been destroyed.

"You don't know anything about the history of the place?" he pressed.

She paused before seeming to decide there was no reason not to answer. He was a paying guest, after all.

"There're plenty of folktales."

He strolled to lean against the stone balustrade that framed the terrace. "Tell me."

"Why?"

"I told you: I'm interested in hotels."

She remained distrustful of his curiosity. "They don't have anything to do with my business."

He arched a brow. "Of course they do. I don't rent rooms to humans. I offer them a fantasy. The opportunity to escape from their dull, humdrum lives, if only for a few days. Or the chance to become rich with the throw of the dice." He gestured toward the lush gardens. "This is a magical retreat for demons desiring the illusion of peace."

She snorted. "It's not always peaceful. I just replaced several chairs in the west wing after a group of fairies decided they needed the wood to build a bonfire. If it hadn't been for Inga, they would have trashed the place."

Chiron nodded. He'd been entranced by the sense of quiet serenity that surrounded the area. Now he realized some demons might choose the location because of its isolation.

He spoke his thoughts out loud. "I suppose some demons consider such an isolated location their private Vegas."

"What do you mean?"

"What happens here, stays here."

A reluctant amusement sparkled in her eyes. It illuminated her beauty and made his gut twist with a strange emotion.

"True."

He clenched the edge of the balustrade. He was trying to find out information that would help in his search, he sternly reminded himself. Later, he would indulge in his fascination for this female.

Always assuming she didn't turn out to be working with the enemy.

"I really am interested," he said.

She studied him, her expression impossible to read. Then she heaved a resigned sigh. No doubt she was telling herself he was just another demanding customer she had to indulge.

"The oldest folklore is that the house rose from the oceans and floated to the wetlands fully formed. A creation of mist and magic. That's my favorite one," she said, her expression softening. Clearly, she loved her home.

Mist and magic. Chiron shuddered.

"What are the others?" he pressed.

"They aren't nearly so nice. One said it was once a lair for the owl people, who would come out at night and sacrifice the local water sprites to fuel their magic. Then there's the one that said this place was built on an ancient burial site and that ghosts walk the grounds." She grimaced. "I haven't encountered any ghosts, so I'm assuming we can scratch that last one off the list."

Chiron wasn't so sure. There were some ghosts who stayed dormant for centuries. There could be a dozen of them sleeping in the gardens without anyone knowing.

"Nothing about witches?" he asked.

She started to shake her head, only to halt, as if she was struck by a sudden thought.

"Actually, there was some weird story about witches dancing in a circle until they gave birth to the barriers that surround the estate. I think I heard it from one of the brownies who came to work on my foundation."

Chiron was intrigued. He wondered if he could track down the brownie who'd told her that story. Probably not. The elusive creatures tended to travel from one area to another, offering their talents for mending stone in exchange for food and shelter. Few of them had permanent lairs.

"Are there any local covens?" he asked.

"I don't think so."

Chiron studied the massive structure. A witch might be capable of creating a small cottage. And a completed circle of witches could potentially manage a stone building. But nothing on this scale.

"Human magic couldn't have done it alone," he murmured.

There was a brief silence as she glanced at him in confusion. "What's your interest in witches?"

Chiron shoved himself away from the railing. This female was already suspicious of him. Unless he wanted to alert her that he wasn't just another guest, he needed to take things slow.

Ignoring the voice in the back of his head that whispered he was way too eager to prolong his stay in this place, he flashed Lilah his most charming grin.

"It's a magical kingdom in the middle of a swamp. All you need is some oversize mice and a princess and a fairy godmother, right?"

She rolled her eyes. "Very funny."

"I have my moments."

"Hmm."

He took another step closer, his fangs aching as her scent teased at his senses. What was she?

"You don't sound like you believe me," he accused in a husky voice.

Her breath rushed between her parted lips. Sweet music to his ears.

"I don't," she told him. She tried to look defiant, but she couldn't hide her reaction to his proximity.

It smoldered in her eyes.

"No?"

"No." She sniffed. "You're not here because you want to learn about my business methods. Everyone knows the best demon hotels and clubs belong to Viper. If you needed advice, you would go to him."

Chiron blinked in surprise. He'd assumed her isolation in the Everglades meant she didn't keep track of the outside world. A timely reminder that he really didn't know anything about this female.

Except for the fact that she was gorgeous and clever and she smelled like ambrosia.

He chose his words with care. "For the past several centuries, Viper and I have not been on speaking terms."

She furrowed her brow. "Why not?"

A smooth lie formed on his tongue, but he found it impossible to speak the words. He told himself it was because he still had no idea what sort of demon she was and what her powers might be. He couldn't risk having her throw him out because she didn't trust him. But a part of him knew it was because he didn't want to deceive her.

A dangerous realization.

"I'm a Rebel."

The name seemingly meant nothing to her.

"I thought all vampires were rebels?"

"My clan was accused of trying to remove the king from his throne, so we were banished."

"That seems very..." She wrinkled her nose. "Feudal."

"Straight out of *Game of Thrones*."

Expecting her to smile at his joke, he froze in shock as she impulsively reached out to lay a light hand on his arm.

"I'm sorry."

Chiron froze in shock. It wasn't just her touch that was sending electric jolts of pleasure through him. It was her sincerity that felt so dangerously real. As if she sensed his lingering bitterness and the wounds that refused to heal.

Careful, Chiron, he silently warned himself. Only a fool would forget that his instincts were scrambled since arriving at the hotel. It was even possible they were being deliberately manipulated.

"I'm not." He kept his tone light. "I've succeeded just fine without the Anasso and his merry band of ass-kissers."

She gave his arm a soft squeeze. "It's lonely without a family."

He took an abrupt step backward as her words brushed a nerve that was still raw and aching.

Beyond a ruthless, gnawing guilt at Tarak's disappearance had been an underlying emptiness. The Rebel clan had scattered without a strong leader, and Chiron had eventually retreated to focus on his own businesses. If it hadn't been for Ulric, he would be completely alone.

"You don't have any relatives?" he forced himself to ask. This conversation was supposed to be focused on discovering information about this hotel. Not wallowing in self-pity.

She shrugged. "None that have reached out to me. Perhaps someday I'll go in search of them."

"I—" He snapped his lips together, his eyes widening as Lilah leaped toward him.

At first, he thought she'd been overcome by lust. Hey, it could happen. He'd had women jump out of windows when he strolled past. But even as he lifted his arms to wrap around her, she was ramming her hands into his chest with enough force to make him stumble backward.

"Look out," she cried.

Oddly, he didn't think for a second she was attacking him. Stupid, really. Why else would she be shoving him around? But he made no effort to fight against the pressure of her hands, allowing her to tumble him back onto the hard stone terrace. At the same time, a pain flared through his shoulder.

What the hell?

He warily watched as Lilah bent beside him. Was that fear etched on her face? Absently lifting his hand, he touched the pain that continued to throb through his right shoulder. There was a sticky moisture he knew was blood, and a slash through his favorite shirt. Damn. He'd been injured.

It wasn't fatal. Already his flesh was knitting together. In less than ten minutes he'd be completely healed. It was just bad enough to piss him off.

"Are you okay?" Lilah demanded.

"Fine." He was on his feet, vaulting over the edge of the railing to search the nearby bushes. A second later, he pulled a wooden arrow from a clump of orchids. *Shit.* This was one of the few weapons that could actually kill a vampire. And if it hadn't been for Lilah, it would have gone straight through his heart. "Go inside," he urged his companion.

Lilah glanced toward the arrow in his hand before meeting his fierce gaze. "What are you going to do?"

He flashed his fangs. "Find whoever is suicidal enough to try to kill me."

Chapter 4

Levet hated vampires. Almost as much as he hated dragons. Oh, and his family. *Oui*, his family topped his list of creatures he detested. They had tossed him out of the nest, then voted him out of the Guild, and when he'd ended up in the hands of slave traders, they'd done nothing to help him.

Not that he had need of them. He'd not only survived, he was an official knight in shining armor, adored by females everywhere. And he had saved the world. How many demons could claim such awesome feats?

None but him.

Unfortunately, his status as a hero meant he was often called upon to rush to the rescue. It was both a gift and a burden. This time, it felt more like a burden.

Chiron had the same nasty temper as every other bloodsucker, and the assumption that he could order Levet around as if he was a servant instead of a big Cheese Whiz.

Feeling full of self-righteous annoyance, as well as several bottles of rum he'd discovered hidden in a locked room next to the kitchen, he waddled his way through the vast hotel.

It was a beautiful building. Glossy wood, stunning murals, and massive stone fireplaces. But he didn't like it.

And worse, he didn't know why he didn't like it.

Maybe it was because his magic felt as sluggish as molasses. Or because his senses were muffled. Or because he wanted to be bathing in lava with a lovely fire imp.

Whatever the cause, his wings were drooping by the time he trooped from the cellars to the upper floors. The key was here. He'd followed the spell to this spot. But there was some strange magic that kept him from pinpointing the exact location.

Finished with a search of the rooms on the top floor, he headed toward a door at the end of the hallway. It was hidden behind a clever illusion of a mirror, but Levet wasn't fooled. He was a master at seeing through magic. Or at least, he was when his talents weren't being rotated with.

No wait…that wasn't right. Screwed. *Oui.* Screwed with.

Reaching the door, he'd just managed to pull it open to reveal a steep staircase when a large form suddenly appeared, heading down the steps like a drunken water buffalo.

"Eek!" Levet flapped his wings, realizing it was the ogress mongrel who'd greeted them when they'd first arrived at the hotel. She was tall and broad, with a face that only a mother could love. Worse, she was thundering down the stairs too fast to stop.

"Get out of the way, you idiot," she barked.

Levet hopped backward to avoid being trampled, waiting for the woman to skid to a halt before sending her an offended glare.

"Why were you fleeing the attics, female? And why did you nearly squish me?"

The ogress whirled around, scowling at him as if he was the one who'd caused the near disaster.

"My name is Inga, and I was not fleeing."

"Then what were you doing?"

Inga glanced toward the open door. "I heard someone running across the roof. I went up to find them, but they disappeared. I intended to make certain they didn't manage to enter the hotel."

Levet followed her gaze. He'd already been on the roof. A gargoyle liked to investigate the outside accommodations as soon as they arrived at a location. There wasn't much to see. Clay tiles. A gutter. A few chimneys. Boring.

"The roof?" he questioned in disbelief.

She made a sound of impatience. "You know, the thing above our heads that keeps us dry when it rains?"

Levet wrinkled his heavy brow. "I know what it is. Why would someone be running up there?"

The ogress folded her arms beneath her breasts. "You should ask your roommate."

Levet was momentarily mesmerized by the swell of her impressive bosom beneath the orange lilies patterned on her dress.

Sacrebleu.

"What roommate?"

"The vampire." Her eyes narrowed. "Unless you have more than one roommate? In which case, you have to pay extra."

Levet shook his head, forcing his gaze to meet her suspicious glare. "Why would Chiron know about the person on the roof?"

"I think he was chasing whoever was up there."

Chiron chasing someone across the roof? Was she drunk? He sniffed the air. He didn't detect any grog on her breath.

"Why would he chase someone across the roof?"

"I don't know and I don't care." She leaned forward, pulling back her lips to reveal her pointy teeth. "He shouldn't be up there, just as you shouldn't be sticking your ugly snout into places it doesn't belong."

"Hey." He spread his wings, just in case she had missed seeing their dazzling colors. "Who are you calling ugly?"

"You."

Levet sniffed. Clearly, the female had trouble with her eyesight. Anyone could see he was an extraordinary creature.

"Have you never heard of the potty calling the kettle black?" he demanded.

She wrinkled her wide nose. "No. That doesn't even make sense."

Levet gave another sniff. Most human sayings didn't make any sense to him, but it was rude of her to point it out. Deciding not to lecture the female on her poor manners, Levet instead gave a wave of his hand.

"What is this place?" he demanded.

She looked confused. "It's a hallway."

"*Non*." He waved his hands again. "This place."

"It's a hotel." She spoke slowly, as if he was too dense to comprehend her words.

Levet gave an impatient click of his tongue. He would have to be more direct. "Why is the magic peculiar?"

"The only thing peculiar here is you."

Levet stomped his foot, even as he revised the most-detested list in his head. His family was no longer at the top. This female ogress was number one.

"I am a guest here," he pouted. "You should treat me as if I am a prince." His tail swirled around his feet. "Which I am, by the way. I have royal blood flowing through my veins."

She wasn't nearly as impressed as she should have been. Indeed, she looked aggravated. Ridiculous creature.

"If it was up to me, I would have you tossed out of here."

"Why?"

"You're trespassing where you don't belong."

"Trespassing?" Levet blinked in confusion. "How can we be trespassing at a hotel?"

She shuffled her feet, obviously incapable of answering the perfectly reasonable question.

"I don't like vampires," she muttered.

Ah, well. That made sense. "Fair enough."

"Or gargoyles," she added, reaching down to grab him by the horn. Before he could protest, he found himself sailing through the air to smack against the wall. He squawked, more embarrassed than hurt, as she stomped past him and disappeared down the hallway.

"Smelly ogress," he groused, rising to his feet and carefully brushing the dust from his wings.

Lost in his mortification, Levet barely had time to notice the frigid blast of air before Chiron was appearing directly in front of him.

"Tell me why I shouldn't rip off your head," the vampire growled.

"Eek!" Levet jumped back, then glared at the demon towering over him. "I wish people would stop creeping around."

Chiron ignored his chiding, pointing a finger in Levet's face. "You tried to kill me."

"What are you babbling about?"

"I was chasing the person who shot this at me." The vampire held up a wooden arrow he had tightly clutched in his hand. "I thought I'd lost him in the maze of hidden passages, but here you are."

Levet parted his lips to demand a tour. He adored hidden passages. Who knew what treasure he might find? But the temperature continued to drop, and there was a tremor beneath his feet that warned Chiron was in a mood.

Typical vampire.

"*Oui.* I am here, but I know nothing about an arrow."

Chiron flashed his fangs. "Do you think I'm a fool?"

Levet stiffened his spine. He'd been threatened by vampires and dragons and trolls. He'd been threatened by the Dark Lord himself. He no longer cowered just because a demon was taller, with big, sharp teeth. At least, not on the outside. Inside there might be a teensy, tiny bit of cowering.

"You are a fool if you believe I would attempt to kill you with such a crude weapon."

"This crude weapon is perfectly designed to kill a vampire," Chiron rasped.

Levet snapped his wings. Stupid demon.

"I am a gargoyle. I could blast you with my magic," he retorted, not bothering to mention that his magic was iffy under the best of circumstances. Right now, it might very well be nonexistent.

Chiron narrowed his eyes, but Levet sensed his anger leaking away. Almost as if the vampire could tell he was speaking the truth.

"Then what are you doing here?" he demanded.

Levet released an exasperated sigh. There was not enough rum in the entire hotel to deal with this vampire as well as Inga, the pain-in-the-derrière ogress.

"I am doing as you commanded. Searching for the key."

Chiron stepped back, impatiently tapping the arrow against the side of his leg. For the first time, Levet noticed the blood that coated his torn shirt and the dirt that clung to the male's slacks.

He didn't appear anything like the immaculate, sophisticated vampire who'd left Vegas. Even his eyes were different. Softer. Distracted. As if...

Hmm.

"Have you discovered anything?" Chiron demanded.

Levet wrinkled his snout. "The magic is very fluid. It flows around me like water, constantly moving."

Surprisingly, Chiron didn't request a more specific explanation. Vampires had no understanding of magic, which meant they were forever demanding the most tedious details.

"Is it human?"

"The spell is human. The magic..." Levet shrugged. It was a question that nagged at him. "There is something unfamiliar about it."

Chiron's frustration layered the nearby mirror in frost. "This has to be the place."

Levet shivered. He'd spent the past months in the company of dragons who were forever spouting fire. Now he was back with vampires who made the air frigid. Why couldn't they leave the temperature alone?

"*Oui*," Levet agreed. "I believe the key might be hidden in the attic."

Chiron glanced toward the door that revealed the stairs leading to the upper floor.

"Then why aren't you searching for it?"

"Because that nasty ogress nearly ran me over," he complained. "Then she tossed me around as if I were a rag dummy."

"Rag dummy?" Chiron stared at him in confusion. "Do you mean a rag doll?"

Levet shrugged, suddenly distracted by the sound of approaching footsteps. "Someone is coming."

Chiron stiffened, his nose flaring as if he'd just caught the scent of something bewitching.

"Lilah." His eyes softened even more. "I'll distract her."

"Lilah?" Levet's wings perked up. There was nothing better than being diverted from his troubles by a female. "I want to meet her."

"No." The vicious word sliced through the air as Chiron sent him a warning frown. "I'll go. You stay here and find the key."

The vampire whirled and whizzed down the hall at a blurring speed. Levet stuck out his tongue. Why should he remain and continue the boring search? A gargoyle had needs.

First, he intended to find a few more bottles of rum, then he would make a quick journey to visit the local sprites. It was only polite to introduce himself to the native demons. And if they desired to have him spend an hour or two in their company, who was he to deny their request?

A gargoyle's work was never done.

Chapter 5

Lilah had grudgingly gone inside the hotel, but not because Chiron had commanded her to do so. She didn't take orders from guests. Not even a vampire who was gorgeous enough to make her blood sizzle with awareness.

It was just that she was as anxious as Chiron to discover who'd shot the arrow. Whether it'd been an accident or an intentional attempt to kill the vampire, it was unacceptable.

She searched through the public rooms, finding her fairy guests sipping nectar in the solarium. They were giggling and dancing around the fountains. It was doubtful any of them had raced back from taking a shot at Chiron.

Next, she found the lone Were who was returning from a run beneath the moonlight. She remained out of sight as he shifted into his human form and headed up the stairs to his room. It was possible he could have been responsible. Weres and vampires were natural enemies. But it seemed odd that he would sneak around and shoot an arrow from a hidden location. Weres weren't known for their devious personalities. They were raw and blunt and sometimes savage. If he wanted Chiron dead, it was more likely he would have shifted into his wolf form and tried to rip off the vampire's head.

She climbed the stairs to the second floor, passing by the rooms. The doors were all closed, but she could sense the newly mated imps in their room. She assumed she wouldn't see them until they decided to return home.

She moved on to the opposite wing, once again walking a long hallway. She was almost at the end when she heard the sound of voices above her. Pivoting on her heel, she hurried toward the staircase that led to the upper floor.

At the same time, there was a faint breeze as Chiron abruptly appeared in front of her.

With a startled gasp, she took an instinctive step backward. *Yeesh.* Vampires needed cowbells tied around their necks. They moved too fast for her eyes to track.

Heat stained her cheeks. She told herself it was because she'd jumped like a dew fairy at his sudden arrival. She was supposed to be a competent business owner who dealt with all sorts of demons. But she knew deep inside that her blush had nothing to do with embarrassment and everything to do with the excitement that sparkled through her like champagne.

It was unnerving.

She'd had hundreds of handsome demons stay at her hotel. Some of them so lovely they didn't look real. As if they were a vision sent down by some benevolent god. But this male...

He wasn't lovely. He was starkly male, with eyes that smoldered with a restless energy. His features were finely carved and his body leanly muscled. At the moment, he'd lost the glossy elegance he'd had earlier, but that only added a spice of danger.

Her heart skidded, as if it'd slipped on ice, then jerked back to beating at a pace that was way too fast.

Had the color in her cheeks deepened? Probably. The vampire could most certainly detect her thundering pulse. It was obvious in the glow of his eyes and the lengthening of his fangs.

Time for a distraction.

She glanced toward his wound, which looked like it had already healed. "Did you find who shot the arrow?"

His lips flattened. "No."

"I don't understand. I've had guests who have been in bloody brawls, and some who have magical abilities that can be dangerous when they're drunk, but none of them have tried to shoot anyone with an arrow."

"Tell me about your current guests."

Lilah frowned. This male might make her feel all ooey-gooey inside, but he was way too fond of tossing around orders.

"My guests have a right to privacy," she told him.

He lifted the hand that held the arrow. The tip was still stained with his blood.

"Even if they tried to kill me?"

An odd horror twisted her stomach. It'd been so close. Too close. If she hadn't spotted a shadow streaking toward them, the arrow might have gone straight through Chiron's heart.

He would have turned to a small pile of ash, and she would have…

Mourned.

Yes. That was the word.

But why? He was sexy, and charming when he wasn't being an ass, and he made her tingle in all the right places. Still, he was a stranger. One who was passing through, like all her guests.

So why did the thought of him dead make her feel almost sick?

A dangerous question she didn't want answered. Not now.

"I'll talk to them myself," she assured Chiron.

Without warning, he reached out to grasp her upper arm. Not hard. In fact, she could tell he was careful to keep his fingers from pressing into her flesh, as if he was afraid he might bruise her.

"No. I don't want you putting yourself in danger."

She blinked at his fierce response. Was he concerned for her? The thought was oddly endearing. But he was still trying to give her orders. That was a habit that needed to be nipped in the bud.

"It's my hotel," she reminded him in the tone she reserved for her most annoying guests. "And have you considered the possibility I was the target, not you?"

A sharp chill blasted through the air as Chiron's fingers tightened on her arm.

"If I thought someone meant to hurt you, I can promise every one of your guests and staff would already be dead."

Her lips parted in shock. "Chiron."

As if realizing he was way overreacting, Chiron dropped his hand and took a step back. His features smoothed into a charming mask, but his eyes continued to glow with a lethal power and his fangs were still peeking between his lips.

"Do you have any demons here who have never visited before?" he asked.

She gave a quick shake of her head. "No. There are only nine other guests besides yourself and the gargoyle. And they're all regulars."

"Any witches?"

She was baffled by his question. "Humans can't penetrate the barriers. They become lost in the swamps if they get near this place."

He nodded. "What about vampires?"

"There's a mated pair here, but they've been coming for years. Even Inga accepts them, and she hates vampires."

His lips curled at the mention of the half ogress. A fairly predictable reaction. Inga was an acquired taste.

"What do you know about your manager?"

Lilah furrowed her brow. He couldn't think Inga had tried to shoot him? The ogress might not be the most charming demon, but she'd been the only family Lilah had ever known. She'd raised her from a child and taught her every aspect of the hotel so that Lilah could run it with the same efficiency as her parents.

Which meant she knew the older female well enough to be certain she wouldn't go around shooting arrows at her guests. Even if they did happen to be vampires.

"I promise you, she's all bluff and no bite," Lilah assured her companion.

He glanced toward the ceiling, as if searching for something.

"I don't suppose you have security cameras?"

"No." She shrugged. It'd never occurred to her that they would need security. She had Inga to deal with any physical threats. Not even a rabid Were was stupid enough to take on an ogress. And the hotel was isolated enough to prevent any outside intruders. "Like I said, we've never had any problems here beyond the random destruction of my property."

He glanced down the corridor, lingering on the nearly invisible break in the wall where there was an opening to a hidden corridor.

"There are plenty of places for an unknown visitor to hide," he murmured, speaking more to himself than her.

Lilah stilled. He'd been furious when the attack had first happened. A perfectly reasonable response. Along with his determination to discover who had shot the arrow. But there was also a strange acceptance. As if it was no surprise that someone wanted him dead.

If she'd truly thought the arrow had been aimed in her direction, she would be a terrified mess.

"Why are you here?" she abruptly demanded. "And don't give me that nonsense about wanting to start your own demon hotel."

He paused, clearly debating how to answer. She'd noticed that before. Was he deciding whether he was going to lie to her?

"I'm searching for my master," he at last confessed.

She furrowed her brow. When he'd told her that he was some sort of rebel, she'd leaped to the conclusion that he didn't have a clan. That he was alone in the world, as she was.

Clearly, she'd been wrong.

"He's lost?" she demanded.

"Something like that."

He was being deliberately vague. Why? Did it have something to do with someone trying to kill him?

"And you think he's here?" she pressed. If there was something that might endanger her guests, she had a right to know.

"I think it's possible he was here."

"I can check the register book if you want."

He shook his head. "It would have been before you were born."

Lilah studied his pale face, sternly refusing to be mesmerized by his dark, compelling eyes. She was trying to make sense of why he would be at the hotel now if his master had left at least a century ago.

Then she remembered something he'd asked when they had been on the terrace. "Oh. That's why you were interested in my parents."

"Yes. I hoped there might be someone here who remembered the past."

Lilah remained confused. "Even if he stayed here, how would that help you find him now?"

He considered his answer. "It's possible he might have decided to live in the area," he finally said.

Hmm. Another vague answer. What was he hiding?

"Then why wouldn't he contact you?"

"As the leader of the Rebels, he was the enemy of the Anasso." There was an unmistakable edge in his voice. There was no denying the sincerity of his bitterness toward his fellow vampires. "He had no choice but to go into hiding."

"And now?"

A portion of his tension eased. "There's a new king. He came to Vegas to assure me that he has no interest in continuing the feud."

Lilah never traveled through the barrier. Not only because it was her duty to take care of the hotel, but because she didn't know just how vulnerable she might be away from the magic of her home. Still, she managed to keep up with the world. Not only did her guests love to share the latest gossip, but she had full access to modern technology.

She'd heard the rumors about Styx, the new Anasso. A few of the vampires had been critical. They admired his enormous power, but they were disappointed he didn't rule with the same iron fist of his predecessor. They assumed that made him weak. Most of the vampires, however, had been pleased by his ascension to the throne. He allowed them to exist in peace as long as they didn't harm another vampire.

Live and let live.

Which seemed like a good philosophy to Lilah.

"You believe him?" she asked.

Chiron grimaced. "I'm willing to give him a chance."

She suspected this vampire's trust was something very difficult to earn. Perhaps impossible.

That thought tightened her chest. What was happening to her? It was as if her emotions were going haywire. And not in a good way.

"So you're here to find your master and tell him it's safe?"

His jaw tightened. "I'm here to take him home."

Vampires were experts at hiding their feelings. Inga said it was because they didn't have any. But Lilah had no difficulty in sensing Chiron's intense need to find his master. "This means a lot to you."

"More than you can even imagine," he said.

Lilah released a small sigh. "Actually, I can imagine it quite easily. I would give anything for the opportunity to see my parents again."

His expression softened, his dark gaze sweeping over her face. "You don't remember anything about them?"

It was her turn to be vague. She didn't tell anyone that she had precious few memories. Especially from when she was young. A human would no doubt assume it was the trauma of being orphaned at such an early age that caused the fuzziness. And that was probably the cause, even for her. But it troubled her that she had no one to ask.

"To be honest, my childhood is pretty much a blur," she said, keeping her tone light.

Of course he wasn't fooled. Instead, he stepped forward and gently touched her face. She didn't know exactly what he was doing. Trying to read her mind? Whatever it was, he wasn't satisfied. At least, if his frown was any indication.

"I'm afraid I can't help with your parents," he reluctantly admitted.

She didn't ask what he thought he could do. They'd died nearly a century ago. And in truth, she didn't want to think about them. It gave her a strange, almost sickening dizziness when she tried to focus on the past.

It was easier to concentrate on the present.

"No, but I can assist in looking for your master," she assured Chiron.

Her soft words promptly stirred his protective instincts. His hand dropped as he gave a sharp shake of his head.

"Lilah, I appreciate your offer, but I'm not going to let you put yourself in danger."

She ignored his predictable attempt to give her an order. They would discuss that later. "What danger?"

"It's obvious someone doesn't want me to find my master."

"Why not?"

He grimaced, as if he regretted his impulsive words. Then he took a step backward, clearly intending to leave. "I don't know. Not yet."

She grabbed his arm. "What are you going to do?"

He shrugged. "Take a stroll around the estate. It's a lovely night."

She flattened her lips. Chiron had created an empire built on bright lights and excitement. He wasn't the sort of male who enjoyed peaceful walks in the middle of nowhere. "Why?"

"There's a chance I might find some clue to where my master is hidden," he smoothly responded.

"I don't believe you."

His lips twitched. "You say that a lot."

Actually, she never said it. Not until Chiron had arrived at her hotel.

"Because it's true," she said.

He pressed his hand to the center of his chest. "I assure you, all I intend to do is take a stroll."

"You're deliberately making yourself a target."

"Why would I do that?"

"To try to lure out whoever shot that arrow."

"If they're stupid enough to try again, I'm prepared to teach them what happens when you threaten a vampire."

She made a sound of annoyance. Males were all the same, no matter what the species.

"What if they don't miss this time?"

Without warning, he stepped close enough for her to feel his icy power wrap around her. His hand lowered to cover hers, still gripping his arm.

"Does the thought trouble you?"

She shivered. There was no way she was going to admit that the mere idea of him being hurt was sending a flutter of panic through the pit of her stomach.

"Of course it troubles me." She forced a stiff smile to her lips. "Having a guest murdered in my hotel isn't going to be good for business."

He wasn't fooled. Not even for a nanosecond. He bent downward, allowing his lips to hover perilously close to her mouth.

"And that's the only reason you're concerned?"

Over the years, Lilah had learned how to avoid unwelcome sexual advances. It had been a necessary skill, considering most males were attracted to her superficial beauty. She didn't take it as a compliment. Not one of those guests had been interested in her thoughts or feelings. She was just an added bonus to their vacation.

So why wasn't she moving away? Her brain was sending out all kinds of alarms, but her feet refused to budge. *Traitors.*

"Why else would I be concerned?" she forced herself to demand.

"Maybe this."

He lowered his head. Slowly enough that she had ample time to avoid his kiss. She didn't avoid it. Hell, she went on her tiptoes to hurry up the contact of his lips. When they finally met, she gasped.

Fireworks were supposed to be a metaphor when people kissed. A mythical promise from the poets that never really happened.

But they were real. And they were going off in her head like the humans' Fourth of July as their mouths connected and clung together. A groan lodged in her throat, her hands lifting to touch his chest. His skin was cool beneath the silk of his shirt, his muscles hard as steel. There was no heartbeat, but she had no doubt he was very much alive.

It was evident in the strength of his hands as they clutched her hips, and the intoxicating power that swirled around them. And the hardening bulge of his arousal.

They mutually pressed closer together as he used the tip of his tongue to part her lips, deepening the kiss.

Time had no meaning as Lilah became lost in the sensations that bombarded her body. Heat. Passion. Need. And a strange tenderness she didn't understand.

Chiron's hands ran a restless path up her body, as if he was equally stunned by the potent desire that sizzled between them. His lips moved to brush over her cheek and then traced her ear before he buried his face in the curve of her neck.

"Lilah," he whispered. "I like the smell of you."

A chuckle was wrenched from her throat. "Are you saying I smell?"

"Yes, and it's intoxicating," he growled, the tips of his fangs scraping against her skin to send a rash of excitement jolting through her. "Lush, warm female." He pressed a kiss to her collarbone. "And something else."

Warning bells clamored in her mind. "What?"

"I don't know what it is and it's driving me crazy," he murmured, misunderstanding her question.

Fear managed to pierce through her haze of pleasure. With a sharp movement, she jerked out of his arms and stumbled backward.

Chiron wasn't the first demon to sense her heritage was puzzling. She'd been asked a thousand times what sort of fey creature she was. And a thousand times she'd dodged the question.

It was something she didn't discuss. Not with anyone.

"I have..." She was forced to stop and clear the lump from her throat.

"You have what?"

"Things to do," she at last croaked, backing down the hallway.

"What things?" he demanded.

"You know. Things." She licked her dry lips. "Try not to get shot."

He watched her awkward retreat with a narrowed gaze. He had to know she was hiding something, but thankfully, he didn't demand an explanation. Instead, he folded his arms over his chest and smiled with a wry resignation.

"I'll do my best."

Feeling flushed and frustrated and wishing a big hole would open up and swallow her, Lilah turned and dashed away.

Why not?

She'd already made an idiot of herself. Might as well reveal she was a coward as well.

Chapter 6

Levet could have gone to the swamp to hunt for his food. No doubt there were alligators and snakes and all sorts of nasty, slimy things. Instead, he'd snuck into the kitchen and gorged on the meat pies he found on a tray in the pantry. He might be a demon, but he had the taste of a true connoisseur.

Then, with his belly full, he'd decided it was time to go in search of the water sprites.

Reaching the edge of the gardens, he'd paused to sniff the air when a tiny breeze stirred his wings. He frowned, glancing around. There was no wind. At least none that was moving the branches of the nearby trees.

Which meant the air was coming from below.

Instantly intrigued, Levet stooped over and wiggled his way into a nearby hedge. There was an odd chill before the illusion of bushes disappeared to reveal the narrow opening in the ground.

Ah. That was where the breeze was coming from.

Sniffing the air, Levet considered his various options.

He could turn around and resume his journey to the sprites. That would probably be the wisest choice. The fey might be fickle and cunning, but they were rarely violent. Even if the males did resent Levet's ability to charm the females.

Besides, what could be better than an evening sipping nectar while being entertained by a lovely sprite?

But when had Levet ever done the wisest thing?

Never.

The thoughts flitted through his brain as he moved forward and slipped into the hole. How could he leave without finding out what was in there? It would be like an itch he couldn't scratch. A thirst he couldn't quench.

Besides, the key might be hidden in the hole. He had to look.

Expecting to discover a small tunnel that an animal had burrowed, Levet was caught off guard when there was nothing below his feet but air.

"Arg!"

Plummeting downward at an alarming speed, Levet gave a desperate flap of his wings. A fall couldn't kill him, but it could hurt like all Hades.

He managed to slow his speed enough that he landed without causing any damage. There was, however, a cloud of dust that made him sneeze, and his eyes watered.

Wrinkling his snout, he held his wings high enough to avoid touching the ground and glanced around. What was this place?

The cavern was large and shaped like an octagon. The ceiling was carved into a dome. The walls had several openings he assumed led to tunnels. And in the very center was a large stone that was flat on top.

It looked like a sacrificial altar.

A nasty ball of dread settled in the pit of Levet's tummy as he moved forward. Why would a hotel have this hidden beneath it? Not that it looked like it'd been used recently. In fact, there was a thick layer of dust and cobwebs on top of the stone.

Forced to go on his tiptoes to see over the edge, Levet blew the dust away. He sneezed again, but he was able to see the runes that had been carved into the granite.

They looked fey with their flowing curves, but he couldn't read them. Strange. He leaned forward and sniffed. Then sniffed again. Salt? Why would there be salt down here?

"You."

Levet squeaked as he turned to confront the large female who was stepping out of a tunnel. Inga the ogress. How could he have failed to hear her approach? Her feet were as big as a barge.

She smirked at his startled reaction. Annoying female. Levet sniffed, tilting his chin to an arrogant angle.

"*Oui.* It is *moi.*" He spread his arms in a grand gesture. "You are welcome."

Her smirk was replaced with a scowl as she stomped forward. "What are you doing here?"

"I am enjoying my vacation."

"Down here?"

Levet shrugged. "I like dank, musty places. Although you might want to do something about the salty smell." He wrinkled his snout. "It is very impotent."

The female halted directly in front of him. "Potent, you idiotic creature, not impotent."

Levet clicked his tongue. Why were people forever correcting him? It was quite irritating. "It is all the same."

"No, it's not," she argued. "One means this." She lifted her hand and stuck up her first finger. It was as thick as a tree branch. She allowed the finger to curl down to touch her palm. "And one means this." She straightened her finger.

Oh. Levet gave a flap of his wings. "I assure you I am potent. *Très* potent."

She shrugged, as if indifferent to the fact that she'd just insulted his manhood. Instead, she planted her hands on her hips, tightening her dress. Levet shuddered. It was hideous.

"This area is off-limits," she snapped.

"You said the attics were off-limits."

"They are."

Levet made a sound of impatience. "I do not believe you have a full understanding of what it means to own a hotel," he informed the ogress. "If you wish to lock your guests in their rooms, you should run a dungeon."

"We have several."

Levet blinked in confusion. "Guests?"

"Dungeons, you dolt."

Levet's tail twitched as his curiosity once again consumed him. First this hidden chamber with a sacrificial altar, and now dungeons. This place became more and more fascinating by the minute.

"Truly?"

"I can show you." The ogress spread her lips to reveal her pointed teeth. Was that a smile? She gestured toward a tunnel across the chamber. "They're down there."

Levet wanted to see them. He really, really did. But while he might be impulsive, he wasn't stupid. When someone offered to show you their dungeons, it usually ended up badly.

"*Non.* This is a trick," he said.

"It's no trick. I assure you there are dungeons."

Levet shook his head, diverting his curiosity to the faint accent he could detect in the ogress's words.

"Where are you from?" he abruptly demanded.

It was her turn to be caught off guard. "Excuse me?"

"Ogres are not native to this country. Most were brought here as slaves."

The female sucked in a sharp breath, her eyes flashing red. "I'm no slave."

"But you were one." Levet moved forward, reaching out to touch her hand. A small burst of power broke through the magic that hid the ugly markings that were branded into the skin of her inner wrist. "Ah."

Inga hissed, jerking her hand from his touch. "Stop that," she snarled.

Levet tilted back his head to study her face. There was anger flashing in her eyes that had gone completely red, but he didn't miss the hint of vulnerability that she couldn't hide.

His tender heart melted. No one deserved to be captured and branded and sold like an animal.

"There is nothing to be ashamed of," he assured her. "I was once held in a slave pen. I was to be auctioned off, before I was rescued by a friend."

She puffed out her chest, her face turning a dark purple that clashed with her dress. "I'm not a slave."

Levet rolled his eyes. *Touchy, touchy, touchy.* Did she believe people would think less of her because she'd been branded?

"I am not judging you," he assured her. "Most of my favorite demons have once been held captive."

Her expression was defensive. "As if I care what you think."

Levet moved closer, brushing his claws over her brand. "Tell me what happened."

She thrust out her jaw, clearly intending to offer a belligerent comment. Then, without warning, she turned her head, blinking rapidly. Was she fighting back tears?

"My mother was captured by a horde of ogres," she finally muttered. "She sold me to the slavers the day I was born."

"*Pauvre bébé.*" Levet clicked his tongue. It should have been a shocking story. Unfortunately, it was one he had heard a hundred times. Demons could be cruel, even to their own offspring. "Who bought you?"

There was a long, painful pause. Levet sensed the ogress wanted to punch him. Or perhaps she was considering the pleasure of tossing him against the wall again. For some reason, demons tended to have extremely violent tendencies when he was around. It was baffling.

But his words had touched a wound that had been festering for a very long time. There came a point where you had to release the poison or be consumed by it.

"First I went to the trolls," she harshly admitted.

Levet's wings drooped. The trolls were vicious creatures who enjoyed inflicting pain. "Were you abused?"

"No more than any other slave." Her words were clipped, warning that she wasn't going to offer any details of the brutality she'd suffered.

"While I was small they used me to squeeze through mine shafts to dig for rubies in Asia."

Levet nodded. He detested trolls. Nasty vermin.

"And after you were no longer small?" he asked.

Her jaw clenched and unclenched as she tried to keep her emotions tightly leashed. At the same time, he caught her light scent. It was clean and sharp. Like wind blowing over the ocean. The female had fey blood running through her veins, he silently acknowledged. Levet sucked in a deeper breath, oddly captivated by the scent.

"They sold me to a goblin who used me as a part of his crew. We traveled from Asia to pillage the gold from the Aztecs," she said.

Well, that explained how she'd gotten to this side of the world. Goblins were like demon Vikings. They used slaves to row their heavy wooden boats from one country to another, pillaging and raping as they went.

"What happened to him?" Levet asked.

"He was killed."

Levet felt a stab of satisfaction. Then he gave a sudden snap of his fingers. There was only one Aztec he knew who would have been capable of killing a full-grown goblin.

"I bet it was Styx," Levet said, easily able to imagine the towering vampire striding through the jungles to rip off the head of an invader.

Inga frowned. "Who?"

"Never mind." Levet gave a wave of his hand. "Was he your last master?"

There was the faintest pause before the female gave a nod of her head.

"Yes. Once he was dead I was free."

Levet sniffed. The female was a skilled liar, but he was beginning to learn her tell. It was the twitch at the top of her pointy ear.

"*Non.* There was more to your story."

Inga went rigid, clearly annoyed that she'd been lured into exposing her past.

"Enough." She sliced her hand through the air, creating a whistling sound. "Leave this place."

Levet pouted. He thought they'd made a connection. Hadn't they both survived painful childhoods? And didn't they both have to deal with the prejudices of others who did not always appreciate the beauty to be found in demons who were different?

Perhaps it was simply because she didn't know that he had not always been the knight in shining armor who was adored by women around the world.

"Do you not wish to hear the story of my childhood?" he demanded. "It is quite fascinating."

"No." Leaning down, she reached out, as if to grab him by his wing. "Leave."

"Hey." Levet scrambled backward. His poor wing was still tender from the last time she'd abused him. "I will not be tossed around like a—"

His words were forgotten as he tripped over something poking out of the hard dirt floor.

"Oof."

He landed on his derrière with a thump. Grimacing in pain, he reached beneath his injured backside to pull out the culprit that had caused him to fall. It was the size of his hand and hard as a rock, but there were ridges in the smooth material and a shimmer even in the darkness of the cave.

"Oh, a seashell. Why is that here?"

His lips parted as he was struck by a distant memory. It'd been shortly after he'd been tossed out of his home and was roaming through Asia. He'd discovered a cavern near the Sea of China that had shells stuck in the ground and the scent of salt in the air. Scrambling to his feet, he turned toward the altar.

"Wait. I know who made those runes," he said in smug tones. He truly was a clever demon. A shame he was not fully appreciated. Intending to reveal his astonishing depth of knowledge, Levet was halted when a ruthless hand grabbed him by the horn and started dragging him across the cavern. "Arg. What are you doing?"

"I tried to be nice," Inga muttered, taking giant-size steps that had them entering one of the tunnels with remarkable speed.

"Nice?" Levet reached up to try to pry her fingers off his horn, his wings flapping. It was hopeless. The female had the grip of a steel vise. A talent that might have been fun in the right circumstances. This, however, was most certainly not the right circumstances. "You are an ill-tempered brute."

She never slowed as they reached a long flight of steps that led even deeper into the earth.

"I didn't want to do this," she said, dragging him down the stairs.

Bang, bang, bang. His heels hit each step, jarring him until he feared his brains might be scrambled.

"Do what?" he demanded as they finally reached the bottom of the stairs and he heard a squeak of a rusty hinge. Turning his head, he peeked over his shoulder to discover they were standing next to a heavy steel door. "Hey, there really is a dungeon."

"Yes." Without warning, Inga swung him around her legs and tossed him through the opening. Levet arced through the air, giving a sharp flap of his wings to prevent yet another painful landing. The door was closing before he ever hit the floor. "I'm sorry," Inga called through the small slit in the middle of the door.

Levet scurried forward, wondering if this was some annoying prank. Ogres did have an odd sense of humor.

"Let me out."

"I can't have you babbling about what you've seen to your vampire friend," the female said.

Levet skidded to a halt, his mouth gaping open. Of course. He had been so stupid. The truth had been staring him in the ear since they'd arrived at the hotel. Wait. Not ear. Face. *Oui*. Staring him in the face.

"You're the one responsible for hiding the key," he accused in sharp tones.

"I'm protecting it," the female argued.

"Fah." Levet tried to decipher the heavy sensation that was making his wings droop. It wasn't fear. Even if he was locked in the dungeon, he could feel the faint breeze that tugged at his wings. Which meant there had to be a way out. *Non*. This was something else. Something that felt disturbingly like disappointment. As if he was bothered by the thought that Inga was the bad guy. He shook his head, trying to dismiss the ludicrous thought. "Did you shoot the arrow at Chiron?"

"I just wanted to frighten him away."

Levet snorted. The ogress clearly hadn't spent much time with vampires if she thought anything could frighten them. They were the most stubborn, irrational of creatures.

"We will not harm the key," he told the female. "Once Chiron has freed his master, you can have it back."

"You don't understand."

"What is there to understand? You give us the key. We free the stupid vampire. Then hand it back to you. Wham. Bam. Buy a ham."

There was the sound of a frustrated sigh. "What?"

Was the female hard of hearing? Levet forced himself to speak in slow, concise tones.

"You give us the key. Free the vampire. And we leave. Simple."

"There is nothing simple about it," Inga told him.

Levet parted his lips to continue the argument, only to snap them together as he heard the sound of her huge feet stomping back up the stairs.

He'd been abandoned.

Heaving an exasperated sigh, he turned to inspect his latest prison.

It was barren, like all good dungeons should be. Stone walls. Stone ceiling. Dirt floor. There were a few ancient torture devices scattered around the large space. None of them looked like they'd been used in the past couple of centuries. Thank the goddess.

Aggravated with the ogress, and himself for being blind to the female's devious nature, he crossed the room and tilted back his head. He could feel the faint breeze coming from a crack in the wall that was hidden beneath a layer of spiderwebs. This would be his way out. Sadly, it looked as if he was going to have to dig through several feet of stone. That meant he would never be out of there before morning dawned. A pain, because he couldn't step into the sunlight or he would be turned to stone.

Unless there was a tunnel leading to the hotel, he was stuck there for at least the next twenty-four hours.

Mon Dieu.

This was the worst vacation ever.

* * * *

It was late afternoon in Vegas. That weird time when the day crowd was filtering out of the casinos and the night crowd hadn't arrived yet.

Usually, Ulric used this opportunity to do a walk-through of the property. He checked hotel rooms to make sure they were being properly cleaned, and then he headed downstairs. Despite having a French chef who cost them a fortune, along with a professional waitstaff, he'd discovered that nothing kept a kitchen running more smoothly than the fear that Ulric might discover something that didn't meet his high standards. And last, he would make a sweep of the casino.

He'd just finished his inspection of the rooms when he was interrupted by one of his guards.

"Excuse me, sir."

Ulric studied the man with a lift of his brows. No one bothered him during his walk-through unless it was an emergency.

"What is it?"

The guard leaned forward, speaking in a low voice. "I was reviewing the security film from the high rollers room, and we have trouble."

"What sort of trouble?"

"I caught one of the dealers stealing chips from a customer."

Furious, Ulric released a low growl. Around him, the air prickled with the heat of his wolf, and he turned his head to keep the guard from seeing the golden glow in his eyes. Working with humans meant he couldn't shift into his animal form and hunt down the bastard. Instead, he had to pretend to be civilized.

"Have him brought to Chiron's office," he commanded, turning to head toward the private bank of elevators.

In less than ten minutes, John Mayfield was being escorted into the penthouse suite. Motioning the guard to leave, Ulric had his fingers around the man's throat and shoved him against the floor-to-ceiling window before the door closed.

In the back of his mind, there was a warning voice that whispered he was overreacting. But it was a voice he easily ignored.

He'd been on edge for hours; now he at last had a productive way to release his frustration. As long as he was capable of keeping his wolf leashed, it was all good. Right?

"Stop, please." The slender human made a gasping sound as he reached up to grasp Ulric's thick wrists. His eyes were bloodshot, as if he'd been crying, his brown hair mussed. He looked pathetic, but Ulric didn't give a shit.

This man had just threatened everything he and Chiron had worked to build.

"How much did you steal?"

"Just a few chips," he rasped.

Ulric growled deep in his chest. The office was filled with the musk of his wolf, but John wouldn't be able to detect it. Not when the stench of his human sweat clung to the air.

"How much?" he repeated.

The man trembled, his heart thundering so loudly, Ulric could hear each frantic beat. John Mayfield might not realize he was in the hands of a Were, but he easily sensed his life was hanging in the balance.

"A hundred." He squeaked as Ulric's fingers tightened. "All right, maybe two hundred."

"When did you start?"

John released a whimper, his face turning a strange shade of blue. "Tonight was the first time ever. I swear."

"Why?"

"My kid is sick and I needed to get some medicine." His voice was harsh with a sincerity he couldn't fake. "The shit costs almost four hundred dollars."

Ulric released his breath with an angry hiss. Chiron might be a demon, but he treated his staff like family. Which was why they had the best, most loyal workers in all of Vegas.

"And you didn't think about asking for an advance on your salary?" Ulric demanded. "Or hell, just asking for some extra cash? When have you ever been told no?"

"I wasn't thinking at all. I was scared out of my mind that my kid…" The man's words ended with a gurgle.

At the same time, Ulric was distracted by the sound of the door opening. He didn't have to turn his head to know who'd entered the private office. A sudden breeze stirred, brushing against him like a physical caress.

Rainn was a rare zephyr sprite, capable of manipulating the air around her. She'd walked out of the desert and into the casino twenty years before. She never talked about her past, or why she'd chosen Chiron to become her new master, and no one pressed her for answers. At Dreamscape Resorts, a person was judged by their competence in their job, and their willingness to work together to forge a better future for everyone.

"Sorry to interrupt your fun, Ulric," the female said in cool tones. "But I need to speak with you."

Keeping his fingers around the dealer's throat, Ulric glanced over his shoulder at the intruder.

Rainn was surprisingly short for a sprite, although she had the usual slender curves and delicate features. Her hair was glossy black and cut in a straight line at her shoulders. Her wide eyes were a misty gray. Her skin was as soft and dewy as a peach and her lips a luscious temptation. She was exquisite, but Ulric never allowed her beauty to blind him.

He knew that beneath her beauty was a spine of steel. This female wouldn't hesitate to kill if she thought it necessary.

"I'm a little busy," he said between clenched teeth.

She strolled forward. She was wearing her usual uniform of a tailored black jacket and matching slacks. Her shoes were black and low-heeled. She dressed to look professional, but the severity of her clothes only emphasized her feminine appeal.

Something he'd cut out his tongue before he'd admit.

"I can see that. Let's talk." She offered him a humorless smile. "Now."

Ulric bristled at her tone, pulling back his lips to bare his teeth. "I told you, I'm busy."

Her gaze flicked toward the terrified dealer. "Pack your things and get out, Mayfield."

Ulric released a warning growl. Rainn could be bossy, but she wasn't stupid. She knew he was in charge while Chiron was gone. "Don't interfere."

Shockingly, Ulric felt the air around him begin to thicken, pressing against him until he couldn't move.

Rainn waved a hand toward the wary human. "Go."

Trapped by the bands of air, Ulric could do nothing to halt John as he cautiously inched along the wall of windows. Then, realizing he had a shot at freedom, he made a mad dash out the door.

The second he was out of sight, Ulric felt the pressure fade. With a snarl of anger, he spun around to glare at the sprite.

"Are you challenging me?"

Rainn held his gaze without flinching, her expression calm. Not much rattled the female. Not even a pureblood Were having a temper tantrum.

"If necessary."

"What the hell is going on?"

"That's what I was going to ask you."

Ulric jutted out his lower jaw. She was eyeing him in a way that made him feel like a...like a damned drama queen.

"He was caught stealing from our customers," he snapped, goaded into justifying his behavior. "Do you know what would happen to this casino if word got out that our staff are a bunch of thieves? We'd be bankrupt in less than a month."

"I took care of it."

His brows snapped together. "How?"

She shrugged. "I returned the money and wiped the memories of the guests who witnessed the stealing," she told him. Along with her talent to manipulate air, Rainn also had the ability to scrub short-term memories from humans. One of the primary reasons she was such a valuable employee. It wasn't something they used very often, but there were times when a customer possessed the innate ability to detect a portion of the staff wasn't human. "They'll wake with a headache, but they won't recall anything that happened tonight."

It was, of course, the most efficient way of handling the problem. But not nearly as satisfying. Ulric folded his arms over his chest, still scowling.

"He needs to be punished."

"Agreed, but stealing a couple hundred bucks shouldn't be a death sentence." She tilted her head to the side, studying him with a curiosity that was thankfully without judgment. "You might be a wolf, but you're not an animal. What's going on?"

Ulric released a heavy sigh, lifting his hand to rub the stiff muscles of his neck. "I'm worried about Chiron."

A sudden breeze swept through the room, the only indication Rainn was troubled by his words.

"Has something happened to him?"

He clenched his jaw, frustration churning through him. "I don't know."

Rainn stepped toward him. "Ulric?"

Ulric reached to pull his cell phone out of the front pocket of black slacks he'd matched with a crisp white shirt. When the boss was away, Ulric forced himself to try to appear civilized. Instinctively, he glanced at the screen. It was the same thing he'd done a hundred times since Chiron left town.

"I expected him to check in last night," he said. "You know how he is when he's away from the office."

Rainn snorted. "He's a pain in the ass. When the two of you went to Hong Kong last month, he called me every ten minutes. I spent two weeks with the phone permanently attached to my ear."

"So why no calls?" Ulric demanded. "Not one."

Concern darkened her eyes to a smoky gray. "Have you tried to contact him?"

Ulric made a sound of impatience. He'd been blowing up Chiron's phone for the past twenty-four hours. "A hundred times."

"No answer?"

"Nope. Straight to voice mail."

She glanced toward the door that connected to the inner sanctum of Chiron's office. Her brow furrowed, the breeze continued to swirl through the room.

It was a rare display of emotion, and Ulric wondered if the mysterious female had feelings for her employer. He hoped not. Chiron had a long history of breaking women's hearts without even trying.

"I'm not sure exactly what he's doing, but I assume it must be important," she said.

Ulric swallowed a growl. He was still pissed that Chiron had taken off without him. "He seems to think so."

"Then it's possible he's too preoccupied to call."

"Maybe."

She narrowed her gaze, studying him with an unnerving intensity.

"What's really bothering you, Ulric?"

He glowered at his companion. What the hell did she think was wrong? Their master was missing. Wasn't that enough to have him upset?

Then, he grimaced. Deep inside he knew what was gnawing at him. He was afraid Chiron had found Tarak and forgotten all about Ulric and his life in Vegas. Not that he was going to admit his petty, childish fear. Not to anyone.

"I'm afraid he's walking into a trap," he said instead.

Rainn didn't bother to ask for details. She accepted Ulric had reason to be concerned. Instead, she squared her shoulders as if preparing to take action.

"Do you know where Chiron is?"

"Florida," Ulric said. He'd been relieved when Chiron had left in one of the cars owned by the casino instead of his private vehicle. That meant Ulric could keep constant track of his movements.

Rainn nodded. "That's a long drive. Do you want me to have the jet fired up?"

Ulric arched a brow. "I was ordered to stay here."

She snorted, well aware Ulric had his own brand of loyalty. He would die to protect Chiron, but he didn't obey commands blindly. Not if he thought they interfered with his ability to fulfill his pledge to guard the male who'd saved his life.

"An hour?" she asked.

"Make it a half hour," he commanded, a sense of relief jolting through him. Sitting around and hoping everything was okay wasn't his style. He needed to find out what was going on. Tonight. Of course, he couldn't entirely forget his duties. "You'll be in charge while I'm gone," he warned.

A slow, dangerous smile curved her lips. "Fine, but I want my paycheck to reflect my extra duties."

Ulric rolled his eyes. Rainn had many talents, but perhaps her finest was her ability to squeeze every penny from her employer. It wasn't greed. She would never cheat or steal. It was more a game where money was the score.

"A grand?" he offered.

"Hmm." She wrinkled her slender nose. "I did several mind wipes and kept you from committing a murder that would have brought in the human police. Always a pain."

"Two thousand?"

Her smile widened. "Why don't we round it up to five thousand?"

Ulric flinched. Chiron was going to shit when he found out what she was demanding.

"You drive a hard bargain, Rainn."

She gave a lift of her hands. "Take it or leave it."

"I'll take it." He headed toward the door.

He'd worry about the cost later. Right now, nothing mattered but finding Chiron.

Chapter 7

Chiron woke the next evening with a sharp sense of dissatisfaction.

It might have been caused by the fact that he'd wasted so much time and was still no closer to finding the key. Or the fact that he'd searched the grounds around the hotel from one end to another and found nothing to indicate who'd taken a shot at him. Or even the realization that the stupid gargoyle wasn't in the room when he woke.

Yep, it might have been any of those things. But when he stepped out of the hotel to glimpse Lilah sitting on a bench at the edge of the garden, he knew precisely what was causing the nagging frustration.

His mood instantly lightened, his feet drawn by pure instinct across the terrace and along the paved pathway. He couldn't resist joining the lovely female. And in truth, he didn't even try.

As he neared, his hunter's eyesight could read the title of the book she was engrossed in.

Shakespeare's sonnets.

He smiled. He liked the thought she was a helpless romantic. He also liked the sight of her sitting as still and lovely as the orchids that surrounded her.

She possessed the lush, peaceful beauty of the gardens. As if she was a part of the magic. And perhaps she was.

"*Who is the maid with silken hair*
By clear Maine Water roaming?
For the fairy Queen is not so fair
As she in the lonely gloaming,'" he quoted in soft tones.

Lilah gave a small gasp as she jerked up her head. Clearly, she'd been too preoccupied with her book to realize she was no longer alone in the garden.

"You like poetry?" she demanded, not bothering to hide her surprise that he might enjoy something besides killing and maiming.

"I'm not a complete heathen," he assured her.

She blushed. "I never thought you were."

He moved to settle on the bench beside her. Close enough to feel her body grow rigid at the brush of his hip against hers.

"I sense your wariness," he told her. "Is it because I'm a vampire?"

She blinked, as if offended by his words. "Of course not. I don't have Inga's prejudices."

"Good."

A silence settled between them, their eyes locked together. At the same time, the air sizzled with an awareness that was tangible.

Lilah's blush deepened, her eyes shimmering with hints of gold in the moonlight.

Delectable.

"Did you find anything of interest during your stroll last night?" she abruptly asked, breaking the sensual spell that was wrapping around them.

He resisted the urge to take advantage of the smoldering hunger he could sense burning inside her. She was too skittish for him to press. He needed to let her take things at her own pace.

"Nothing," he admitted, recalling the frustration that had blasted through him as he'd circled the extensive grounds around the hotel and even probed through the wetlands.

He'd caught the scent of sprites and fairies and even the stupid gargoyle, but none of them had led to the roof of the building. Which meant it had to be one of the guests or staff who'd taken the shot at him.

"Perhaps whoever it was ran away," she suggested. "They would know you're searching for them."

He curved his lips into a smile. No reason to share that he suspected someone in the hotel. "Perhaps."

"Hmm." She wasn't fooled. "You think they're still here."

"If they are, I'll deal with them." He shrugged, eager to distract her. "Tonight I'm on a different mission."

She studied him, almost as if afraid to ask. "What's that?"

"I'm searching for Levet," he told her.

Something that might have been relief fluttered over her face. "The gargoyle?"

"Yes. He didn't return to our room. Have you seen him?"

She shook her head. "No, but Inga has. She complained earlier that he'd stolen an entire tray of meat pies and she chased him into the swamps."

Chiron rolled his eyes. On their journey to Florida, Levet had pillaged food from every bakery and farmhouse they'd passed. For such a tiny thing, the creature had the appetite of a full-grown troll.

"That sounds about right," he muttered, wondering where the creature had spent the daylight hours. And, more importantly, why the hell he wasn't busy searching for the key. "Irritating chunk of granite."

She tilted her head to the side. "If you find him irritating, why would you travel with him?"

"A debt to an old friend," he smoothly answered.

"He must be a very good friend."

The familiar ache pulsed in the center of Chiron's soul. He'd never considered Tarak a friend. He'd been his leader, his teacher, and the only family he'd ever had.

"He's like a father to me," he said in low tones.

She heaved a small sigh. "I can understand that."

Unable to resist temptation, Chiron reached to trace her lower lip with the tip of his finger. He didn't want to hurt her. Hell, that was the last thing he wanted to do. But he needed to know the truth about her past.

Not just because it might unravel the reason the witch's spell had led him to this location. But because...

Chiron grimaced. He didn't want to consider the fact that he wanted to know every intimate detail about this female because there was a voice whispering in the back of his mind that she was more than a passing acquaintance.

Much, much more.

"Lilah."

She trembled beneath his light touch. "Yes?"

"Tell me who you are."

He heard her breath catch at his soft question. "An owner of a demon hotel in the middle of the Everglades," she said. "Pretty boring."

"I didn't ask what you did. I asked who you are."

"Nobody."

He continued to stroke his finger over her mouth, his fangs lengthening in anticipation. He ached to taste her. No. It was more than that. He ached to *consume* her.

"That's not true," he argued. "'*Shall I compare thee to a summer's day? Thou art more lovely and more temperate....*'"

"No," she interrupted, sending him a scowl. "You're cheating."

He chuckled, savoring the small tremble of her lips. She could pretend annoyance, but her reaction to his touch was pure lust.

"Why?" he asked.

"I love poetry."

He leaned forward, allowing his fingers to trail down the curve of her neck. "Tell me who you are."

She swept her lashes downward, hiding her expressive eyes. "I can't."

Chiron allowed the tips of his fingers to linger over the pulse that raced at the base of her throat. "Can't? Or won't?"

"Can't," she breathed.

"Look at me," Chiron entreated.

She gave a sharp shake of her head. "I might be isolated here, but even I know better than to gaze into the eyes of a vampire."

His fingers skimmed up her neck, cupping her chin so he could tilt back her head.

"I'm not attempting to compel you," he assured her. Compulsion was a trick used by vampires to lure humans into being willing prey. There were also a few vampires who could use it on demons.

"Then what do you want?" she demanded.

"The truth." He waited for her to reluctantly lift her lashes. "Please, Lilah."

"There is no truth," she muttered.

He held her gaze, his powers still strangely muffled. Not that he intended to force his way into her mind.

He told himself it was because he had to earn her trust. If she realized what he was doing, she might very well throw him out, and the opportunity to find the key would be lost. Once she understood he wasn't a threat, he could try to convince her to allow him to peer into her thoughts.

Perfectly reasonable and not at all self-delusional. Right?

"Truth is the only certainty in this world. It is stubborn and unwavering, even if others, or yourself, try to bury it beneath a fog of lies," he said, speaking as much to himself as to his companion.

"A poet and a philosopher." She tried to sound mocking, but he was acutely aware of her vulnerability.

His heart twisted. She was so unbearably young and innocent. And he was so old and cynical. The knowledge should have horrified him. Instead, it only intensified his craving for her.

"No, I'm just a male who's survived long enough to appreciate the finer things in life," he told her, his gaze lingering on the earthy beauty of her features.

She trembled, but even as his head started to lower, she was abruptly surging to her feet.

"All right. The truth is, I don't know what I am," she confessed in harsh tones.

Chiron lifted himself off the bench, unnerved by his inability to resist the impulse to reach out and grasp her hand. As if he was being manipulated by a force beyond his control.

Magic? No. Something far more dangerous.

Fate.

He hurriedly slammed shut the door on his disturbing thoughts. There was nothing he could do to halt the inexorable tug of awareness between them. Nothing except try to concentrate on more important things.

"You don't know anything about your heritage?" he pressed.

"No."

"What about Inga?" He studied her tense expression. He didn't need his powers to know she was telling the truth. She knew nothing about her dead family. "Surely she recognized the species of your parents?"

She shrugged. "She told me they were both mongrels. That's why they were willing to hire a half-breed as a nanny."

Chiron frowned. Mongrels weren't unusual in the demon world. But it was odd that Inga hadn't been able to determine their bloodline.

Was it possible the female was hiding something?

"That's all?" he demanded.

Her wary expression returned. "Does it matter?"

It should. Unless Levet managed to locate the key with his dubious skills, Chiron needed information about the past to determine where it might be hidden.

But even as the knowledge seared through his mind, he was stepping forward. At the same time, his fingers trailed up her arm and over her shoulder.

"No. It doesn't matter," he said in husky tones, his curiosity captured as her thick curls brushed the back of his hand. "Your hair is damp."

"I just finished my bath," she explained.

"In the swamp?"

"Not quite." Her lips twitched at his horror, then, taking a step back, she motioned toward a dark corner of the garden. "Would you like to see?"

A flare of excitement raced through him. There was a hint of uncertainty in her voice that told him she rarely shared her secret place. Not with anyone.

"Very much," he said, readily following her as she pivoted to lead him toward the shadowed spot between two towering cypress trees. They paused, and he peered into the darkness with a sudden grimace. He was a vampire who'd lived in the desert for the past fifty years. The sight of black mud and slimy moss wasn't particularly appealing. Clearly he should have left his expensive leather shoes at home. "It looks...boggy."

She chuckled, reaching for his hand. "It's magic. Come with me."

Chiron hissed, his fangs throbbing as her simple touch sent a rash of electric awareness dancing over his skin. He didn't know a damned thing about magic, but he knew he was being trapped ruthlessly in this female's sensual spell.

Right now, he couldn't make himself care.

In fact, he was an eager participant.

An icy chill raced over his skin, and once again, he caught the strange scent of salt. What the hell? On the point of asking Lilah if the bog had access to the ocean, he was distracted as the sticky mud and moss were suddenly replaced by a white marble grotto.

His brows arched as they climbed the shallow steps and passed through the fluted columns towering twelve feet in the air. Most astonishing, a spill of bright sunlight surrounded the grotto, as if it was noon instead of midnight.

Chiron instinctively flinched before accepting the golden glow was a part of the illusion. Amazing.

Entranced by the light he hadn't seen in a millennium, Chiron allowed Lilah to lure him toward the center of the grotto, where a rectangular square was cut into the marble floor. It was filled with impossibly blue water sparkling in invitation.

He moved to study the statues, which had clearly been carved by the hand of an extraordinary artist. There were both male and female marble figures in flowing gowns with their hands outstretched toward the water.

"Did you create it?" he asked, his tone hushed. There was an atmosphere of peace in the grotto that touched even his jaded soul.

She smiled, obvious pleasure on her face as she glanced around the open space. "No. It must have been the original builders. I couldn't see through the illusion until Inga brought me here."

He turned to study his companion. If Inga had only been at the hotel for a brief time before the death of Lilah's family, how had she known about this place? As far as he knew, ogres had no talent for sensing illusions.

"Inga," he murmured. "I think I might need to have a few words with her."

Lilah snorted, clearly amused by the thought of him trying to have a conversation with the large, ill-tempered ogress.

"I wouldn't suggest it. Not unless you're willing to risk another brush with death."

He stepped toward her. "I thought you claimed she didn't murder your guests."

"As long as they leave her alone." She gave a lift of her hands. "If you start forcing your company on her, I make no promises. Her temper can be very ogrelike when she's provoked."

He shrugged. Inga might be dangerous to most demons, but she was no match for a vampire. Not unless she had some devious traps set around the hotel.

He had every intention of cornering the female before the night was over, but for now, he wanted to enjoy a brief moment of solitude with Lilah.

Taking a step toward her, Chiron was caught off guard when the water suddenly began to spin in the middle of the pool and then shot upward in a spray of droplets that glittered like diamonds.

"This is stunning."

"It's my favorite place," she told him with a small, satisfied sigh. "I could stay here and never leave."

The water settled back into the pool, and Chiron turned his head to study Lilah's delicate profile. He appreciated her love for her home, but he didn't like the thought that she preferred to stay here forever.

Especially if it meant she would be here without him.

"It's magical, but there are other beautiful places beyond the Everglades," he told her.

She turned to meet his gaze. "Any particular location?"

"Vegas. Monte Carlo." He shrugged. "Paris."

Her lips curled into a grin, amusement sparkling in her eyes. "Isn't that where your resorts are?"

Bewitched by the sight of her rare smile, Chiron moved to stand mere inches from her. Her scent filled his senses, heating his blood so it started to flow to parts of his body that tingled and hardened in reaction.

"A few of them," he admitted. "You should visit."

"Hmm." She pretended to consider his suggestion. "Perhaps I will. One day."

Chiron wasn't satisfied. He didn't want vague promises. He wanted to know beyond a shadow of a doubt that he would see Lilah strolling through his casino while he worked, and sharing his bed when he slept.

The realization rocked through him, making it feel as if the ground had just shifted beneath his feet.

He reached up, framing her face in his hands. "When?"

She stood quietly beneath his touch, the sound of her racing heartbeats a sweet melody to his ears.

"I'm not sure," she breathed.

"Soon?"

"I…" Clearly sensing he wasn't going to be satisfied until she agreed to his demands, she gave a slow nod. "Yes, soon."

"Do you promise?"

She licked her dry lips. "I've never traveled away from here."

His gaze was locked on her damp mouth. It looked as luscious and edible as a ripe berry. "I swear you'll be safe in my hands."

"I'm sure I'll be protected," she murmured, "but I'm not sure I'll be safe."

"I'm not going to pretend I don't want you," he rasped.

He heard her suck in a sharp breath. "As dinner?"

"I want to nibble you from head to toe and everywhere in between," he said, taking a step forward, and then another. He was subtly herding her toward a nearby column. "I want to run my fingers through your hair, and savor the sweetness of your lips. I want to strip away your robe and run my hands over your naked body. And I want to feel my fangs sliding into your flesh as I sip your blood."

She made a strangled sound as her back hit the marble column.

"Dangerous," she muttered.

"More dangerous than I ever imagined possible," he agreed, wondering if she felt the same tug of destiny.

She shivered. "Chiron."

He allowed his gaze to skim over her face. Her honey skin was luminous in the faux sunlight, and her eyes were pools of molten gold.

Stunning.

"I'm beginning to understand the allure of staying in this spot and never leaving," he told her. "It's like the world outside doesn't exist. In here, it's just the two of us."

Their gazes locked, awareness pulsing in the air between them.

Then, as if unnerved by the sheer intensity of their mutual passion, Lilah lifted a hand to press it against the center of his chest.

"You'll soon be bored and ready to leave."

He frowned. Was she trying to convince him or herself? "How can you be so sure?"

"You have a business to run."

He did, of course. And under normal circumstances, he refused to spend more than a few hours away from the office. And that was when he was traveling from one resort to another.

A successful business empire didn't happen by accident.

Since arriving at the hotel, however, he'd barely spared a thought for work. He was too bewitched by Lilah to spend time worrying about costs and profits.

He lifted his hand to brush his finger down the clenched muscles of her jaw. "I pay an enormous staff an obscene amount of money to keep things running smoothly for me."

"What about your master?" she demanded.

"What about him?"

"You're here to find him, aren't you?"

Chiron flinched at her direct hit. She was right. He was allowing his primitive hungers to distract him from the reason he'd traveled to this hotel.

"Yes," he forced himself to agree. "It's my duty."

She studied him with a steady gaze. "Because he's your master?"

"Because it's my fault he's missing." The words slipped from his lips before he could halt them.

He never discussed the past. Only Ulric knew the full truth of what had happened to Tarak.

But somehow, the urge to share his sense of guilt was overwhelming. He needed to see her reaction to his confession. As if her opinion of him was of the utmost importance.

She frowned in confusion. "I thought you said it was because of the previous Anasso?"

"It's a long story," he warned.

"I'd like to hear it." Her hand slid up his chest to brush the side of his neck. The light caress sent a sharp tremor through his body. "Please."

Chiron smiled wryly. There was no way he could resist her soft plea. Hell, he would probably dance naked in the middle of the Vegas Strip if she begged him to.

"I don't even know where to start."

"At the beginning," she suggested in that same, soft voice.

Chapter 8

The beginning?

He stepped back, eyeing her with a wry smile. Did she have any idea he was over a thousand years old?

Not wanting to remind her, he settled for the condensed version.

"Like most vampires, I was abandoned by my sire after I was turned," he said, his voice carefully devoid of emotion.

Vampires were feared predators. And with good reason. They were savage warriors who sat firmly on top of the demon food chain. But they began life as vulnerable as any baby. Perhaps even more vulnerable. When they woke from being turned, they had no memory of their previous life. And because most sires didn't bother to stay around and assist their creations, the new vampire didn't even know what he or she was, or what might kill them.

Most vampires perished during their first few hours by walking into the sunlight, or being killed during their initial hunt for blood.

"Thankfully, I woke deep in a cave, so I didn't stumble into the sunlight," he continued. "But I spent years alone, never realizing there were others like me. It was Tarak who eventually found me, and taught me who and what I was."

"Tarak." She tilted her head to the side. "That's your master?"

"Yes."

"Did he make you a member of his clan?"

Chiron turned to pace toward the pool, the emotions he'd kept locked away for centuries churning through him.

He could remember the precise moment Tarak had entered the cave. Chiron had been like a feral animal, attacking the intruder with every intention of destroying him. Tarak had easily overpowered him, but instead of striking the killing blow, he'd taken Chiron back to his own lair.

Over the next decade, the older male had taught Chiron everything he knew. How to hunt. How to fight. How to lure his prey with minimal effort. And how to interact with other vampires.

That last lesson had been the toughest for Chiron. After so many years alone, it had been next to impossible to learn to trust anyone beyond Tarak.

"At that time, he was a devoted follower of the Anasso," he told Lilah, pivoting back to meet her curious gaze. "Once I was moderately civilized, we began to travel with the king to help him maintain his hold on the throne."

She arched her brows. Obviously, she was fully aware of the irony of his words.

"The one he was hiding from?"

"At the time, the Anasso was striving to unite the vampires. Before then, we were so busy killing one another with our clan wars, we were blind to the dangers of evolving human technology."

"That sounds like a good thing."

"It was. In the beginning," he agreed.

Most vampires had been impervious to the threat of the humans who were starting to band together and build cities. They'd become complacent in their belief they were indestructible. The Anasso, however, understood the bows and arrows used by the humans were only the beginning.

"Did he become power hungry?"

Chiron rolled his eyes. The Anasso had been arrogant, bossy, ill-tempered, and consumed with his lust for power.

A typical vampire.

"He started that way," he told his companion.

Her gaze lowered to his hands, which had clenched into tight fists. "Then what happened?"

Chiron didn't try to ease his tension. Why bother? As long as he was digging through his ancient memories, he was going to be on edge.

"Over the centuries, he started to become more aggressive," he explained. "And unstable."

"Unstable?"

"Violent mood swings."

She looked confused. "Is that unusual?"

Chiron narrowed his eyes. "I think I was just insulted."

She blushed. "Sorry."

Chiron waved aside her apology. It wasn't unusual for demons or fey who didn't spend time with vampires to assume they were still the brutal savages they had been in the beginning.

Now, vampires tended to be cold, cunning creatures who used their intellect rather than their brawn to maintain power.

"At first, it was bursts of temper that might be expected from any leader who's under constant pressure from challengers to his throne," he continued. He wanted to be done with his story. "Not to mention being the arbitrator between an endless parade of squabbling vampires to prevent clan wars."

"That sounds awful."

Chiron grimaced. It'd been more than awful. They'd had to be on constant guard to prevent assassins from sneaking into their current lair, while the Anasso spent his days listening to one whining complaint after another. The grim discipline became grinding after a few centuries.

The memory made him shudder.

"Yeah, I can't imagine why any vampires would want the job."

"I assume there was more than frustration with his job bothering the Anasso?"

"I started to notice strange bouts of euphoria," he said. He could still remember the occasion he'd walked into the private baths to discover the Anasso leaping across the floor and singing at the top of his lungs. And when the idiot had locked himself in the dungeon and it'd taken them three days to find him. "Like he was drunk."

She made a sound of surprise. "Vampires can get drunk?"

"Only if they ingest the blood of a creature who's been drinking or doing drugs."

"A lot of demons enjoy imbibing substances that aren't always good for them," she pointed out in dry tones. "At least half my yearly budget is used to repair the damage done by inebriated guests."

Chiron struggled not to be distracted by her words. Later, he would ponder his sudden aversion to Lilah dealing with dangerous demons in this isolated location. It didn't matter if it was her birthright. Or if she had a half ogre to offer her protection.

He didn't want her here. Not without…

Him.

"Vampires can quickly become addicted," he said, pretending the treacherous thought hadn't just wiggled through his brain. "That's when the true damage happens."

"What damage?"

"The corrupted blood begins to rot their brain. Eventually, they go completely mad."

"And that's what happened to your Anasso?"

He gave a sharp nod, forcing himself to return to the past.

"Yes, but it starts slowly. I began noticing a change in him, but everyone dismissed my fears." He'd been furious when Tarak had refused to listen to his suspicions. More than once, the older vampire had threatened to have Chiron driven from the lair. "To be honest, I don't think anyone wanted to accept that anything was wrong. They'd all devoted their lives to the Anasso's dream of a united vampire nation. I was relatively new to the clan, so I didn't have much invested."

She nodded in understanding. "So you could see more clearly."

A humorless smile twisted his lips. "That's what I told myself."

She allowed her expression to soften, as if able to sense his lingering bitterness. "But?"

He glanced back toward the pool. The old emotions continued to churn to the surface. Raw regret and frustration. But there was also an unexpected sense of healing taking the sharp edges off his pain.

Was it simply sharing the story with Lilah? Like lancing an infected wound? Or was it something to do with this place?

Impossible to know for sure.

"I think there was a part of me that resented the Anasso's sway over my master," he admitted.

"You were jealous."

He gave a reluctant nod. It sounded so childish. But at the time, he'd been a relatively young vampire who'd begrudged Tarak's fierce devotion to the older vampire. He wanted Tarak to leave the Anasso so they could create their own clan.

"Looking back, I think I was," he said.

"What did you do?"

"I started following the Anasso in secret." Chiron had been embarrassed by his compulsion to sneak around. He was a warrior, not a dirty gremlin. But he had to know the truth. "Eventually, I discovered the secret stash of drug-addicted humans and demons he was holding like cattle in pens to feed on."

She lifted her fingers to her mouth, her eyes darkening with anger. "The bastard."

Chiron had been equally horrified. Vampires might be predators, but they used their skills to hunt their prey. They didn't trap and torture them. Unfortunately, he hadn't dared to release the prisoners.

It wasn't until after Tarak had disappeared that he'd gone on a rampage, smashing open the pens he could find to release the pathetic captives. Including Ulric.

"That was my reaction, along with Tarak's, when I told him what I found," he told her.

"Good."

His lips twitched at her fierce tone. She was genuinely upset by the thought of demons and humans being mistreated. The knowledge pleased him. It revealed her heart was as tender as he'd suspected.

"Not entirely." He made a sound deep in his throat. When Tarak disappeared, he'd realized he'd made a tactical error. "I assumed Tarak must have discovered something that proved I was telling the truth, and threatened to denounce the Anasso as his king, probably in front of the entire clan."

"That's when he went into hiding?" she asked in sympathetic tones.

Chiron hesitated. He didn't want to lie. Then again, he wasn't prepared to reveal the complete truth. Not until he'd found the key and released Tarak.

"He disappeared," he hedged.

She hesitated, as if choosing her words with care. "How can you be sure he wasn't killed?"

Again, he fudged the truth. "I would sense if he'd been destroyed," he said, not revealing he'd had a brief peek into the Anasso's perverted mind. It'd been just enough to be assured Tarak was still alive, along with the vague sense he'd been taken captive.

She thankfully jumped to the conclusion he had a connection to his master.

"At least you know he has survived," she murmured.

"And now I have the chance to bring him home again," he steered the conversation away from Tarak's disappearance.

She reached out to lightly stroke her fingers down his arm. "I get it."

The painful memories were abruptly shattered. Like a glass being struck by a hammer.

Her touch was light, and if he was being honest with himself, given more out of pity than passion. But it still sent pleasure zigzagging through his body.

He swallowed a self-derisive urge to laugh. He was a male who'd had the most beautiful females in the world try to capture his attention. They flirted, they followed him around the casino, they occasionally stripped off their clothes and threw their panties at him.

This female had barely allowed the tip of her fingers to brush his sleeve and he was giddy with pleasure.

Pathetic.

"Do you get it?" he asked, his voice husky as he stepped toward her.

She made a tiny sound in the back of her throat. Was she being distracted by the same awareness that sizzled through him?

"You feel like it's your fault he was forced to leave," she murmured.

"Yes," he agreed, taking another step forward.

Close enough to feel the heat of her body through his clothes. A growl rumbled deep in his chest.

He wasn't a Were, but tonight he felt as if there was an animal trapped deep inside him. It was wild and hungry for a taste of this female.

"And the only way to make it right is to have him back where he belongs," she continued, her own voice lowering with a breathless rasp.

He studied her upturned face. Her words captured his feelings with a perfect simplicity. "You're very perceptive."

"Not really." A troubled frown tugged at her brows. "There are times when I feel…"

He touched her cheek, sensing she was about to share one of her deepest secrets. "Tell me."

"Blind," she at last confessed. "As if there's something I should see that remains just out of sight."

Chiron felt a flicker of hope. There were witches who could create a revulsion spell to safeguard their objects of power. Perhaps they'd done the same thing to hide the key.

"Magic?" he demanded. "An illusion?"

She wrinkled her nose. "Never mind. It's ridiculous."

"No, I don't think it is." He allowed his fingers to glide over her cheek. "I'll help if you want me to. I have a gift that allows me to peek into the thoughts of others. It might help you to recall where—"

With a jerky motion, she reached up to knock his hand away. "Don't."

"Okay," he said in soothing tones. "Easy."

The sharp tang of her fear filled the air. "I don't want anyone poking around in my head."

Chiron was caught off guard by her intense reaction. It was one thing to be annoyed by having someone rummaging around in her brain. Most people were reluctant to open their minds to a foreign invasion. But she wasn't annoyed. She was terrified.

Why?

Refusing to push the issue, he leaned down to lay his forehead against hers. "No poking. I promise."

As if realizing she'd overreacted, Lilah released an unsteady sigh and allowed her tense muscles to relax. Then, once again catching him by surprise, she offered him a tentative smile. "What about biting?"

A better vampire would have ignored the subtle invitation. Not only was she obviously too young and innocent for him, but he was still hiding his true reason for being there.

He was taking advantage of her vulnerability.

But he wasn't a better vampire. There was no way in hell he could resist his urgent need to touch her.

Lifting his hand, he slid his fingers beneath her curls, cupping her nape in a possessive grip.

"Only if you ask very, very nicely," he assured her.

He caught the scent of her excitement, laced with a lingering fear. This time, however, he was confident it wasn't fear of him, but of the heat combusting between them.

He didn't blame her.

The intensity of his need for this female was more than a little unnerving.

She sucked in a deep breath, as if gathering her courage. Then she allowed her gaze to lower to his mouth. "What about kissing?"

The earth shifted beneath Chiron's feet. Three simple words, but there was nothing simple about the hunger that lengthened his fangs and twisted his gut into a painful knot.

"You don't even have to ask."

He leaned down, using the tip of one fang to scrape against her cheek. He wanted Lilah to know who he was. *What* he was.

Her excitement spiked, making his nose flare, but her fear vanished. A tension he hadn't even realized was clenching in his muscles eased.

She obviously wasn't bothered by the fact he was a vampire.

He moved in closer, caging her with his big body. He ached for a taste, but he contented himself with a lick of her parted lips. Chiron groaned. She tasted of summer. Lush raspberries. Golden heat. Sensual enticement.

Her hands reached out to tug at the buttons of his shirt, parting the silk material to lay her palms flat against the bare skin of his chest.

"Are you messing with my mind?" she demanded, the words more a plea than an accusation.

He chuckled. "I promised I wouldn't," he reminded her.

"Then why can't I stop touching you?" she demanded, her fingers tracing his flat nipples.

He hissed an electric excitement tingling across his skin. As if he'd been plugged into a circuit.

"Because I'm irresistible," he suggested.

"And so modest."

He kissed her. Or at least it was meant to be a kiss. Two mouths touching, clinging…deepening. But it was so much more. A primitive need to brand her as his own.

Lifting his head, he studied her flushed face with a brooding gaze.

"Whatever this is, it has nothing to do with mind control, or even the magic of this place." The air snapped and sizzled between them, as if it were alive. "It's us. The two of us."

Her fingers explored down his chest to the rigid muscles of his stomach. "I'm not sure that makes me feel better."

If Chiron had a heartbeat, he was certain it would have stopped. It was a struggle to concentrate on her words when his mind was clouded with the image of her wandering fingers reaching the hard length of his erection. Would they curl around his cock and stroke him with a soft caress? Or would she squeeze him with impatient desire?

"Why?" he managed to choke out.

"You're a guest."

"And?"

"Here today. Gone tomorrow."

He frowned. She was right. His time at the hotel was no more than a brief visit. A few nights, and then he would be on his way to free Tarak from his prison. From there, he would return to his lair in Vegas. Or Paris.

But the thought of walking away from this female refused to form. As if the image was so incomprehensible, his mind couldn't accept it.

"I'm here now," he told her, peering deep into her eyes. "No yesterday. No tomorrow. Just now."

She hesitated, as if torn between common sense and lust.

Lust won.

Thank the goddess.

"Yes." The word was so low, only a vampire could have heard it.

Chiron groaned, tilting his hips so his erection was pressed against the gentle curve of her stomach.

"So soft. And sweet," he murmured. "Like a luscious berry."

Her breath rasped between her lips as she continued to explore his rigid body, her fingers trailing up and down his torso.

"There's nothing soft about you," she told him. "You're like steel. All hard muscles and cool skin."

"You sound surprised."

"I am, a little," she told him. "I've never touched a vampire before."

"Never?"

"There have only been a few who chose to stay here, and they've all been mated."

Chiron felt a surge of satisfaction. It pleased him to know she'd never been with another vampire. Why? He had no idea.

He was beginning to think the magic in this place had completely scrambled his brain.

Right now, however, he didn't give a crap.

All that mattered was the faint flush of anticipation on her cheeks and the smoldering passion in her golden eyes.

"Does it bother you?"

"No." She gave a small shake of her head. "It's exciting."

She trembled, and he could feel the hard tips of her breasts press against the thin material of her robe. She was as aroused as he was. A growl rumbled in his throat. The fingers he had cupped around her nape tightened. A claim of ownership?

Damn. He was in trouble.

He stroked his lips down the curve of her cheek, nibbling at the edge of her plush mouth.

"Exciting, yes," he agreed. He stole a lingering kiss before moving to trace his tongue down the line of her jaw. "Exhilarating. Addictive."

She moaned, arching her body against him. "Keep talking."

He released a soft laugh. She was surprisingly demanding as a lover.

"Intoxicating. Glorious." He readily obeyed her command, his fangs scraping against the tender skin of her neck. "Unique."

She shivered, pulling back to send him a questioning gaze. "I'm not sure I like that one."

He held her gaze, his fingers threading through her curls. They felt warm and silken and vibrant with life.

Just like Lilah.

"It's easy to be like everyone else," he told her. "You're special."

She released a sigh, her expression rueful. "You're very good at this."

He shook his head. "I'd like to take the credit, but sparks like this aren't created by skill or experience," he told her. And it was the truth. He'd been seduced by the most experienced courtesans in the world. None of them had been capable of creating the enchantment Lilah could induce with a mere touch.

"Magic," she said.

"Fate." The word slipped past his lips before he could halt it.

For a second, they gazed at each other with a shocked awareness. Somewhere deep in their souls, they knew he was right. This sort of driving, ruthless passion wasn't just animal lust. It was destiny.

"Shh." She lifted her hand to press the tips of her fingers against his lips. "No yesterday. No tomorrow."

Either indifferent or unaware that there was no escaping the danger brewing between them, she once again allowed her hand to drift down his chest. Chiron muttered a rough curse, pressing restless kisses over her face.

"Only now," he agreed.

Her nails scraped his skin, sending flames of pleasure searing through him. "Chiron."

He nudged aside the neckline of her robe, exposing one full, rose-tipped breast.

His mouth watered. He could already imagine the sensual delight of allowing his fangs to sink into her pillowy flesh.

With an effort, he resisted temptation. The pang of denial was a small price to pay to avoid the potential for disaster if they shared blood. He'd feasted off thousands of hosts over the centuries, but not one of them had made him consider the possibility that they might be his true mate, bound together for all eternity.

Lilah was different. From the top of her glorious curls to the tips of her tiny toes.

He'd told her she was unique.

And that's exactly what she was.

He forced himself to use his hand to explore the soft temptation of her breast, his lips gliding down the curve of her neck.

She trembled, suddenly grasping his shoulders. As if her knees had gone weak.

"More," she commanded.

He absorbed the evocative scent of her arousal, using his thumb to tease the tip of her nipple. He didn't need to feel between her legs to know she was wet and slick in anticipation of his possession.

He wrapped one arm around her waist, pressing her tightly against his aching body.

"You're a perfect fit," he murmured. "As if you were created for me."

She went on her tiptoes, nipping his bottom lip. "More likely you were created for me."

"Yes." Chiron shuddered in bliss.

It felt as if the magical sun had somehow crept inside him and was scorching him from the inside out.

Continuing to caress her breast, Chiron returned his lips to her mouth. He was desperate to quench his thirst. Both for her blood and her body.

A damned shame he wasn't going to be able to do either.

Not until Tarak was released and he could be honest with her.

As if determined to test his self-control, Lilah nibbled a path over his chest. A moan was ripped from his throat. Her touch was light, almost teasing, but it was sending bursts of fire through his veins.

He slid his tongue into her mouth, sweeping through the moist warmth. He could taste her sweetness, and the hunger that churned inside her.

And something else.

An echo of power that seemed separate from her.

Strange. Lifting his head, he grimly struggled to leash his need. As much as he ached to lay her on the marble floor and lose himself in the pleasure of her body, he needed to understand what he was sensing.

"Lilah."

He waited for her to tilt back her head and meet his searching gaze.

"What?"

"There is a—" His words were rudely interrupted by the sound of a female voice bellowing like a drunken troll.

Or, more accurately, an angry ogress.

"Lilah," Inga called out.

The air seemed to shudder, as if a delicate spell had just been shattered. Giving a small gasp, Lilah grasped the neckline of her robe and hurriedly pulled it together.

"It's Inga," she warned, as if Chiron hadn't recognized the sound of the female's voice, or the stomp of her heavy footsteps.

"Send her away," he urged.

She frowned, no doubt assuming he was frustrated because their privacy was being interrupted. And he was. Painfully frustrated.

But right now, he was equally anxious to learn more about the strange power. Was it a spell? Some parents wrapped their children in magic to protect them. But he shouldn't be able to sense it.

"I can't," she said, her hands pressing against his chest. "She wouldn't be looking for me if she didn't need something."

Chiron wasn't so easily convinced. The ogress clearly hated him. And if she thought he was alone with Lilah in this secluded grotto, she would do whatever was necessary to interrupt them.

"I'm sure it can wait," he said, too distracted to think through his words.

A mistake.

Instantly, Lilah was offended, and her hands gave a rough shove against his chest.

"This hotel might not seem like much to you, but it's important to me," she snapped.

"I didn't mean it wasn't important, but there's something I sensed inside you—"

Her outrage swelled to pure fury. "You promised you wouldn't rummage around in my head."

Chiron grimaced. He was going from bad to worse. Where was his usual charm? There was never a situation he couldn't smooth over with a few diplomatic words and a dimpled grin.

Ulric would be laughing his ass off if he were here.

Or worse, Levet could have witnessed his awkward fumbling.

He shuddered at the mere thought.

"It wasn't in your mind."

She scowled. "What are you talking about?"

He gave a helpless lift of his hands. "I'm not sure, but I think it might be important."

"Important for whom?" she demanded.

Well, hell. How could he explain his urgent curiosity? It was impossible without confessing the truth of why he was at the hotel.

She made a huffing sound at his hesitation, slipping around his body to head toward the stairs.

"Lilah," he called out.

She never slowed as she left the grotto, her stiff spine warning she wasn't in the mood to discuss the issue.

Chiron clenched his hands at his sides. He'd managed to blow that in spectacular fashion.

"Dammit."

Chapter 9

Lilah was acutely aware of Chiron's frustrated glare burning into her back as she hurried out of the grotto. She kept her pace swift and her spine stiff. She wanted him to know she was thoroughly annoyed.

Not because Chiron had kissed her. What woman in her right mind would be upset to be in the arms of that magnificent male? Not even the onslaught of hunger that had hit her like a tidal wave had managed to make her regret giving in to her passion. And if there was an opportunity to continue where they'd left off, she was 100 percent onboard.

But while she was willing to offer her body, she'd become increasingly convinced she couldn't offer him her trust.

Why was he here? There was sincerity in his words when he spoke about his master. She believed he desperately wanted to find Tarak. But it made no sense that he would stay at the hotel. Why not make a sweep of the area, interview the local demons, and then move on if he couldn't find him? He was doing nothing to actually search for the vampire that she could tell.

And then there had been the attempt on his life.

Who would want him dead? Certainly no one who worked for her. Which meant he'd brought the danger with him.

So was he hiding from his enemies? Or hunting them?

Or was it something completely different that had brought him to this hotel?

The fact she didn't know pissed her off.

Her whole life was one of shadows and unanswered questions and elusive memories.

She didn't want any more mysteries.

Smoothing her riotous curls away from her face, she pressed her way through the illusion that guarded the grotto and stepped into the garden. Instantly, she was shrouded in the velvet darkness of the night.

The scent of orchids filled the air with a sweet perfume and the mossy ground was soft beneath her feet. Above her head, the sky was dappled with sparkling stars.

She paused, pretending she needed a second for her eyes to adjust. The truth was, she had a sudden, almost overwhelming impulse to turn around and rush back to the grotto.

The raw scent of Chiron's power clung to her robe, and her skin still tingled from his cool touch. Chiron was out of sight, but he most certainly wasn't out of mind. In fact, she would swear she could sense him whispering to her, urging her to return to his arms.

It wasn't a voice that spoke to her brain. But to her heart.

Destiny...

"Lilah."

The sharp voice of her onetime nanny sliced through her dangerous thoughts, and Lilah swallowed a sigh. It was too late for regrets. And it wasn't as if Chiron was going to disappear in a puff of smoke. Was he?

There was time to explore the passion that continued to heat her blood.

Lilah stepped forward as the large female barreled toward the hidden grotto.

"I'm here, Inga," she said. "What's wrong?"

The ogress came to an abrupt halt, glancing over Lilah's shoulder with a suspicious expression.

"I noticed the vampire was missing and I was worried he might be bothering you."

Lilah frowned. Inga had always been insanely overprotective. And she'd never hidden her hatred for vampires. But she'd never been quite so...smothering. As if she had a special fear of Chiron.

"Why are you so worried he might hurt me?" she demanded.

Inga folded her arms over her massive chest, her vibrant muumuu blowing in the gentle breeze. Tonight, it was a painful shade of purple with yellow pineapples.

"All vampires are cold-blooded killers," she said.

"Many demons are killers, including the Sylvermyst who visited last week with his pack of hellhounds and the Were we currently have staying here," she pointed out. "You've never worried they were plotting some evil."

Inga revealed her opinion of Lilah's argument with a sniff. It was loud enough to scare the dew fairies playing among the ferns.

"What's your interest in the leech?" the older woman asked, clearly deciding offense was the best defense.

Lilah abruptly turned to walk up the pathway. It was the only way to hide the hot flush that stained her cheeks. "Besides the obvious?"

Inga was quickly at her side, her strides twice as long. "What's that mean?"

Lilah gave a lift of her shoulder. "He's gorgeous. Any woman would be fascinated by him," she admitted.

"He's dangerous," Inga chided. "You need to stay away."

Just seconds ago, Lilah had rushed out of the grotto, unnerved by the fear that Chiron was hiding something from her. But the moment Inga tried to warn her away from him, she had a perverse need to charge to his defense.

"He's interested in the history of the hotel," she said, not bothering to argue his potential threat to her.

It was a waste of breath. He was a powerful vampire. There were few things more lethal.

Oddly, Inga's suspicion only seemed to deepen. "Why would he be interested in the hotel?"

"Something to do with his master. He thinks he might have stayed here when my parents were still alive," Lilah explained with a grimace. It sounded even more lame when she said it out loud.

Inga's eyes widened before she was giving a fierce shake of her head. "Impossible. Your parents never catered to vampires."

Lilah blinked in confusion. She'd expected her companion to question Chiron's assumption he'd be able to locate his master after so many years. But she hadn't expected her to claim her parents hadn't allowed vampires into the hotel.

"How do you know?" she demanded.

The ogress faltered, as if caught off guard by the question. Then she jutted out her lower jaw. "They made their feelings clear."

Lilah studied the older woman. Was that why Inga was prejudiced against vampires? Because of her parents? But if that was the case, why hadn't she told Lilah when she first took control of the hotel?

Just as importantly, what else hadn't Inga shared with her?

"You never talk about them," she said in soft tones.

Inga abruptly turned her head to scan the garden, as if searching for some hidden danger. Or, more likely, to give herself time to consider her words.

The ogress was always reluctant to discuss the past, especially when Lilah asked about her parents.

As a rule, Lilah respected her aversion. She'd told herself it was because she loved this oversize female who'd taken care of her since she was a child. Certainly, Inga hadn't had to stick around. She could easily have abandoned Lilah and run as far as possible from the plague.

That's what most demons would have done.

But suddenly, she realized her natural curiosity was as muffled as her memories. As if it was being deliberately dampened by some unseen force.

The knowledge made her stomach twist with a strange unease.

"Because I didn't have the opportunity to get to know them," Inga told her. "Not beyond their rules for the hotel and how they wanted me to take care of you. They were very particular about that."

Lilah furrowed her brow, trying to force her way through the fog in her mind. "Were they?"

"Of course. They loved you."

Familiar frustration bubbled through her. "I wish I could remember."

They walked around one of the garden's prized fountains. It was twelve feet across and had a sculpted replica of Poseidon in the center that sent water spraying from the tips of his trident. The tinkling sound wasn't as soothing as her hidden pool in the grotto, but it pleased the guests, who liked to strip off their clothes and run through the sparkling droplets.

"There's no point in living in the past," Inga growled. "Trust me, it's best to forget."

It was Inga's routine response. One Lilah was tired of hearing. "It's different to deliberately shove away your memories. It's another thing to have them stolen."

"Stolen?" Inga came to a sharp halt, her eyes narrowed. "Why would you say that?"

Lilah nearly stumbled over the larger female. Jumping to the side, she turned to study her companion. Clearly, Inga was bothered by Lilah's words. Why?

"They were stolen by whatever it is that makes my mind so fuzzy," she explained, carefully watching the muscles of Inga's face relax.

"It's from the cleansing spell I used after the plague." Inga shrugged, her tone offhand. "It lingered in the area for years."

Lilah flattened her lips. The explanation no longer had the ability to ease her frustration. In fact, tonight it rubbed her nerves raw. Or maybe her nerves were already raw, and the worn excuse was like pouring salt on them.

"Whatever the cause, it's frustrating," she said between clenched teeth, struck by a strange yearning. "There are times when I wonder if I traveled away from this place it might clear away some of the fog."

"Travel?" Inga jerked, as if she'd just been hit by a bolt of lightning. "Where?"

Lilah glanced around the garden, trying to act casual. Until tonight, the mere thought of leaving this place would have sent her into a panic. Now she felt a tiny tingle of excitement.

And she knew exactly who was responsible for that excitement.

She gave a vague wave of her hand. "Just away."

Inga looked like she'd swallowed a lemon. "You have a duty here."

Lilah stiffened, annoyed by Inga's words. She'd devoted her whole life to this hotel. "I understand my duty."

"Do you?" Inga pointed toward the large building at the end of the garden. "This place isn't going to run itself."

"I could close it down for a few days."

"And what would happen to your guests? We aren't so overrun with visitors we can turn them away."

Lilah hesitated. Inga had a point. They barely scraped by, and if she closed down for any length of time, the few guests they had might decide not to return.

She considered her options before landing on the most obvious one.

"You're capable of taking care of things while I'm gone," she said.

Inga scowled. "You intend to travel without me?"

Lilah shrugged. "Why not? I'm a big girl."

"You have never been beyond the barrier."

Lilah waited for the fear to hit, but once again, she felt nothing but a tiny tingle of anticipation.

Perhaps she'd finally matured to the point where she could face the outside world, she decided. Or it could be the temptation of spending time with Chiron overcame her natural anxiety.

He could lure a dryad from her tree.

"That's my point." She nodded toward the edge of the garden. "Maybe it's time."

Inga turned on her heel and began stomping her way up the pathway. The ground shook beneath the impact of each step, the paving stones crumbling to dust.

Lilah sighed as she hurried to keep pace with her companion. She had to replace the pathway every year or so. Inga's temper tended to require a lot of repairs around the place.

"It's that vampire, isn't it?" the ogress snapped as Lilah managed to catch up. "He's trying to seduce you into leaving."

"He invited me to visit his resorts," Lilah admitted.

Stomp, stomp, stomp. Three more flagstones crushed to dust.

"I knew he was going to be trouble," the female muttered.

Lilah held up her hands in a gesture of irritation. "Why is that trouble?" she demanded. "It's hardly a crime for a handsome male to ask me to spend time with him, is it? I can't imagine why you aren't happy for me. Do you want me to be alone forever?"

The ogress sent her a pained glance, as if Lilah had hurt her feelings.

"You're not alone," she reminded Lilah. "And I can't protect you if you leave here."

Lilah's irritation faded as swiftly as it'd risen. There were many things in her life she questioned, but this female's devotion to her wasn't one of them. It wasn't fair to vent her frustrations on the only person in the world who cared about her.

"Protect me from what?" she asked, truly curious.

"Demons. Humans." Her expression tightened, genuinely afraid for Lilah. "Everything."

Lilah instinctively reached out to place a comforting hand on the woman's arm.

"Inga, nothing's going to hurt me."

"You don't know that." The ogress's voice was gruff. "Without knowing your bloodline, we have no way to fully understand any vulnerabilities you might have."

"True," Lilah readily agreed. "And there's only one way to find out."

Inga gnashed her pointed teeth before she finally heaved a resigned sigh. "You're not leaving tonight, are you?"

"Of course not."

"Then we'll discuss it later."

Lilah didn't press the issue. Who knew whether she'd actually have the courage to travel away from the hotel when it came time? Or if Chiron was even serious in his offer to have her stay with him?

Instead, she turned her attention to Inga. "What about you?"

The ogress sent her a puzzled frown. "Me?"

"Don't you ever want to travel away from here?"

The female shuddered, her face paling. "Never. I know what's out there."

"What?"

"Evil."

Lilah felt a pang of sympathy. The ogress refused to discuss her past, or what had brought her to the hotel, but it was obvious something terrible had happened to her.

"The entire world can't be evil," Lilah protested.

"As far as I'm concerned, it is."

"But what about your family?"

The sound of the female grinding her teeth filled the air. "I've told you. I have no family."

Lilah shook her head. "You said you didn't have any connection to them. That's not the same thing as not having any family. Perhaps it's time you consider a reunion."

Inga turned her head, her eyes flashing red. "They threw me away like a piece of trash. If I ever decide to have a reunion, it will be to rip out their hearts."

Lilah grimaced. *Okay, then. Scratch the whole reunion thing off the to-do list.*

"Yeah, maybe it's better you stay here," she murmured, her hair blowing around her face as a puff of wind swirled through the garden. Then she frowned as she caught the unmistakable scent of granite that seemed to be coming from Inga. "Why do you smell like the gargoyle?"

"I..." The ogress coughed, as if she had something stuck in her throat. "His scent must have gotten on me when I chased him into the swamps."

Lilah glanced toward the nearby bogs. Many of the guests enjoyed spending time with the native demons who lived in the area, but they were full-size creatures who could protect themselves. "That was hours ago," she said, more to herself than her companion. "Maybe I should go look for him."

"Why?"

"He might be lost. Or even hurt." Lilah shrugged. "He's tiny for a gargoyle."

"He's fine," Inga muttered, her expression angry.

Lilah wondered just what else the gargoyle had done to stir the ogress's temper. Surely it had to be more than stealing a few meat pies.

"How can you be so certain?"

"He was headed toward the nest of the water sprites. I'm sure they're keeping him entertained."

"Hmm." Lilah wasn't so convinced. It seemed odd that he would take off without telling Chiron where he was going.

As if realizing Lilah was genuinely worried about the small demon, Inga paused beneath the weeping willow, turning to meet her gaze.

"If he doesn't return in a couple of hours, I'll go look for him."

"If you're sure." Lilah gave an absent nod, suddenly distracted.

"I am…" Inga's words trailed away as Lilah walked past her to lay her hand against the trunk of the tree. "What are you doing?"

Lilah barely heard the question. She didn't know what she was doing. There was a buzzing in her ears and a strange sensation in the center of her mind. It was as if a curtain was being pulled aside and she was being sucked backward in time.

Her breath tangled in her throat. What was going on? She could see herself walking across the garden with perfect clarity. She was wearing a white, flowing gown and her hair was long enough to brush her lower back. Slowly, she bent down and placed something in the ground. Was it a seed? Yes, she was carefully covering it with the mossy ground and speaking a soft word. Within the blink of an eye, tiny sprouts shot through the dirt, and with a smile of satisfaction, she straightened.

Was it a dream? Or something that had been placed in her memories?

Inga grasped her arm, digging her fingers into the soft flesh. "Lilah, tell me what's wrong."

Lilah gave a shake of her head, pulling herself out of the illusion.

"I had a sudden memory of planting this tree," she said. "But that's impossible. It's hundreds of years old."

Inga sucked in a sharp breath, her eyes once again flashing red. "What did the vampire do to you?"

Lilah frowned. What did this have to do with Chiron? "Nothing."

"Did he touch you?"

"He kissed me," Lilah admitted without apology. Why should she be ashamed of her perfectly natural desire?

Inga continued to glare. "Did he use his compulsion on you?"

"He didn't have to. But…"

"What?"

Lilah hesitated, not wanting to stir up Inga's anger. Then again, she wasn't going to hide the truth. She hated secrets. They caused nothing but trouble.

"He has the ability to see into people's minds," she admitted.

As expected, Inga hissed in fury. "That bastard."

Lilah patted the thick fingers still wrapped around her arm. "He swears he didn't use his powers."

"He must have," Inga argued. "It's too soon."

Lilah's queasy uncertainty was distracted by the bizarre words. "Too soon? Too soon for what?"

Inga released her arm and took an awkward step backward. As if she realized she'd said more than she'd intended.

"He's clearly been embedding fake memories in your mind," she tried to bluster.

Lilah snorted. "Why would he embed the memory of me planting a willow tree?"

It took a second for her to come up with an answer. "It was just a first step. Eventually, he'll use his powers to convince you to leave me."

"That's ridiculous."

"Is it?" Inga narrowed her crimson gaze. "He's already tried to seduce you. The next step is to lure you away from here."

Lilah allowed Chiron's image to form in her mind. It was remarkably easy. The glossy dark hair that begged for her touch. The smoldering ebony eyes that offered all sorts of wicked pleasures. The finely carved features and lips that had created complete chaos when they touched her mouth. Even his glistening fangs were imprinted on her brain, as if she was harboring a dark hunger to feel them sliding deep in her flesh.

A rash of tingles spread through her body. She wanted him. Desperately.

"He doesn't need mind control to encourage women to join him at his expensive resorts," she assured her companion, all too easily able to imagine the flock of women who would eagerly rush to share his bed. "And even if he did, why would he choose me? I'm nothing special."

A strange expression rippled over Inga's bluntly carved features.

"You're more special than you can possibly imagine, Lilah."

Lilah snorted at Inga's fierce tone. Had the female been dipping into the grog? Lilah knew she kept a stash of the powerful brew hidden somewhere in the swamps. Not that she blamed the ogress. There were days everyone needed a shot of liquid courage.

"I think you might be a little prejudiced," she said dryly.

Inga reached out to lightly touch her shoulder. "You have to trust me, Lilah."

"I do. It's just…" Lilah's words trailed away. What could she say? She didn't know what was wrong. Her mind felt scrambled, as if someone had tossed it into a blender. And there was a ruthless ache in the center of her being. Almost as if being separated from Chiron was causing a physical reaction. Just what she needed, more problems. She heaved a sigh. "I feel like there's so much hidden from me. I want my mind to be clear."

Inga squeezed her arm, her expression oddly pained. "Why don't you go eat your dinner? The cook made your favorite lemon tarts."

Realizing her words were hurting this female who'd raised her as if she were her own daughter, Lilah forced a stiff smile.

"I am hungry," she lied, her stomach cramping at the mere thought of food. Taking a step forward, she halted when Inga continued to stand in the middle of the pathway, her nose flaring as if she'd caught some nasty scent. "Aren't you coming?"

"I have something I need to take care of," the ogress muttered.

"It can wait."

"No, I need to deal with it now," she insisted, waving her hand toward the hotel. "Go on. I'll join you as soon as I'm done."

Chapter 10

Chiron remained in the shadows as he watched Lilah scurry into the hotel. His body was clenched tight with frustrated desire, and his fangs ached to taste the blood of his female. But it was the grim urge to rush forward and toss her over his shoulder so he could take her to his lair that worried him.

There was no way he could avoid the truth any longer.

Not when it was seared into every fiber of his being.

He battled against his instincts, watching the ogress who had turned to glare in his direction. Could she see him? Maybe. He didn't care. He had a few questions for the female who'd been here with Lilah's parents.

Stepping forward, he frowned as the female abruptly hurried toward the far side of the garden. She clearly was on a mission. Chiron shrugged. He would track her down later.

For now...

Chiron stiffened, his brows snapping together as he caught an unmistakable scent.

He turned on his heel, glaring toward the thick clump of cypress trees.

"Show yourself, Ulric," he drawled. "I know you're here."

The Were stepped into the moonlight, his golden eyes glowing and the musk of his wolf stronger than usual. He was dressed in a black tee that was stretched tight over his bulging muscles and a pair of worn jeans with heavy shitkickers on his size fourteen feet. Chiron's lips twitched. He might as well have tattooed *badass* on his forehead.

"How did you find me?" Chiron demanded.

The Were shrugged, strolling forward. "I have a tracker on all our cars."

Chiron felt a jolt of shock. He was willing to endure Ulric's habit of fussing over him like a mother hen, and even his tendency to believe Chiron was incapable of protecting himself. But he'd be damned if he allowed his guard to trace his every movement.

"You have a tracker on my car?" he growled.

Ulric shook his head. "Not your personal car, but you used one of the casino vehicles, and I have all of those tagged."

Ah. Chiron had almost forgotten he'd grabbed one of the fleet cars when they'd left Vegas. There was no way he was allowing Levet into his Jag.

"I followed the trail to the edge of the swamp, then it disappeared," Ulric continued. "I had to use my finely honed senses to actually locate this hotel."

Chiron folded his arms over his chest. His annoyance wasn't entirely appeased. "I thought I told you to stay in Vegas. You don't obey orders very well."

Ulric didn't bother to act contrite. A good thing. He was terrible at it.

"I obey them with spectacular skill if I happen to agree with them," the Were assured Chiron with his typical arrogance.

"I'm not sure you have a firm grasp of what *obey* means."

"My pledge is to protect you," Ulric reminded him. "That comes above any orders. Even from you."

Chiron knew he was wasting his breath. Well, not his breath, because he didn't have any, but at least wasting his time protesting Ulric's belief he was in Chiron's debt.

Still, he couldn't help himself.

"How many times do I have to tell you, there is no pledge? Any obligation has long ago been repaid."

The Were was as unimpressed with Chiron's reprimand as he'd been the thousand other times Chiron had tried to convince him to forget the past.

"That's my decision."

"You know, I'm beginning to wonder who's the boss."

"I don't want the job."

Chiron released a sharp laugh. Most people assumed he kept Ulric around because he was loyal and smart and capable of dealing with any enemy who might try to harm Chiron. All those were true. But the reason he kept him as his personal guard was because he enjoyed his company.

A rare friendship for a vampire and a Were.

Of course, Chiron was legendary for his preference in choosing his own path. Since Tarak's capture, he hadn't needed to please anyone but himself.

"Smart hound," he commended his companion. He glanced around the garden, ensuring they were alone. "Now that we've established how you found me, tell me why you're here."

"I've been trying to call you, but I didn't get an answer."

Chiron frowned, reaching into his slacks to pull out his cell phone. It was on, but he didn't have any missed calls.

"Damn, the magic must be interfering with my service," he muttered. He felt a stab of guilt. He should have checked in with Ulric the minute he'd arrived at the hotel. He'd never been away before when he wasn't in constant communication with his staff. He could blame his distraction on his fierce desire to free Tarak, but he knew deep inside it had everything to do with Lilah. "Is there anything wrong?"

"Beyond the fact that I had no idea if you were alive or dead?"

Chiron grimaced. "Okay, I'm sorry. I should have checked in. Now, tell me what's been happening."

There was a pause while Ulric clearly struggled not to continue his chastisement, then he gave a resigned shrug. "I got a call from Hong Kong. The triads paid a visit to our new hotel."

Chiron nodded. He'd worked among humans long enough to anticipate that any new enterprise was going to encounter the usual greed, corruption, and local protests. Mortals were depressingly predictable.

"Protection racket?"

"Yeah. Jayla took care of it."

Jayla was a female vampire who'd been part of the Rebel clan when they'd been banished. She looked as fragile as a lotus flower and was as lethal as a striking cobra. Perfect to open his new venture in Asia.

Not that his choice wasn't without dangers. Jayla had the cold logic of most vampires, but when her temper was roused she would destroy anyone standing in her path.

"How many are dead?"

"Just two," Ulric said, his tone revealing a complete lack of sympathy for the humans who were stupid enough to try to strong-arm Jayla. "Three more are in the hospital, but they're expected to live."

Chiron was equally unconcerned with the criminals, but he didn't want any hassles with the government. He'd worked for years to get the proper permits to build the hotel. "Any trouble with the human authorities?"

"No, I think they're eager to turn a blind eye."

"Good." He studied his friend's unreadable expression. "Anything else?"

"A blackjack dealer was stealing chips from our guests in the high-rollers club."

"Has it been handled?"

"Of course." Ulric looked oddly uncomfortable. As if he didn't want to discuss exactly how he'd resolved the issues.

Strange.

"Is that all?" he prompted.

Ulric shrugged. "It's early."

That was true enough. Running a business empire meant constant headaches. Which was why he'd insisted Ulric remain in Vegas while he was away from the office.

"Who did you leave in charge?" he demanded.

"Rainn."

Chiron grimaced. Rainn was the perfect choice. Except for Ulric, she was his most trustworthy employee. But she was never slow to take advantage of any opportunity to bleed him dry. "How much?"

"Five thousand."

Chiron muttered a curse. "And the clock is ticking. I'm sure the price goes up every night you're gone." He sent his companion a pointed glance. "I assume you plan to leave now you know I'm still alive and kicking?"

Ulric glanced around, not at all intimidated by Chiron's stern tone. The truth was, Ulric did exactly what he wanted, when he wanted. "I haven't decided."

"I don't need a babysitter," Chiron warned, conveniently forgetting he'd nearly taken an arrow through his heart.

Okay, he hadn't forgotten it. He just had no intention of sharing that little tidbit of information with his companion. Ulric would tear the hotel apart searching for the assassin.

The last thing Lilah needed was rumors she had a rabid Were terrorizing her guests.

"It's not that," Ulric denied, thankfully unaware that Chiron wasn't being entirely honest. "I'm intrigued by this place."

Chiron stilled. He didn't fully believe his companion. Ulric was here because he thought Chiron needed his protection. But it was obvious the male was truly fascinated by his surroundings.

"Why?"

Ulric tilted back his head, his nose flaring as he sucked in a deep breath. "The magic calls to my wolf."

That explained why the male's musk was so strong. And the glow of gold in his eyes. His animal was close to the surface.

Chiron took an eager step forward. "Do you recognize the spell?"

Ulric sniffed, then gave a shake of his head. "No. I've never felt anything like it before," he said, a visible shiver racing through his big body. "But it's powerful."

Chiron had never given magic much thought. He couldn't sense it, so he tried to avoid it whenever possible. Now he hated the knowledge that he was stumbling through the dark.

"Could witches create a spell that would incite your wolf?"

Ulric considered in silence, his gaze continuing to scan the shadowed garden. As if he could spot the person responsible for creating the magic.

"I've heard of witches who could force a cur to shift, so I assume it's possible a coven could band together to create a spell that would force a Were into his animal form," he said, his voice revealing his skepticism. "But it would have to be extremely focused and for a limited amount of time."

"You're saying the magic belongs to a demon and not a witch?" Chiron asked in confusion.

Had Levet brought them to the wrong spot?

A growl rumbled in his throat.

"Or a natural occurrence," Ulric said.

Chiron was jerked out of his dark thoughts, not sure if he'd heard his companion correctly. "Natural?"

Ulric offered a patronizing smile. "Unlike vampires who are dead to magic, Weres are primal creatures. We have the talent to absorb power from nature."

Chiron snorted. "Now I understand why vamps and Weres spent the past centuries trying to kill each other, mangy dog."

Ulric bared his teeth, but there was no real threat in it. The two males had a bond that had survived wars, famines, and a voyage around the world. Nothing could break it.

"We're far more attuned to the mystical powers that are an essential part of the world," he told Chiron.

Chiron considered his words. It was true vampires were as impervious to the earth as they were to magic. No surprise there. In the truest sense of the word, they were dead. It was the power of their inner demon that kept their bodies from disintegrating into dust.

"So you believe this is all a trick of nature?"

"No." Ulric glanced toward the edge of the garden. "The barrier is definitely a spell. And it's quite possibly a witch's spell. But there's something else here that's infused in the ground." Chiron watched another shiver shake his friend's body. "Either natural, or created so long ago it's become a part of its surroundings."

Chiron clenched his hands into tight fists. Around him, the temperature dropped by several degrees. "More mystery."

Ulric grimaced, no doubt sensing the need to distract Chiron from his mounting irritation. "What have you discovered?"

Chiron leashed his surge of impatience. He'd waited centuries for the chance to find his master and release him from his prison. He wasn't going to risk Tarak's freedom because he couldn't maintain control of his emotions.

"Levet traced the scroll to this location," he told his companion. "But once we arrived, he discovered his ability to pinpoint the key was muffled. I assume it has something to do with the magic that surrounds this place."

Ulric looked pained at the mention of the gargoyle. He still hadn't forgiven Levet for managing to sneak away and plunder Chiron's private stash of cognac. He took it as a personal insult to his skill as a protector.

"Where is the lump of stone?"

"I was told he was caught with his hand in the meat pies and was chased into the swamps."

"Of course he was," Ulric muttered. "Worthless gargoyle."

"So far," Chiron agreed. "Unfortunately, he's the only one who can help me."

Ulric looked confused. "Why? If the key is here, we should be able to find it."

"I don't think it will be that simple," Chiron warned, wishing it was as easy as searching through the hotel for a stray key. "It's probably hidden behind an illusion. Which means the gargoyle will have to use his magic to reveal it."

Ulric snapped his teeth. "Then why is he off in the swamp while you're wandering around the gardens as if you're lost?" The male leaned forward, drawing in another deep breath. "And why do you smell like a female?"

Chiron's lips parted. He intended to deny the accusations. He wasn't wandering around like he was lost. Was he? That would be...pathetic.

But meeting Ulric's steady gaze, he conceded defeat. There was no point in lying. Not to his companion, or to himself.

"I've been distracted," he admitted.

"You could have been distracted at home," Ulric pointed out. "And in a lot more comfort."

Chiron tried to conjure up the image of the bevy of beautiful women who worked at his casino. He couldn't. Not one of them.

It was as if Lilah filled so much of his brain, there wasn't room for any other female.

"This distraction is quite unique," he conceded.

The Were studied him with a hint of alarm. The big bad wolf could face any enemy, but Chiron sensed his one fear was having his position as Chiron's most trusted servant threatened.

Ulric was a pack animal. He needed the security of knowing exactly where he stood in the hierarchy of Chiron's life.

"How unique?"

"As unique as it gets."

The Were scowled. "You're starting to worry me."

Chiron's short laugh echoed through the garden. "Yeah, join the club."

Ulric paused before forcing himself to ask the obvious question. "You think she might be your mate?"

"I do."

"Damn." Ulric looked just as troubled as Chiron felt. Then, with surprising speed, he was squaring his broad shoulders and staring at Chiron with a grim acceptance. "Is she a guest here?"

"No, she's the owner."

"Good. You should have a lot in common." Ulric studied him with a steady gaze. "What are you going to do about it?"

Chiron blinked. Well, that was quick. There'd been a tiny fear inside him that Ulric wouldn't accept any mate he might bring home.

Now he realized the Were had adjusted far more easily than Chiron had. Probably because it wasn't his life being yanked apart.

"What can I do?" Chiron cringed at the sound of his whining. "She's a part of this place."

"So?"

"There's a reason the witches would have chosen to hide the key here."

"And what is it?"

Chiron made a sound of impatience. Hadn't the Were been listening? He'd been searching for the connection to the witches since he arrived.

So far, he'd come up with nada.

"I don't know."

"Did you ask?"

Chiron frowned. "Ask Lilah?"

Ulric gave a lift of his shoulder. "Is that the woman who you think might be your mate?"

"Yes."

"If she owns this place, she seems like the logical person to question about the whereabouts of a mysterious key."

Chiron's gaze was drawn toward the hotel, where the lights blazed from a dozen windows. What was Lilah doing in there? Was she dealing with some troublesome guest? Or meeting with the staff? Or was she alone, remembering their passionate kisses in the grotto?

Abruptly, his cock was hardening with need.

"It's not easy, without giving away the true reason I'm here," he muttered, fiercely trying to distract himself from the erotic images that crashed through his mind.

Right now, Ulric was respecting Chiron's discomfiture as he tried to adjust to the thought of possessing a mate, but soon enough the Were would be unable to resist the temptation to tease him. The last thing he wanted was to give his friend additional ammunition.

"Why not?" Ulric demanded.

Chiron studied him in confusion. "Why not what?"

"Why haven't you told her the truth?"

"Because I can't be sure whether I can trust her," he snapped.

Was Ulric deliberately trying to piss him off?

If so…mission accomplished.

"She's your potential mate and you don't trust her?"

Chiron frowned. "I think she's hiding something from me," he clarified.

Ulric wasn't impressed. "Just as you're hiding something from her?"

Yep. The Were was clearly trying to piss him off. "It's not the same."

Ulric arched his brows. "Let me see if I have this straight. She's supposed to trust you, even though you haven't told her the full truth," he drawled. "But you should wait until she's revealed everything before you'll decide whether to offer her the same trust?"

The words made Chiron cringe. He'd been so consumed with his own fear he might jeopardize his opportunity to rescue Tarak, he hadn't allowed himself to consider the situation from Lilah's point of view. Now he felt his unbeating heart squeeze with guilt.

"Stop being so damned logical," he growled. "It's annoying."

Ulric released a bark of laughter. "To state the obvious, you have trust issues, amigo."

He did. What vampire wouldn't? He'd been abandoned by his sire in a damp cave, then abandoned again when Tarak was taken prisoner. That didn't even include the Anasso blatantly lying to him before he was banished from his clan.

His first instinct was to assume he was going to be betrayed.

"And you don't?"

Ulric held up his hand. "Hey, this isn't about me. It's all about you and the fact that you're too scared to share the truth with your mate."

Chiron snapped his brows together, but he couldn't argue. Well, he could. He could point out that Tarak's life hung in the balance. And that he'd only known Lilah for a couple of days. And that the mysterious magic might be screwing with his mind, convincing him that Lilah was his mate. And that...blah, blah, blah.

Instead, he grimaced. "You're right."

"Of course I am," Ulric readily agreed, his hands on his hips. "What am I right about this time?"

"I've avoided revealing why I'm here because I'm terrified she might have something to do with the witches," he confessed. "And that I'll have to make a choice between her and Tarak."

Ulric's features eased, as if he hadn't considered that particular consequence. "Tell me about her," he urged.

Chiron's gaze once again strayed toward the hotel. There was a ruthless ache inside him. As if the distance between them was causing a genuine sense of withdrawal.

Like she was a drug and he was the addict.

"She's young. Unbearably vulnerable," he told his friend. "And so beautiful it hurts my heart to look at her."

A cryptic emotion flickered over Ulric's face. Something that might have been envy, if it wasn't so ridiculous. The Were had made it quite clear he had no intention of settling down with a mate and producing a litter of pups. Chiron had always assumed it was because he'd dedicated his life to serving him. Now he wondered if it was something else.

Perhaps the male had already loved and lost his female.

The thought made Chiron's stomach clench. Losing a mate...

That would be intolerable.

"Don't break her," Ulric said in soft tones.

Chiron's lips twisted. "It's more likely she'll break me."

"Go talk to her."

Chiron quivered. He desperately wanted to charge toward the hotel like a madman. With an effort, he forced himself to glance toward his friend. "What are you going to do?"

Ulric rolled his eyes. "Find that stupid gargoyle and force him to look for the key."

Chiron reached out to place his hand on Ulric's broad shoulder. He'd been pissed when he realized his servant had defied his orders. Now, he accepted he'd been foolish to leave this male behind. There was no one he trusted to guard his back. No one but this male.

Now he felt an unmistakable sense of relief.

While he concentrated on Lilah, Ulric could hunt down the gargoyle and force him to focus on the reason they were there.

"Thanks, amigo," he said with blunt sincerity. "As usual, you've managed to see through all the bullshit to the heart of the problem."

Ulric offered a smug smile. "It's what I do."

"Don't eat the gargoyle," Chiron warned, already turning toward the hotel. "We need him for now."

"No promises."

Chapter 11

Chiron chuckled as he rushed up the pathway at a speed that made him little more than a blurred shadow to anyone who might be watching. He had a brief flicker of confusion as he noticed the busted flagstones. They hadn't been broken earlier. What the hell had happened?

His bafflement was forgotten as he entered the hotel from a side door. Lilah's sweet scent instantly filled his body, luring him toward the kitchen. He slowed his pace as he stepped into the long, narrow room that was filled with the rich odors of meat roasting over the roaring fire and dried herbs that were hung from the open-beamed ceiling. There was also the tart citrus smell of lemons.

No doubt the aromas would make most demons' mouths water, but it was only the enticing perfume of Lilah's warm blood that captured Chiron's attention.

His gaze skimmed over the wooden cabinets that framed the room and the large farm sink piled with dishes. The floor was tiled and there was a long table in the center where Lilah was currently staring at a plate of tarts.

She was still wearing the robe that clung to her curves, and her hair haloed her face in a tumble of golden curls. *Stunning.*

Best of all, she was completely alone.

No hovering ogress. No guests. No staff.

Just him. And her.

Perfect.

Silently moving forward, he was standing next to the table before her senses could warn her that he was approaching.

"I'm sure Inga would tell you to clean your plate," he murmured.

Her head jerked up in surprise. "Chiron."

Chiron stilled. Her eyes had widened in shock, revealing the fear that lurked in the golden-green depths.

He crouched next to her chair, forgetting about everything but his need to provide comfort for his female. "Is everything okay?"

"I don't know."

His brows snapped together. If someone had hurt her, he would rip out their heart. "What's wrong?"

She paused, as if she wasn't entirely sure she wanted to answer. Then she heaved a small sigh.

"I feel like the ground is crumbling beneath my feet," she said. "Nothing is the same since you arrived."

Ah. His tension eased, replaced by a piercing bolt of joy. She wasn't upset because someone hurt her. It was because she was terrified of the same tumultuous feelings that plagued him.

He reached out to tenderly brush a stray curl from her cheek. "Is that bad?"

She trembled beneath his light touch. "I haven't decided."

He smiled, anticipation tingling through his body at the feel of her soft skin. Was she silky smooth all over? He couldn't wait to find out.

"Maybe I can help you make up your mind," he offered in husky tones.

She swayed forward, their gazes locked. "I'm sure you could. I'm just not sure if it's wise."

His fangs lengthened, his cock already hard, but he forced himself to slowly straighten. This wasn't the place to do what he wanted to do. Not when someone might stroll through the door at any moment.

Besides, he hadn't sought her out with the intention of seducing her. Not that he would protest if they happened to end the night with her wrapped in his arms. But first, he intended to be fully honest with her.

She had a right to know why he was there.

"Can we go someplace private?"

Tilting back her head, she studied him with an anxious gaze. "Now?"

"I have a confession to make."

Without warning, she surged to her feet, the chair scraping against the tiles. "Are you mated?"

He gave a sharp shake of his head, caught off guard by the question. Most demons could sense mated pairs. A good thing. It saved a hell of a lot of bloodshed.

"No, of course not," he assured her. "This is about my master."

"Oh." She released a shaky breath, nodding toward a narrow door on the far side of the room. "Follow me."

Chiron nodded, just a step behind her as she led him out of the kitchen and up a narrow flight of stone stairs. He was once again struck by the age of the place. It weighed down on him like a physical cloak. Not threatening, but boundless. Like the endless waves of an ocean.

In silence, they headed into Lilah's private quarters, in the wing opposite his own room. There was a large sitting room with the sort of shabby furniture chosen for comfort, not fashion, and a window that overlooked the back garden. There was also a large stone fireplace that was currently empty. Thank the goddess. Vampires and fires didn't mix.

Closing the door behind him, Chiron turned his back on the opening on the other side of the room. A quick glimpse was enough for him to catch sight of a wide bed that was covered with a handmade quilt. A silent invitation his body was eager to accept.

His gaze instead roamed over the walls of the sitting room. They were covered from floor to ceiling with the same frescoes he'd noticed in the hallways of the hotel. He leaned forward, reaching out to touch a vibrant orchid that looked real. On one leaf, a small fairy was sprinkling dew that appeared to glisten in the moonlight.

"Exquisite," he murmured. "Did you paint these?"

Lilah moved to stand next to him. "No, it was Inga."

"Inga?"

Chiron's mouth fell open. Stupid, really. He'd known trolls who could eat babies and yet sing with the voice of an angel. Or goblins who lived in a hole in the ground but could carve a chunk of marble into a masterpiece. He supposed he shouldn't be surprised that an ogress could create masterpieces on the wall of an isolated hotel.

"She's really very talented," Lilah gently chided.

She was. No arguing with that. Against his will, he found his opinion of the prickly female softening. No one could be all bad and create such beauty.

"This place is just one surprise after another," he said.

"It's my turn to ask if it's a good or bad thing."

He straightened, turning to face her before she could pull away. They were close enough that he could watch her eyes dilate with instant awareness.

"Nothing will ever be the same," he told her in husky tones.

Her lips parted, her breath releasing on a soft sigh. Then, with an obvious effort, she was stepping back.

"You mentioned your master?"

Chiron clenched his hands at his sides. It was that or reach out to haul Lilah against his aching body.

"I told you that I was here to look for him," he said.

"You're not?"

"It's a little more complicated."

She studied him with an expression that was more stoic than surprised. "I suspected it was."

Chiron grimaced. Obviously, his hidden agenda hadn't been so hidden. Was it because he'd had an instant connection to this female? He hated to think he was losing his ability to deceive and manipulate others.

That would just be sad.

"What I told you about my past is all true. I was rescued by Tarak and he was a devoted disciple of the previous Anasso."

She tilted her head to the side. "But?"

"But he didn't go into hiding after he denounced the king," he revealed. "He was taken captive."

Her eyes widened. There were few creatures daring enough to try to hold a vampire prisoner.

"How?"

Chiron shrugged. "I can only assume he was lured into a trap by the Anasso."

"Your own king took him captive?"

Chiron gave a sharp nod, the ancient anger still burning deep in his gut. "After realizing Tarak was missing, I went directly to the Anasso. The older male claimed my master had threatened to battle him for the crown and he'd been forced to banish him, but I knew he was lying."

Chiron shuddered. It made his skin crawl to recall his brief glimpse into the vampire's decaying thoughts. It'd been like being dipped in acid. The dark, ruthless hunger was all-consuming.

"What did you do?"

"I tried to rescue him," he said, his voice rough with regret. "I even went on my knees and begged for his release."

Her expression softened with sympathy. "What did the Anasso do?"

Chiron felt his stomach twist as the memory of his final meeting with the Anasso crashed through him. The large male had arrived without warning at Chiron's lair, along with several of his guards. Looking back, Chiron recalled that Styx hadn't been with him. Which was odd. At that time, the Anasso rarely left his private castle, and when he did, it was never without Styx at his side.

But that night he'd stormed into Chiron's lair, warning him that he was being exiled, along with every other vampire who'd called Tarak master.

"I was put on a ship and told never to return," he told Lilah. "Thankfully, I was able to smuggle Ulric aboard before we were being shoved out to sea."

She looked confused. "What's an Ulric?"

Chiron smiled. "A pureblooded Were who happens to be my most trusted friend."

She nodded, not questioning his rare friendship with a Were. Perhaps because that was the least weird part of his story.

A scary realization.

"No one believed you when you told them the king had imprisoned Tarak?"

"No, not even Styx, who was his top lieutenant back then," he said. "The bastard swore Tarak had been a traitor, that he was forced to leave the clan. He even accused me of lying to cause chaos among the vampires."

"Styx." She repeated the name, as if trying to place it. Then she blinked in surprise. "The new Anasso?"

"Yes."

"He lied to you?"

"That's what I believed for centuries."

"And now?"

"I'm beginning to accept he was as blind to the faults of his master as Tarak had been," he conceded. "When he came to my casino in Vegas, he brought a scroll he'd found hidden among the previous Anasso's belongings."

"What kind of scroll?"

"A map." He grimaced. "Of sorts."

"Oh." She lifted her brows. "Did it reveal the location where they're keeping your master?"

Chiron shook his head. If only it could have been that simple: Get a map. Locate Tarak. Free him.

"Not exactly," he drawled. "It had a spell used to hide the key that will unlock his prison."

She looked baffled by his explanation. Hell, *he* was baffled.

Which was why he hated magic. And witches.

"There's a key?" she demanded.

"I'm hoping so."

Her confusion only deepened. "Then why are you here?"

He studied her pale face. Her bewilderment seemed utterly sincere. And he was an expert at reading people. Or at least, he'd always thought he was. That was what made him so successful at running a casino.

Surely she would have given some clue she was aware of the key?

"This is where the scroll led us," he told her, continuing to regard her with an intense scrutiny.

"Here?"

"According to Levet." He didn't bother to hide his opinion of his traveling companion. "He's the one who's following the spell. I have no ability to sense magic."

Her lips suddenly twitched. "That at least explains why you're with a gargoyle."

"It certainly wasn't by choice," he dryly admitted.

"Is that where he is now?" she asked. "Getting the key?"

Chiron frowned, abruptly glad Ulric was looking for the absent gargoyle. If he hadn't been so distracted by Lilah, he would have been concerned by Levet's absence long before now.

"I haven't seen him for hours," he reminded her. "I truly don't know what he's doing."

"I don't understand. If you know where the key is, why not get it and leave?"

"That was the plan, but Levet claims the magic of this place is muting his powers."

She wrinkled her nose. "I've heard that a lot," she said. "For some demons, the magic seems to intensify their abilities; for others, it dampens them." She shrugged. "There's no rhyme or reason to it."

Chiron thought about Ulric and the restless glow of his wolf in his eyes. Obviously, his friend was on the *intensified* side of the magical spectrum, while Levet was on the opposite end.

"He's supposed to be finding a way to locate it, but who knows what the hell he's doing?" he said, giving a shake of his head. "Probably stealing someone's priceless cognac."

Thankfully, she turned the conversation away from the gargoyle and his aggravating habits.

"What's the key look like?"

Chiron shrugged. "I have no idea."

"But you think it's here?"

"This is where the spell brought us."

She paused, as if considering the possibility of having a mystical key lying around the hotel.

"I haven't seen it," she said.

"It might be hidden behind an illusion."

"That's true. This place is filled with them," she agreed, reaching out to grasp his arm. "I can help you search."

Chiron kept his gaze focused on her lovely face, but his body was acutely aware of the feel of her fingers lingering on his arm. Her touch seared through the thin material of his shirt, her scent teasing at his nose. His heroic attempt to concentrate on Tarak and the need to locate the key was swiftly crumbling. Who could blame him? He was alone with the female who'd stirred his lust to a fever pitch. The fact that he hadn't already scooped her off her feet and headed toward the nearby bed was nothing less than a miracle.

"You have an idea of where it might be?" he asked, his tone distracted.

"No, but Inga would," she said, her cheeks darkening with a fascinating blush. Could she sense his escalating hunger? "She has explored every inch of this hotel and even the swamps. Plus, she has an ability to see through illusions."

Chiron grimaced. He didn't want to think about the ogress. Not now. Talk about a buzzkill. "I knew I needed to find time to question the female."

She licked her lips. A conscious provocation? Probably not. She was too innocent to realize the impact the swipe of her tongue would have on his body.

As if to prove his point, she stepped back in a flustered movement.

"Do you want to go now?" she asked, her voice breathless. "She should be in the kitchen."

He gave a slow shake of his head, his gaze resting on her damp lips that glistened in the moonlight.

"I should, but no. I don't want to go." He stepped forward, brushing his fingers down the side of her throat. "I want to stay here."

She trembled beneath his touch, her breath leaving her lips on a shaky sigh.

"What about your master?"

The familiar guilt twisted his gut, but this time it was overwhelmed by his urgent need to sate his hunger for this female.

"I will free him. I swore an oath the day he was captured," he rasped, speaking more to himself than Lilah. "But now there's something more important."

She regarded him with wide, dazed eyes. "What?"

"You."

Chapter 12

Lilah reminded herself to breathe. *Air in. Air out.*

It was a lot harder than it should have been, and it was all due to the male who was stroking his fingers up and down the curve of her throat.

She'd been a fool to bring him to her private rooms. She might be young, but she wasn't stupid. She was acutely aware that the passion that smoldered between them needed only a spark to ignite into a raging inferno. And what could be more certain to create a spark than being completely alone in a place where they were guaranteed privacy?

No doubt a part of her had been well aware of what she was doing. That secret part that had taken one glance at Chiron and decided she was going to be his lover. Regardless of the cost.

Now she gave a rueful shake of her head. "You're supposed to be a guest," she tried to remind herself. "Here today, gone tomorrow."

He stepped even closer, his icy power wrapping around her. Oddly, it didn't scare her. It should, of course. He could destroy her with pathetic ease. Instead, it sent jolts of excitement through her.

"We're way beyond that," he assured her, his soft voice brushing over her raw nerves and sending a shiver down her spine.

"Are we?"

"I can only speak for myself." His thumb stroked across the pulse at the base of her throat. "But the thought of walking away and never seeing you again is unbearable."

Her heart fluttered, her mouth suddenly dry. *Air in. Air out. Air in. Air out.*

"You have your businesses to run," she said, as if he'd somehow forgotten his resorts spread around the world.

Or, more likely, she was reminding herself of all the reasons this male couldn't possibly settle for a mongrel demon like her.

His head lowered until they were nose to nose. "I do. And I'm eager to have you as my partner."

"A partner." The word trembled in the air between them.

His eyes darkened, his power brushing a delicious chill over her skin.

"I've been alone a long time," he told her, his voice edged with an ancient pain. "I didn't even realize how alone until I looked into your eyes and felt the emptiness inside me."

His words touched her deepest vulnerability. She understood loneliness. And the aching need to fill the void in the center of her soul.

"You won't be alone once Tarak returns," she forced herself to remind him.

"He's my leader, not my partner." He held her gaze, his power continuing to swirl through the air. "He owns my loyalty, not my heart."

"Your heart?"

He reached to wrap his fingers around her wrist, lifting her hand to press it to the center of his chest.

"It doesn't beat, but it's in there," he assured her in a husky voice.

She shivered. His body was as hard and cold as a marble statue beneath her palm, but that wasn't what was sending quivers of pleasure through her. At least, not entirely.

Instead, it was the sensation that she was sharing Chiron's emotions. As if they were tangled with her own in a way that was inexorably binding them together.

Tenderness. Lust. And a vast need that was too large to be named.

"I feel it," she breathed. "I don't know how or why, but I feel it."

His other hand moved to touch the sensitive skin between her breasts. "Just as I feel yours."

Her mouth went dry, the awareness that had been lurking in the depths of her subconscious mind rising to the surface.

"Is this…" Her words trailed away.

"What?" Chiron demanded.

"Is this a mating?" she asked before she could lose her courage.

His brooding gaze swept over her face. "I believe it is."

She licked her dry lips. "So we'll be bound together for an eternity?"

"Yes."

Pure joy curled through the pit of her stomach. The thought of being forever bound to this male wasn't frightening, it was exhilarating. But still, she found herself hesitating.

Chiron was clearly caught up in the passion that sizzled between them. Had he truly considered what it would mean to be mated to her?

"We don't even know what I am," she reminded him.

"I don't care."

"But—"

Her words were cut short as he lowered his head and kissed her with a need that scorched an erotic path of pleasure from her mouth to the tips of her toes.

"Do you want this, Lilah?" he asked against her lips.

Did she? Hell yeah. With every fiber of her being. And yet a tiny seed of unease continued to plague her.

"I'm a little scared," she whispered.

He slowly lifted his head, his eyes glowing with an ebony heat that was at complete odds with the frost that was beginning to crawl over the walls.

"I'm a lot scared, but I've never been more certain of anything in my life." His voice was rough with an unmistakable sincerity. "You belong to me."

His fingers traced the vee of her robe, his cool touch sending jolts of anticipation through her body.

The sound of her jagged breath echoed softly through the room, a vivid reminder of another difference between her and Chiron. Not that his lack of breathing bothered her. Honestly, his *otherness* added fuel to her excitement.

As if she needed any fuel. Already, she was shivering, her palms sweating. She felt like her entire body was on fire.

"You have that backward," she said, her voice husky. "You belong to me."

"Hell yeah, I do," he growled.

Lilah shivered as his fingers traced the soft mound of her breast.

"Does that mean no other females?" The question left her lips before she even realized the worry had been gnawing in the back of her mind.

After all, it didn't take much imagination to see him in one of his lavish resorts, surrounded by females who knew exactly how to please a male. How could he possibly be satisfied with a mongrel who'd never traveled away from her isolated home in the swamps?

His fingers slid downward, curling around the belt of her robe. At the same time, he pulled back his lips to reveal his fangs, fully extended and glistening with lethal sharpness in the moonlight.

She should be terrified. Instead, a biting need raced through her.

"It does," he assured her, unraveling her belt before grasping the edges of her robe and yanking it apart. "Just like there won't be any other males."

The cool air brushed her skin as he peeled off her robe, allowing it to slide down her body and pool at her feet. She trembled, her mouth oddly dry as his hands lightly skimmed over her shoulders and down the line of her collarbone.

She struggled to think through the sensual pleasure that was threatening to cloud her mind. As much as she wanted to drown in desire, there was still a part of her that remained wary.

Her existence seemed filled with layers of illusion. What if this was just another one?

And even if it was real, was she really prepared to turn her life upside down? She'd been so isolated, she wasn't even sure what the world was like beyond her barriers.

"What about my hotel?"

His brooding gaze slid over her bare breasts, lingering on her nipples, tightly furled, as if begging for his lips.

"I have to travel to keep track of my resorts, but we can stay here whenever you want."

She blinked. His tone was casual. As if he didn't find anything odd in the thought of secluding himself in the middle of the Everglades.

"It's nothing like the places you're used to living," she felt compelled to warn him. As if he couldn't see the lack of bright lights and chattering crowds.

He chuckled, his hands smoothing down the curve of her waist. "Lilah, I spent the first years of my life in a cave wearing rags and drinking the blood of goats when I couldn't find a human. This place is paradise in comparison."

Her eyes narrowed. She wasn't sure she liked having her hotel compared to damp caves and smelly goats. "Are you poking fun at my home?"

His fingertips explored upward, brushing the sides of her breasts.

Oh…

Sparks of bliss danced over her skin.

"Not at all," he assured her. "I find it peaceful. I wouldn't mind running off your guests so we could use this as our private retreat."

Her heart melted. *Yes.* Could there be anything more romantic than spending her nights completely and utterly alone with this male? No guests, no staff, no interruptions.

As Chiron had said…paradise.

Her fantasy was briefly shattered when she recalled that running off her guests wasn't without consequences. "What about Inga?"

Chiron didn't hide his grimace. No surprise. Inga was like a fine wine. An acquired taste.

"I think she would love my new hotel in Hong Kong."

Lilah's lips twitched. Was he going to be the one to tell the ogress she was moving to Hong Kong? If so, he had more courage than she did.

"That's not very nice," she chided.

His eyes smoldered with a wicked humor. "Then I doubt you want to hear my other suggestions," he warned.

Her breath tangled in her lungs. He was always gorgeous. Drop-dead gorgeous. Yes, a terrible pun, and yet completely true. But when he smiled... She was lost.

Her hand lifted so she could lightly press her fingers against his cheek. His skin was as cool and smooth as silk. She had a sudden urge to lick him from head to toe and all the yummy places in between.

"So, are we going to do this?" she asked in husky tones.

He gazed down at her, his expression suddenly somber. "One step at a time," he said gently. Had he been able to sense her wariness? Probably. He seemed to know her better than she knew herself sometimes. "First this," he murmured, lowering his head to press their lips together. She quivered. The taste of him hit her tongue like the finest aphrodisiac. A primitive enticement sizzled through her body. "And this." He scraped the tip of his fang along the line of her jaw. Then he cupped her breast. "What about this?"

She wrapped her arms around his neck, not bothering to try to sort through her tangled emotions. Relief. Disappointment that the mating wasn't going to happen in that moment. And a breathless anticipation.

Right now, all that mattered was that she was naked in Chiron's arms. She didn't want to waste one more second.

"It's not bad," she teased.

He released a low growl before he was scooping her off her feet and heading across the room to the nearby bed. "Ah, a challenge."

A flare of triumph raced through her at the hunger that tightened his features as he gently lowered her onto the mattress. She wasn't alone in this staggering awareness. Bending down, he claimed her mouth in a kiss of fierce possession.

"Are you up for it?" she demanded, nipping at his lips.

He released a sharp bark of laughter. "Oh, I'm not only up for you, I'm already hard and aching," he said against her lips.

She made a sound low in her throat, her hands grasping the lapels of his shirt. With one yank, she sent the buttons flying.

"You have on too many clothes," she complained.

He glanced down at his ruined shirt with a rueful smile. "I should have packed more."

Her laugh tangled in her throat as her gaze skimmed down his naked torso. In the silvery moonlight, his skin had the sheen of ivory and his tousled hair was as glossy as ebony. He appeared a creature of mystical power. A beautiful monster that had strayed into the swamp and captured her heart.

"I like you better without them," she murmured.

He growled his approval at her words, his eyes burning with a savage hunger as he kicked off his shoes and stripped off his slacks. Then, with liquid speed, he joined Lilah on the bed, wrapping an arm around her trembling body.

"Good, because you're going to be seeing me without them." He pressed a line of kisses down her throat. "A lot."

"I love the feel of your skin," she whispered, her fingers stroking over his chest.

He pressed his lips to her brow before trailing down the line of her nose. Lilah shivered, well aware the scent of her arousal was filling the air.

"There's plenty more to touch," he assured her, his lips trailing over her cheek, pausing to nuzzle the corner of her mouth. "Feel free to explore."

She chuckled. "So generous."

"You'd better believe it." Chiron buried his face in the curve of her neck, his fingers not quite steady as they skimmed up and down the arch of her spine. It was a light caress, but it was unbearably erotic. "And I intend to return the favor."

Before she could respond, his hands slid over her shoulders and cupped her breasts in his palms. A moan was wrenched from her throat.

"Yes," she hissed between clenched teeth.

"So lush and yet so fragile." His voice was filled with awe, as if he were touching a female for the first time.

"Chiron." His name was torn from her lips as he gently rolled the tip of her nipple between his fingers.

"Hmm?" he prompted, kissing a path down her throat.

She stirred restlessly, feeling the sharp points of his fangs scrape her neck. There was no fear. Just need. A dark, aching need.

He made a soft, tortured sound. As if he'd sensed her hunger and was fighting his own urge to sink his fangs deep into her flesh.

With grim determination, he lifted his mouth back to her lips, teasing at them until they parted in welcome. He dipped his tongue into the moist heat while his hand brushed down her naked thigh.

Melting in pleasure, she wrapped her arms tightly around his neck. Now wasn't the time to dwell on their potential mating. Now was the time for heat and passion and searing bliss.

"You were right," she breathed. "Fate must have brought you to me."

Chiron continued to stroke his fingers in a lazy pattern along her thigh, nipping at her lower lip.

"Our meeting was etched in the stars," he agreed. "'All days are nights to see till I see thee, and nights bright days when dreams do show thee me.'"

Her fingers clutched at his hair, her body arching with an unspoken plea.

"It's not fair to use poetry," she chided.

With a soft laugh, he pressed his cock against her lower stomach. It was thick and hard as a rock.

"I'm beginning to think you must possess the blood of a siren," he rasped.

Lilah's lips curved into a pleased smile. She liked the thought of being a siren. At least when it came to this vampire.

"Perhaps I do," she murmured.

Chiron captured the tip of her nipple between his lips, his finger dipping through the moist cleft between her legs. "So beautiful."

Lilah gasped in pleasure and released a soft laugh as he circled the hard tip of her nipple with his tongue.

She intended to tell him that she wasn't beautiful, at least not in comparison to the females she'd seen on the TV and internet, but the words died on her lips as his finger slid with gentle insistence into her welcoming body. A sensual tempest raged through her as he stroked his finger in a slow, tantalizing tempo.

"More," she commanded in a hoarse voice.

He nipped at the pulse that raced at the base of her throat, careful not to pierce her skin.

"My demanding lover," he teased.

"I like to be the boss," she warned. Her nails lightly scored down his back.

"When we're in bed you can boss me all you like," he rasped, his lips claiming hers in a kiss of fierce anticipation.

A flare of triumph raced through her as she willingly met the thrust of his tongue, her back arching as her body sought relief from her mounting tension.

"Then give me more," she murmured.

"Aye, my lady."

With one smooth motion, he rolled on top of her. His firm weight settled against her. Lilah gave a groan of sheer relief.

Yes, this was what she'd needed.

Spreading her legs, she gave a small moan as Chiron reached down to stroke her sensitive clit. The male had skills, she acknowledged as she squirmed in bliss.

"Now, Chiron," she muttered.

Chiron continued to stir her hunger as he situated his cock into the opening of her body. Then, with a loud groan, he entered her with one slow thrust.

Her mind threatened to shut down at the shocking pleasure of having him lodged deep inside her. It wasn't just a physical connection. Not just body to body, or lust to lust.

It was hearts and souls and promises of eternity.

Nearly overwhelmed by the intensity of her emotions, Lilah tangled her fingers in his hair. Their mouths crashed together, both lost in the sensations that thundered through them.

Slowly, Chiron pulled back his hips and plunged into her slick channel. His fingers stroked down her throat, the scent of their passion drenching the air.

Lilah lifted her legs to wrap them around his waist. She might not possess Chiron's experience, but she could match him in enthusiasm.

Their soft moans filled the air with sweet music as they moved together in a tempo that was slow and deep and steady.

Perfection.

Lilah broke free of the kiss, sucking in a lungful of air. Clearly she would have to remind Chiron that she wasn't a vampire when they were making love. Unlike him, she actually had to breathe.

Satisfaction sizzled through her as she realized the ease with which she'd assumed this was only the first of many times she would be spending the night in Chiron's arms. She might remain wary of being hurt, but she was increasingly certain she was destined to be this male's mate.

Unaware of her life-altering thoughts, Chiron buried his face in the curve of her neck. He increased the tempo of his thrusts, his hands shifting beneath her hips to angle them upward. Her nails dug into his flesh, her body arching as she neared her climax.

"Chiron," she groaned. "Come with me."

"Yes," he agreed in thick tones. "I'm with you."

Scattering kisses over the curve of her breast, he lowered his head to suckle at the tip of her nipple, his hips maintaining the ruthless pace as she held on tight.

Lilah cried out, her womb clutching at his cock as the shattering climax slammed through her at the same time Chiron gave a shout of pure rapture. The world outside the bedroom faded from thought as the tempest of pleasure assaulted her.

For breathless minutes, Lilah floated in a cloud of pure bliss. Then, with a low groan, Chiron wrapped his arms around her quivering body and rolled to the side, pressing her against his chest.

A silence filled the room, broken only by her heavy breathing as they both struggled to recover.

Lilah released a small sigh, not sure whether to laugh or cry.

Chiron was right. Nothing would ever be the same again.

Chapter 13

Ulric took his time as he strolled through the lush gardens.

He'd been wary when he'd followed Chiron's scent and discovered the towering wall of mist in the middle of the Everglades. He'd quickly determined the magic wasn't dangerous, but there was the possibility that it might be the prison that held Tarak. Was he possibly about to become another captive? Just like in those stupid human horror flicks, where people kept creeping into the dark despite the fact that their friends were disappearing one by one.

Then he'd forced himself to step through the barrier and realized it cloaked a demon hotel.

His wariness had only deepened. Why was Chiron staying here? And why hadn't he called?

Deciding to check out the grounds before entering the actual building, Ulric had shifted into his wolf form and padded through a tangle of lush ferns. A potent shiver of pleasure had raced through him. There was a primitive magic pulsing through the air that had nothing to do with the barrier. It'd urged his wolf to howl in raw wonderment as he raced beneath the moonlight.

Instead, he'd crouched low as he caught sight of the ogress speaking with a beautiful young female. He'd sniffed the air, baffled by the realization he couldn't tell what species the woman was. Odd. Then the ogress had taken off in one direction, and the female had headed into the hotel.

About to continue his sweep, Ulric had been halted by the sight of Chiron's sudden appearance. It looked as if he'd stepped out of thin air, which meant there must be something at the edge of the garden wrapped in illusion.

Ulric had studied his master, easily determining Chiron wasn't hurt. And he didn't appear to be an unwilling captive. In fact, he was staring toward the hotel with an expression of aching need.

He'd known in that moment why Chiron hadn't bothered to check in. A male in the throes of the mating heat could barely remember his own name, let alone anything else. Until Chiron had claimed Lilah, he would be worthless.

Which meant Ulric would have to take care of forcing the gargoyle to locate the key.

Of course, first he had to locate the gargoyle.

Remaining in his human form, Ulric strolled around the gardens until he picked up the gargoyle's scent. He frowned as he followed it to a hole hidden behind the illusion of a bush.

The gargoyle was down there. But why?

Ulric hesitated. Unlike Chiron, he wasn't a gambler. Long ago, he'd learned a hard lesson in following your heart, not your head. It wasn't until he'd spent several cautious minutes making sure there were no other scents in the area that he finally wiggled his way through the opening and dropped into the cavern below.

He remained crouched in a position where he could easily defend himself, his head tilted back as he sniffed the air.

Granite. And salt.

The granite was the gargoyle. The salt? He didn't have a clue.

Slowly straightening, he glanced around the large space. It was empty except for the long table in the center of the floor. He didn't bother to investigate it. He didn't care what weird ceremonies the locals might indulge in. He just wanted to get Levet and find the key.

Moving toward a nearby tunnel, he followed the gargoyle's scent, baffled when it began to fade. Backtracking, he tried to pinpoint the precise spot where the smell was the strongest. Where was the stupid creature?

"Gargoyle," he at last snapped. "Come out where I can see you."

"Hush, you mangy hound," Levet retorted, his voice muffled.

A growl rumbled in Ulric's throat. "I'm going to…" His threat trailed away as he leaned forward and pressed his nose against a crack in the smooth stone. "Are you in the wall?"

"*Oui.*"

"Why?"

"Because I'm attempting to escape."

Ulric glanced around. There was no one in the caves. Not unless they could hide their scent from a pureblood Were. Highly unlikely. "Escape from what?" he demanded.

There was the sound of Levet heaving a harsh sigh. "Are all dogs so dense, or are you special?"

Ulric felt a jolt of shock. Was the gargoyle insane? Or just suicidal?

"Come out and I'll show you how special I am," he snarled. "I'll start with ripping off those frilly wings and shoving them down your throat."

Ulric was accustomed to full-size trolls fleeing in fear when he used that tone. The gargoyle, however, heaved another sigh.

"Do not be a hater. You could only wish you had wings as glorious as mine."

"You—" Ulric bit off his words. It was ridiculous to argue with the three-foot pain in the ass. "Why are you in the wall?"

"I was locked in a dungeon and I am attempting to dig my way out."

Ulric blinked. There was a dungeon here? That wasn't what he'd been expecting.

"How did you get locked in the dungeon?"

"That annoying ogress," Levet explained, his tone edged with frustration.

Ulric recalled Chiron's explanation for the gargoyle's disappearance. "She threw you in the dungeon for stealing meat pies? That seems harsh."

There was a brief silence. "How did you know about the pies?" Levet finally demanded, sounding surprised.

Ulric snorted. "A better question is, why did you steal them?"

"I didn't," the gargoyle protested. "Well, I might have borrowed a few, but I am a guest. She should be delighted I enjoy the meals."

Ulric glared at the wall. Was the demon joking? If so, he wasn't funny.

"You don't *borrow* meat pies," he snapped.

"What do you care?" Levet groused. "Are you the meat pie pupu?"

"Pupu?" Ulric shook his head. What the hell was the gargoyle talking about? Then he abruptly realized what he was trying to say. "Do you mean po-po?"

There was the sound of stone cracking, as if the gargoyle had kicked the wall.

"Why are you so obsessed with pies?"

"Because they got you locked in a dungeon."

"The pies did not lock me in the dungeon," Levet argued. "I told you, the ogress did."

Ulric balled his hands into tight fists. He was going to kill him. It was that simple.

"Because of the pies." The words hissed between his clenched teeth.

"*Non.*" Levet sounded confused, as if he couldn't believe anyone would be stupid enough to think pies could have gotten him thrown into the dungeons. "It was because she is hiding the key."

"The key?" Ulric shoved aside his pulsing need to claw his way through the stone until he could get his hands on the aggravating demon. The gargoyle had just said the magic word.

"The item we came here to find," Levet said, in slow, concise tones. As if he was afraid Ulric couldn't understand.

Ulric counted to ten. "I know what it is."

He heard the gargoyle click his tongue. "Then why did you ask?"

Ulric felt his claws pop through his skin, even as the power of his wolf thundered through his body. He shuddered, struggling to control his beast.

Focus on finding the key, he sternly reminded himself. Later, he could teach the gargoyle just what happened when you taunted a Were. And he would savor every agonizing minute of the lesson. "Why didn't you tell Chiron?"

"Because I was locked away before I could."

"Where did she hide it?"

"I don't know."

Hmm. Did Ulric believe him? It sounded like a convenient excuse.

Still, there didn't seem to be any logical reason for the gargoyle to lie. Unless this truly was a trap devised by Styx.

"But you're sure the ogress has it?" he pressed.

"*Non,* but I am certain she knows where it is hidden," Levet said.

Ulric turned, heading back toward the large cavern. "I need to find the ogress," he said, speaking more to himself than the gargoyle. "That shouldn't be too difficult. She's as big as a barn."

"Hey! Wait!" The gargoyle's voice floated through the air, edged with a hint of panic.

Ulric's long strides never slowed. "What?"

"You are not going to leave me stuck in the wall, are you?"

A genuine smile curved Ulric's lips. "With the greatest of pleasure."

"Stupid dog. You need me."

"Like I need a hole in my head," Ulric muttered, enjoying the thought of the creature being trapped in the stone for an eternity.

Maybe he would return and seal up the various cracks…

"That can be arranged," Levet called out.

Distracted by the ridiculous gargoyle, Ulric was caught off guard as he entered the chamber to discover the towering form of the ogress standing a few feet away.

"Inga." He stepped forward, momentarily pleased it had been so easy to locate the female.

He'd expected to waste an hour scouring the grounds and then the hotel looking for the ogress. Instead, she'd just appeared.

Like magic.

Too late, he realized it wasn't luck or magic that had brought Inga into the cavern. She'd obviously followed him. Now she bared her pointed teeth, and before Ulric could shift into his wolf, she lifted a fist and smashed it into his face.

Ulric's eyes rolled back in his head and pain exploded in his brain.

His last thought was that he hoped the punch actually killed him. Nothing could be worse than waking to discover he was trapped in the dungeon with that damned gargoyle.

Chapter 14

Lying in bed with Lilah wrapped in his arms, Chiron savored a rare sense of contentment.

Not that he wasn't still anxious to release Tarak from his prison. Or that he couldn't feel the soul-deep ache to complete the mating with this female. But for the moment, he intended to enjoy the sensation of her lush, warm body pressed against him.

How could he ever have considered his life complete without a mate? Obviously, he'd had no idea what he was missing. Like a blind man walking through the world for centuries, then suddenly being given the gift of sight.

Everything was more intense, more vivid, more exhilarating.

He couldn't imagine what it would be like once they'd actually completed the mating. He wasn't sure his poor old heart could stand the excitement.

Nuzzling soft kisses over her tangled curls, Chiron shivered as her fingers lightly traced the muscles of his bare chest.

She abruptly broke the peaceful silence. "Tell me what happened after you were banished."

Chiron lifted his head to gaze down at her flushed face. He'd spent a long time trying to put the past behind him. Now, it felt like he was being forced to dig through memories he'd rather forget.

Still, he understood her curiosity. He was asking her to bind her life to his for the rest of eternity. She needed to know what she was getting.

"It's not a very exciting story," he warned.

Her nails scraped against his skin, sending darts of pleasure through him.

"I'll be the judge of that," she informed him.

He dropped a kiss on the tip of her nose. "Bossy."

"Is there a reason you don't want to talk about it?" she asked, clearly able to sense his reluctance.

Chiron grimaced. "It was a dark time for me."

Her fingers lifted to touch his cheek. "You were alone?"

"No, thank the goddess. Ulric was with me. If he hadn't been there..." He allowed his words to trail away, knowing exactly what would have happened to him without the steadying influence of his faithful companion.

He would have been dead.

"Tell me," she urged.

His lips twitched. Lilah had already discovered he could deny her nothing when she used those soft, pleading tones.

Dangerous female.

"My first decades of life, I was little more than a feral beast who survived by cowering in a cave," he said. "The only time I left was when my hunger drove me out to hunt for blood. Then I became a loyal soldier in the Anasso's clan. Everything was regimented, including where I slept and how far from the lair I could travel. I never had any true sense of freedom."

She looked puzzled at his words. "And after Tarak was captured you felt free?"

He shook his head, realizing she'd misunderstood his words. "Not free. I felt lost," he said, although *lost* didn't adequately capture his sense of being adrift. It was as if the floor had dropped from beneath his feet and he was plummeting through an endless darkness. "And with no barriers, I charged from one reckless decision to another. It didn't matter how dangerous or stupid it might be."

Her fingers drifted down the line of his jaw, her expression troubled. "Were you trying to kill yourself?"

"Not intentionally."

"But unintentionally?"

He considered the question. At the time, he'd been desperate to distract himself from the bitterness that simmered inside him like a toxic brew. The easiest way to accomplish that goal was to put himself at constant risk. Whether it was taking on a pack of trolls in a bar fight, or standing in the middle of a field until the cresting sun would send him fleeing for shelter, his skin raw and painful. Nothing like facing death to make you forget your troubles.

"It didn't seem to matter," he admitted. "I had nothing to lose."

Her fingers moved to press against his lips, her scent sharp with distress. "Don't say that."

He grasped her wrist, kissing her palm before tugging her hand away from his mouth. A part of him was fiercely pleased by her reaction. She was obviously upset by the thought he had been so reckless with his life, but another part hated the knowledge that he'd upset her. He swiftly attempted to distract her. "One good thing came out of that chaotic time."

"What?"

"I realized I had a talent for gambling."

Her tension eased, a hint of humor dancing in the golden shimmer of her eyes. "Hardly a talent if you can read people's minds."

He pretended to be aghast at her implication that his epic winning streak had been a result of cheating. "Not always."

She arched a brow. "Hmm."

He chuckled. He'd made a fortune fleecing unsuspecting humans and demons. "I'll admit it's a bonus."

She studied him with a curious expression. "Is that why you chose to go into the resort business?"

His fingers skimmed down her arm, bathed in the fading moonlight. She'd been vivid and beautiful in the magical sunlight, but in the darkness, she possessed a mystical charm.

A temptress who'd firmly woven him in her spell.

"It started as a fluke," he said, his fingers continuing to drift over her bare skin. It was addictive. Like stroking pure silk. "I won a decrepit hotel in Paris in a card game. Ulric challenged me to turn it into a profitable business." He gave a rueful shake of his head. The building had been on the point of collapse and in an area of the city no respectable guest would willingly choose. So he'd created a private gambling club for aristocrats that catered to their deepest fantasies. Within less than ten years, he had to turn customers away. "I could never resist a dare."

"I believe that." She rolled her eyes. "Why humans?"

"I was still technically banished. I wasn't supposed to be in Europe." He shrugged. Ulric had been furious when Chiron had traveled around the world only to return to one of the numerous countries from which he'd been formally banished. For Chiron, it had been a necessary act to regain his self-respect. "I thought a human casino would draw less attention from the Anasso."

"Obviously, he didn't find you."

Chiron shrugged. "By the time I returned, he'd already started to retreat from the world, rarely leaving his lair. I suspect Styx had taken over the duties of the Anasso, although he was careful to keep his master's illness hidden."

Lilah fell silent, as if mulling over a new, unexpected thought.

"Do you resent him for that?" she abruptly demanded.

He stared down at her, not sure what she was trying to ask. "Resent who?"

"Styx." She moved so she was perched on her elbow, her hair bouncing over her shoulders and brushing against the pillow. Chiron swallowed a growl. He'd spent a lot of time running his fingers through those curls. Just the memory was enough to make him hard and aching. "It sounds as if your master was next in line to become king. The two of you could be ruling the vampires."

Her unexpected words promptly killed his surging desire. Okay, it didn't kill it. Nothing could do that. But it put a severe damper on it.

"Not me." He gave a dramatic shudder. "I have no desire to babysit a bunch of whiny, psychopathic demons who are constantly bickering over who has the bigger territory." Even when he'd suspected the Anasso was lying to them, Chiron had pitied him. After an hour of listening to the various vampires who'd come to plead their case to the king, Chiron had a throbbing headache. "I'd rather deal with humans."

"What about Tarak? Will he challenge Styx when he's released from his prison?"

Chiron started to shake his head. Tarak had never once indicated a desire to sit on the throne. But that was before he'd been betrayed and imprisoned. Who knew what the hell had happened to his friend during those long centuries.

"I'm not sure," he admitted. "Tarak was always a team player. At least, when he believed in the Anasso's vision for our future. But now?" He shook his head. "I'm afraid."

"Of what?"

"That he might be consumed with the need for revenge. Or worse."

She looked confused. "What could be worse?"

Chiron's throat threatened to close shut. He didn't want to speak the words that had been haunting him for years. As if he could avoid the worst-case scenario by simply pretending it couldn't possibly happen. Now that he was on the point of actually finding a way to release his master, however, he couldn't continue to stick his head in the sand.

"He could be completely mad when he comes out of his prison," he forced himself to admit, his stomach clenching with dread. A crazed vampire was one of the most lethal creatures on earth. Tarak could massacre thousands of humans and demons before they could stop him. "Styx would have no choice but to destroy him either way."

Lilah grimaced. "You still want him released?"

Chiron nodded without hesitation. "Yes. No one deserves to be caged."

Sympathy flared through her eyes, making Chiron regret his choice of words. He was beginning to realize Lilah possessed her own painful frustration at the sense she was trapped. Her chains might not be as tangible as Tarak's, but they were just as crushing.

"Then we'll find the key and get him out," she assured him, abruptly rolling to the side and slipping out of bed.

He frowned as he watched her quickly tug on her robe. "What are you doing?"

She turned back to face him. "Inga should be in her rooms by now. We can ask her what she knows about the mysterious key."

Chiron wanted to argue. He'd barely taken the edge off his hunger for this female's luscious body. But dawn was swiftly approaching, and if they were going to question Inga before he was forced to return to his wing of the hotel, they had to do it now.

"I'd rather stay here, but once Tarak is released, we can concentrate on our mating," he said, speaking more to himself than Lilah as he crawled off the mattress and pulled on his clothes.

"Yes," she breathed, the sweet scent of ambrosia lacing the air.

Chiron shuddered, his fangs fully extended as his instincts screamed for him to claim his female.

"Damn," he muttered, wrapping his arm around Lilah's shoulders and steering her toward the door. "Let's go before I forget about everything but you."

* * * *

Levet was fuming as he wiggled through the small cracks in the stone. Dogs were always ill-tempered beasts. And especially the purebloods. But Ulric was clearly sadistic as well.

How dare the hound leave him trapped in the wall? Not that he wouldn't eventually escape, but that was not the point. Did Ulric not realize that Levet was a hero who had saved the world? More than once. The Were should have considered it an honor to be the one to assist Levet in his time of need.

Clearly, he needed to find a PR person. Perhaps if the word was spread about his heroics, demons would be properly impressed when they met him.

Digging another few inches, Levet froze when he heard the sound of pounding footsteps below him. Only one creature was heavy enough to shake the earth when she walked.

Poopy. Inga had returned.

Remaining as still as the stone around him, something gargoyles excelled at, Levet listened to the sound of something being dragged into the cell below him. Then there was a string of curses as the female realized her prisoner was missing.

"Gargoyle!" Inga's roar echoed through the cave, making Levet's ears ring. "You can't escape."

Levet remained frozen in place. Then the thunder of rocks being pulverized by massive blows made his pulse race. She was battering her way toward his hiding spot.

"There is no one here," he called out.

"Annoying creature," she muttered.

A breeze swept through his cramped tunnel before he felt her fingers wrap around his ankle.

"Eek! Release me." Levet kicked his feet, even knowing it was futile. The ogress was too big and too strong.

"Get back here."

Inga's fingers tightened until Levet feared she would crush his bones as she yanked him out of the tunnel. He sputtered in outrage. "There was no reason to be so rough, you oversize cow. My wings are very delicate."

The female dangled him upside down, as if he was a sack of potatoes and not a powerful demon.

"I should have killed you and the vampire as soon as you arrived," she snarled.

Levet frowned, debating whether to punish her with his awesome magic. He could turn her into a toad. That would teach her to treat him with a little respect. Unfortunately, his powers were not entirely stable, and there was the teeniest possibility he might bring the roof down on their heads.

He was forced to content himself with a stern glare. "I do not blame you for wanting to kill the leech. He is, after all, an arrogant pain in the derrière. But I have done nothing wrong." He was suddenly distracted as he caught an unexpected scent. "Why do I smell dog?" Inga spun him around until he had a view of the large male sprawled on the ground. "Oh. That explains the dragging sound."

Inga made a sound of disgust. "I caught sight of him in the gardens with your master."

Levet flapped his wings. "Chiron is not my master," he protested. "Indeed, I have no master. I am an independent contractor."

The ogress ignored his chiding words. "It was obvious he was another troublemaker. As if I don't have enough to deal with tonight."

Levet pointed out the easy solution to her troubles. "Give us the key and we will leave you in peace."

"I can't."

Levet clicked his tongue. Why was the female being so difficult? "Why not?"

"It's mine to protect." Her eyes flashed red. "And I will do whatever is necessary to keep it safe."

Levet shivered. Whatever was necessary? That couldn't be good.

"What does that mean?" he pressed.

"You shouldn't have come here," she said, tossing him across the cell with a flick of her wrist.

Levet squealed as he hit the ground with a painful thump. *Mon Dieu.* One day he was going to show the ogress she was messing with the wrong gargoyle.

Perhaps he would put a very large boil on the tip of her nose. One that could never be cured.

With a sniff, Levet forced himself to his feet and glared at the female as she used her massive foot to collapse the tunnel he'd spent the past hour digging. Then, stomping across the floor and stepping out of the cell, she slammed the heavy steel door behind her.

For a moment, Levet studied the pile of rubble that had been his escape tunnel. It was possible he could dig through the debris. But not before daylight.

Was Inga headed back to the hotel at this moment to crush Chiron? Did he care? Hmm. Not particularly, but Styx was certain to be all pussy—no wait, pissy—if he allowed the vampire to be killed on his watch.

Perhaps he should at least attempt to save him.

It was, after all, what he did best.

Heaving a sigh, Levet turned to make his way to where Ulric was snoring loud enough to wake the dead.

"Get up," he commanded.

More snoring. Levet leaned over the male, slapping his swollen and bloody face. It looked like he'd run into a brick wall.

Or Inga's fist.

He slapped the male's face again. And again. And again.

He'd just fallen into a nice rhythm when Ulric's hand shot up to grab Levet's fingers in a punishing grip.

"Stop that."

Levet scowled, pulling his fingers free as he took a step back. "Hey, no need to be a jack butt," he said.

Ulric slowly sat up, giving a shake of his head, as if he was trying to clear his thoughts.

"Jackass," he snapped. "Not jack butt."

"Whatever." Levet waved his hand toward the crumbled wall across the cell. "Because of you, my escape attempt has been ruined."

The Were scowled, clearly trying to figure out where he was and how he'd gotten there. "What happened?"

"Inga," Levet said.

Ulric looked momentarily confused, then his eyes smoldered with the golden heat of his inner wolf.

"She hit me in the face," he growled, reaching up his hand to gingerly touch his cheek. "I think she broke my jaw."

Levet shrugged his indifference. The dog deserved everything that had happened to him.

"*Oui.* And then she brought you down here and discovered me in the tunnel I had dug. Just look at what she did to it." He turned back to glare at his companion. "And it is all your fault."

Ulric muttered a curse as he forced himself to his feet. He wobbled, as if he was about to collapse, and Levet scrambled backward. The Were was large enough to squash him. Then, with a visible effort, Ulric managed to remain upright.

"How have you survived so long?" he groused.

Levet blinked. Was that a joke?

"I may be small, but my powers are as fearsome as they are wondrous," he informed his companion. "And my charm is—"

"Shut up," Ulric interrupted, glancing around the dungeon with an impatient expression.

Levet folded his arms over his chest. "Typical dog. Always growling and snapping."

Ulric pretended he didn't hear the insult, his hands balling into tight fists. "The ogress must be working with the witches."

Levet wrinkled his snout. "If she is, they are no longer in the area. I have not sensed a human since we arrived."

Ulric considered for a moment. "So either they don't care about the key, or they assume Inga is an adequate guard."

Levet shrugged. Neither explanation fully satisfied him. Vampires hated witches. Why would the Anasso work with the humans to create the spell if they were going to walk away? Why not work with Inga directly?

It was all very confusing.

"I suppose you can ask her when she comes back to kill us," Levet suggested.

Ulric jerked his head around, his eyes narrowed. "Did she say anything?"

Levet's wings twitched. Weres didn't produce the same heat as a dragon, but they did amp up the temperature when they were in a mood. Which was always.

"Only that we were interfering in matters we know nothing about, and that she will do whatever is necessary to protect the key."

Ulric peeled back his lips, his teeth lengthening as the smell of wolf filled the cavern. "Chiron is in danger."

Levet parted his lips, about to point out that it was more important that *he* was in danger than the stupid vampire. Then he swallowed his words. The Were was far more likely to get them out of there if he was anxious about his friend's safety.

"*Oui.*"

On cue, Ulric swiveled toward the door. "We have to get out of here."

Levet made a sound of impatience. "What do you think I have been saying?"

"Yap. Yap. Yap," Ulric said, his tone distracted. "At least that's what it sounded like to me."

Of all the conceited, ill-mannered mutts...

Levet raised his hand and extended one claw. "Dogs." He extended a second claw. "Ogres." Third claw. "Family." Fourth claw. "Vampires and dragons."

Ulric glanced over his shoulder with an annoyed expression. "Now what are you babbling about?"

"It is my most-disliked list," Levet informed him. "You are first."

Ulric didn't appear nearly as crushed as he should have been. Indeed, he gave a dismissive lift of his shoulder.

"Good. I like to be first."

Levet blew a raspberry in his direction. "How do you expect to get out of here?" he demanded.

Ulric halted in front of the only exit. "Like this."

Without warning, the large male began smashing his fists against the door, driving huge dents into the steel.

"Yikes." Levet scurried backward, his eyes wide.

Perhaps he should not be quite so quick to annoy the Were. He was clearly filled with all sorts of pent-up aggression.

Chapter 15

Lilah led Chiron into the hallway, attempting to squash the strange premonition that sent a rash of goose bumps over her skin. As much as she might want to remain wrapped in Chiron's arms, she couldn't pretend the outside world didn't exist.

Not only did Chiron need to return to the vampire wing of the hotel before dawn, but she wanted to help him release Tarak from the witches' prison. When they eventually completed the mating, she wanted to ensure he wasn't distracted by his gnawing need to rescue his master.

She wanted his full attention.

Telling herself the shiver snaking down her spine was one of excitement, she continued to the end of the hallway.

"This is her room," she said, reaching up to knock on the door. She frowned as it swung inward. Poking her head into the room, she tried to see through the gloom. Unlike most demons, she didn't have the ability to see at night. "Inga?" she at last called out. There was no answer and she straightened, turning back to meet Chiron's steady gaze. "Strange. She's usually preparing for bed at this hour."

Expecting him to shrug and turn away, Lilah watched in confusion as he brushed past her and pushed the door wider. Then, without hesitation, he stepped into the room and glanced around.

"Salt," he muttered.

She frowned in confusion before forcing her feet to carry her forward. She rarely entered Inga's private space, and never when the older female wasn't there. "What about salt?"

"I keep smelling it." He turned in a circle, as if trying to pinpoint the source. "I assumed it must have something to do with the witch's spell, but it's much stronger here."

"Oh." She gave a wave of her hand toward the walls. Each of them was painted with a dazzling display of an underwater scene. "It's the murals."

He remained confused as he moved toward the nearest wall and studied the fish that appeared to be swimming through the lacy coral. The colors were so vivid, so enchanting, they never failed to take Lilah's breath away when she saw them.

Chiron straightened. "Why would the murals smell like salt?"

"She told me it makes them more realistic."

He walked to the center of the room. Beyond the murals, it was remarkably barren, with one cushy chair that was large enough to fit Inga's oversize body, and a long cedar chest that had the top open to reveal neat stacks of leather-bound books.

Chiron shook his head and crossed the floor to shove open the wooden door set in the far wall. "No. This isn't from the murals."

"Chiron." Lilah hurried toward the male, cringing at the thought of Inga's horror if she discovered them. Never in all the years they'd lived together had Lilah dared to trespass beyond the front room. "What are you doing?"

"I think your manager knows more about the key and my missing master than she's willing to admit," he said, as if that explained everything.

"We can't just barge through her rooms," she protested, trying to grab his arm.

As if she'd ever be able to prevent a vampire from doing whatever he wanted to do. She'd have more luck stopping a freight train.

He easily shook off her hand. "You can't, but I can."

"No."

He shoved open the door and entered the attached bedroom. Instantly, fairy lights sparked to life, dancing across the ceiling to spread a soft golden glow through the small space.

In silence, they both glanced around the stark space. A large bed consumed most of the floor and a wood armoire was lovingly polished. That was it. There were no knickknacks, or pictures, or personal items. It looked like a cell rather than a bedroom.

Chiron circled the room. "She has a very austere style."

"She's also very large and very mean when someone invades her privacy," Lilah warned.

"I'm not invading."

She frowned as he circled the bed, then headed toward the armoire. "Then what are you doing?"

"Glancing."

"Is there a difference?"

"Of course there is." He stopped in front of the armoire and pulled open one of the doors. Lilah's mouth dropped open. It was bad enough to trespass into Inga's rooms, but to actually paw through her belongings was unforgivable.

Lilah stepped toward him. Enough was enough. They needed to get out of there before Inga returned and decided to twist Chiron's head off his body.

"Chiron, you can't—"

"Shit," Chiron interrupted, reaching into the armoire to pull out an object that had been hidden inside. "Did you know Inga owned this?"

Lilah's eyes widened as Chiron pulled out a bow and arrow. Of all the things she'd expected him to find in the armoire, a weapon was at the bottom of the list.

After all, Inga was big and strong enough to kill most things with her bare hands. Why would she need to shoot something?

"I don't ever remember seeing her with one," she said, her brain trying to land on a reason for the older female to have the strange object. "She might use it for protection when she goes into the swamps."

"Or to kill vampires."

Her gaze jerked up to search his tightly clenched features. She'd been surprised by the weapon, but it hadn't occurred to her that it might have been the one used to shoot at Chiron.

"No way." She gave an emphatic shake of her head.

He held out the arrow, pointing at the distinctive red fletching. "This is a replica of the one that nearly turned me into a pile of ash."

Lilah couldn't deny his accusation. The arrow did look the same. But Inga? Okay, the female might hate vampires. And she might have an extra dose of dislike for Chiron. But Lilah simply couldn't imagine the large ogress creeping onto the roof and waiting for the vague opportunity to shoot one of their guests through the heart.

Of course, there had to be some reason the weapon was in her armoire.

"Someone could have taken it from here." She grasped at the only straw that wiggled its way through the dazed fog in her brain. "We just proved she rarely locks the door."

He arched a brow. "It would have to be someone who knew she had the weapon in here. Who's closer to her than you are?"

There was no one. Inga didn't have friends. Not among the staff or any of the guests. And as far as Lilah knew, the older woman had never taken a lover.

Lilah wrapped her arms around her waist. That terrible sense of premonition wasn't just a tingle. It was thundering through her with unnerving force.

"It's impossible," she breathed.

"Why?"

"Because she has no reason to want you dead," Lilah desperately pointed out.

"Are you sure?"

The question was obviously rhetorical as Chiron turned away and tossed the bow and arrow onto the bed. Then, with long strides, he was across the room and placing his hand on the narrow door to the closet.

She pressed a hand to her churning stomach. "Now what are you doing?"

He continued to stroke the wood, as if he was capable of sensing what was on the other side. And maybe he was.

"Don't you think it's curious she doesn't lock the outside door, but she has this one double bolted?"

Lilah had been too distracted by the discovery of the weapon to pay much attention to the closet. Now she could see the heavy locks drilled into the door.

Odd.

"Perhaps she keeps her valuables in there," she suggested.

Chiron glanced over his shoulder. "Let's find out."

Lilah hurried forward. Did the male have no sense of boundaries at all? Clearly, the answer was no. "Please, let me just ask her."

He turned to face her, his expression grim. "Do you think she would be honest? Has she never lied to you?"

The questions slammed into Lilah with a physical force. Against her will, she recalled her earlier frustration with Inga. Not only because she was so reluctant to allow Lilah to travel beyond the barrier, but her insistence that she knew nothing about Lilah's parents. There was a mystery surrounding her past. She'd known it in her gut, even before Chiron had arrived and stirred up her suspicions. Still, she refused to think Inga was somehow evil. "She only wants to protect me," she said, speaking more to herself than to Chiron.

"From what?"

"I…" She gave a helpless shake of her head. "I don't know."

He reached to grasp her hands, clearly sensing her distress. "Lilah, I've seen you with Inga. Whatever she might be hiding, there's no doubt she's utterly devoted to you."

She released a shaky sigh. Could he sense how desperately she needed to trust in her former nanny? Inga had been the bedrock of her life. "She's all I've ever had."

"I understand." He squeezed her finger. "I truly do."

There was a fieriness in his voice that puzzled her. Then her breath caught in her throat. He was remembering Tarak, and how the older vampire refused to accept the truth that his beloved Anasso was addling his mind with tainted blood. Even when the truth was no doubt staring him straight in the face.

"I suppose you do." She heaved a small sigh. "I'm just like your master, attempting to convince myself that nothing is wrong."

He grimaced, as if he was suddenly regretting his words. "And I'm the same impatient fool who pushes without considering who I'm hurting." He lifted her hands to press her fingers against his lips. "I'm sorry, Lilah. Why don't you go back to bed? We can speak later."

Lilah hesitated. She wanted to obey his soft command. Why not crawl into her bed and pull the covers over her head? She didn't want to pry into Inga's privacy. And she didn't want to have her heart broken by the knowledge that the older female didn't deserve her trust.

Then she gave a sharp shake of her head. Wasn't she just whining to Inga that she wanted the fuzz cleared from her mind? Now that she had the opportunity, she wasn't going to run and hide. Even if it broke her heart.

"No." She stiffened her spine. "Denying the truth won't make it go away. I can only hope Inga will forgive me."

He continued to study her with obvious concern. "I don't want you hurt."

She nodded toward the door. "Right now, all we have is a suspicion that my friend might know more about the key than she's willing to admit. It's quite likely there's nothing behind the closed door beyond her stash of muumuus."

His brows arched. "Is that what you call those dresses she wears?"

"She does have a unique style," Lilah agreed, rushing to the defense of her friend. "As I recall, you said you liked unique."

He shrugged. "No doubt Levet is unique as well, but I don't want to think about him in a muumuu."

Lilah chuckled at the thought of the gargoyle in a muumuu, at the same time struck by a sudden thought.

"They both appear to be misfits among the demon world. Perhaps the two of them—"

"Stop." Chiron held up a hand. "I beg of you."

Lilah's brief amusement faded as she glanced toward the closet. She didn't know where Inga was, but the ogress would soon be returning. The last thing Lilah wanted was a physical confrontation between her onetime nanny and her soon-to-be mate.

"Let's get this over with."

He nodded, turning back to the door. "I'll try the easy way first," he told her.

He reached out to grasp the doorknob. Lilah took an instinctive step backward as she heard the screech of metal on metal. Vampires didn't have to be as large as trolls to have extraordinary strength. But surprisingly, the locks held. They were either reinforced or magically enhanced.

Chiron released the knob and sent her an apologetic glance. "Looks like it's going to have to be the hard way."

"Hard way? What's that mean?" she demanded. He didn't answer. Instead, he lifted his leg and with one fluid motion, kicked the center of the door. Lilah threw up her hands to protect herself from the wood splinters that blasted around her. "Chiron."

"Sorry."

Cautiously, she lowered her arms, studying the jagged opening that used to be a door. Beyond it was nothing but darkness, along with a sense of a wide, empty space. This was no mere closet.

"My life was so peaceful before you showed up."

Chiron flashed a charming grin. "You mean boring?"

Lilah had heard about knees melting, but hers had never done it. Not until now. That smile…That glorious smile. It could make any woman a little wobbly. With a stern effort, she managed to stay upright.

"Maybe."

His lips parted even farther, deliberately revealing a hint of fang. Her pulse went haywire; then he ruined it all by opening his mouth.

"Stay here. I'll be back in just a few minutes."

Lilah planted her fists on her hips. "Excuse me?"

He glanced around, as if surprised by the edge of annoyance in her voice. "We don't know what Inga might be hiding."

She wasn't impressed with his logic. "This is my hotel. And Inga is my employee."

With staggering speed, he was standing in front of her, his hands lightly gripping her upper arms. "And I need to protect you."

She tilted back her head, fighting against the urge to be blinded by his male beauty. "Because I'm a female?"

"Because I'm a vampire and I assume no one is stronger or faster or more lethal than I am."

His simple honesty stole her surge of resentment. This wasn't about him being a male. It was about him being a vampire.

"Arrogant," she muttered.

"Without a doubt." He reached out to frame her face in his hands, his cool skin sending jolts of heat through her. How did he do that? "Please let me make sure there's no hidden danger."

She scowled. Her pride told her to refuse. He was the sort of domineering male who would take a mile if she gave an inch. Then again, she wasn't stupid. They didn't know what was lurking inside. And she didn't have the sort of powers to battle against monsters.

"Fine. But we're going to have a conversation about your assumption I can be treated like some helpless victim," she warned.

"Can't wait." He bent his head to press their lips together.

Another jolt of heat blasted through her. Before she could reach up to yank him closer, he was pulling away. She sighed, watching as he disappeared through the shattered door and was swallowed by the darkness.

She wasn't afraid for Chiron. There were few things in the world that could actually harm a vampire. Besides, what lethal creature could possibly be hiding in a closet?

But she was afraid of what he might find.

The temperature in the room abruptly dropped. Lilah rubbed her arms. She recognized that chill.

She took a step forward. "Chiron?"

"Yeah, I'm here," he called out, reaching up to brush over the fairy lights so a bright glow spilled out of the opening.

Lilah took another step forward. "What did you find?"

Chiron appeared, using his foot to sweep aside the broken pieces of wood before he gestured for her to join him. "I think you need to see this for yourself."

"Okay."

It was impossible to read any emotion in his voice, but Lilah didn't hesitate to move forward. Chiron wouldn't urge her inside unless it was absolutely safe.

She stepped through the opening, instantly shocked by the sheer size of the room. She'd already suspected it was much bigger than a closet, but this was three times as large as the other two spaces combined. She turned in a circle, taking in the rough wooden floors and bare walls. The space was devoid of furniture, but it wasn't empty. There were stacks of framed canvases leaning against the walls, and shelves that held Inga's various painting supplies.

An artist's studio.

Lilah absently moved toward the nearest pile of canvases. She really shouldn't be surprised Inga would have converted her rooms to create a space to indulge her love for painting. The older woman never discussed her passion for art, but it was evident in the beauty she created throughout the hotel.

She waited for her unease to fade. There was nothing sinister in here. Was there? But Chiron was staring at her with a strange expression. As if there was something in the room she wasn't seeing.

Not the most pleasant sensation.

Unsure what she was supposed to do, Lilah reached out to grab the top canvas. Her brows arched as she realized it was a portrait of her. In the painting, her curly hair was pulled on top of her head and she was wearing a long green gown with a white ruff collar. It looked like a costume worn by humans attending a renaissance fair.

Strange.

She reached for another canvas. This was another one of her. Only she was wearing a bright yellow gown over wide hoops and a straw hat. Like the woman from that movie *Gone With the Wind*. Lilah had watched the movie a hundred times, always wishing she could be Scarlett O'Hara but fearing she was more like poor Melanie.

Lilah shook off the ridiculous thought as she shuffled through the canvases.

"They're all portraits of me," she said.

"Exquisite, but they raise a number of questions," Chiron said, moving to stand directly beside her.

"What questions?"

He reached for the painting that had her in the elegant green gown. "How could she have painted your portrait four hundred years before you were born?"

Lilah scowled. "Why would you assume it was painted four hundred years ago?" she demanded, pointing toward the fireplace in the portrait. It was clearly the one in the lobby downstairs. And on the mantel were the same vases and delicate jade figurines. "Inga could easily have created it last week."

"Do you have that gown hanging in your closet?" he demanded.

"Of course not, but clearly, Inga wanted some variety in the paintings and used her imagination."

He tossed the picture back on the pile. "Why not just paint you at different ages?"

Her mouth felt oddly dry. Why? It wasn't fear. Not exactly. But Chiron's question struck a nerve.

Why would Inga have so many portraits of her? And why put her in costumes she'd never owned? It would make more sense to have a series of paintings that followed her growing from a baby to a grown woman.

"I don't know," she admitted. "I never realized she had these."

Without warning, Chiron grasped her arms and turned her to meet his dark gaze. "Lilah."

"What?"

"I can feel the age in these." He nodded toward the stack of canvases. "They weren't painted a week ago. They're old. Really old."

She wanted to argue. It simply wasn't possible. But she assumed he could truly tell the age of the portraits. Which meant...

"Wait." A desperate explanation formed in her foggy brain. "Then they must be of my mother. Inga has always claimed I look just like her."

"You would have to be an exact duplicate of her," he pointed out in gentle tones. "And didn't she say she didn't arrive at the hotel until after you had been born?"

"Then maybe Inga didn't paint them."

"Lilah."

She swallowed a sigh. There was no doubt the portraits had been done by Inga. She was just grasping at straws.

Warily, she met Chiron's steady gaze. Was that suspicion she could detect deep in his dark eyes? The thought made her heart clench with pain. "Do you think I've been lying to you?"

He gave a slow shake of his head. "No. Not intentionally."

A sharp laugh was wrenched from her lips. "That's not very reassuring."

He stepped closer, wrapping her in his icy power. "You told me you don't remember much about your childhood."

"So?"

"Tell me what you do recall."

She tilted back her head. She didn't bother to try to force the memories. It was a wasted effort. "I can't."

"You don't know anything about your childhood?"

"Everything in the past is fuzzy." She shrugged. "I think I tried to block out the deaths of my parents. Plus, memory loss is a side effect of the cleansing spell Inga used after the plague."

His eyes narrowed. "Did Inga come up with that excuse?"

"Yes."

His hands lifted to lightly brush his fingers over her furrowed brow. "Will you let me try to discover the truth?" he asked.

"How?"

"I can look into your mind," he reminded her. "If there are any memories, I should be able to retrieve them for you."

She shivered, but not from the chill Chiron created in the air. No, it was the mere thought of digging through the mysterious layers in her brain.

What if she was blocking something horrible that happened in her past? Or worse, what if the memories had been truly destroyed so she would never, ever be able to recall her childhood? "What if you can't?"

His fingers threaded through her curls, his expression somber. "There's only one way to find out."

She grimaced. "I'm afraid."

"Do you trust me?"

Did she? The question came without hesitation. Completely and utterly. It didn't matter that she barely knew him. Or that he'd hidden his reason for coming to her hotel.

This male was her mate. And her faith in him was unshakable.

"Yes." She lifted her hands to place them against his chest. "What do I have to do?"

"Just relax."

"Relax?" she demanded in disbelief. "I feel like my life is being turned upside down and you want me to relax?"

"Shh." He allowed his fingers to stroke over her cheeks, bending his head until they were nose to nose. "Look into my eyes."

She released a choked laugh. "Isn't that a little clichéd?"

"You already know I have a fondness for cheesy lines."

His teasing managed to ease the tight bands of tension around her chest. At least enough so she could suck in a breath.

"Yes."

His fingers continued to stroke over her face, his eyes unfocused as the temperature in the room dropped. That was the only indication he was using his powers.

She didn't know what she'd expected. Lightning bolts through her head. Or the feel of his mind poking into hers. Or even a few sparks and tingles.

Instead, there was nothing.

Minutes ticked past, then more minutes. On the point of accepting he wasn't going to be able to penetrate the fog, Lilah heard him mutter a low curse.

"Chiron?"

"There's something there," he muttered.

"What?"

"A barrier." His fingers pressed against her temple. Not hard, but insistent. Did his touch help him connect to her thoughts? "It's trying to keep me out."

"I'm not doing it."

"I know," he assured her. "It's the same thing I sensed before."

Lilah tried to clear her mind. Could the barrier be from the cleansing spell? Or had it been placed there by someone else?

Maybe...

Her spinning thoughts were interrupted by the strange *pop* that echoed through her skull. It was like the snap of a rubber band. Or a crack in the barrier Chiron was attempting to break through.

The breath was yanked from her lungs as her knees went weak. A darkness was swirling through her mind, dragging her downward.

No. Not downward.

Backward.

"Lilah. Lilah."

Distantly, she could hear the sound of Chiron's frantic voice, feel his arms wrapping around her. But while her body remained in Inga's hidden studio, her mind was being sucked into the past...

Chapter 16

Lilah walked through the elegant home. In a hidden part of her mind, she understood this was a memory, but it all felt vividly real.

She battled back the urge to shake herself out of her strange, dreamlike state. How long had she yearned to know about her past? Now she had the opportunity to relive what had happened. She'd worry about the how and why later.

Focusing on her surroundings, Lilah took in the wooden floor and the whitewashed stucco walls. Overhead were heavy open beams, while the windows were small with diamond-shaped grills.

She passed by a flickering candelabra set near a framed mirror on the wall. Her gaze cast a quick glance to the side before skittering away.

She should have been shocked by her reflection. This was supposed to be the past. But instead of a younger version of herself, she'd glimpsed a woman who looked to be in her mid-sixties, with thick curls faded to a dull gray and her face heavily lined. She was wearing a shabby dress that brushed the floor and a red woolen apron wrapped around her waist. It looked like something a gypsy would wear centuries ago.

It wasn't shock she felt at the image, however. Instead, it was a weary acceptance that included her slight limp from an old injury to her hip.

In this past, she was a human witch who had spent most of her life hiding from ignorant peasants who were forever blaming her coven for whatever disaster happened to befall the village. Plagues. Miscarriages. Too much rain. Too little rain.

Ignorant fools.

Still, they'd managed to avoid being burned at the stake. The villagers might fear them, but they were also quick to seek out their spells and potions when they were in need of assistance.

At least until the castle built high on the hill had been besieged and taken over by a rival family. Lord Batton had brought with him a slew of aristocrats, along with a large number of soldiers. As well as a blatant hatred for witches.

Lilah had scrambled to find a way to safely lead her coven away from the area. A difficult task. Relocating thirteen women along with their livestock took money.

Money she didn't have.

Then, this morning, disaster had struck. Which was the only reason she'd agreed to meet with Sir Travail when he'd sent a note promising assistance. He was one of the noblemen who'd moved into the finest home in the village, which meant he was loyal to Lord Batton. But what choice did she have but to listen to his offer?

Limping forward, she entered a distinctly masculine room. The furniture was heavy wooden chairs with a few tables devoid of knickknacks. The walls were paneled, and there was a brick fireplace where cheery flames danced.

The warmth of the room was a welcome relief to her aching hip. At least until her gaze landed on the male standing in the center of the room.

Her muscles tensed. Sir Travail was exquisitely handsome, with his lean, perfectly chiseled features and deep, startling blue eyes. His brown hair was cut short and his goatee was neatly trimmed. This evening, he was wearing a green velvet doublet with a pair of thick hose and pointed shoes. He'd thankfully forgone the codpiece that was all the rage among men.

At her entrance, he strolled forward to grasp her hand, performing an elegant bow.

"Ah. Lilah. I am so pleased you accepted my invitation."

Lilah pulled her fingers free with a sharp tug. Unlike most females in the area, she hadn't allowed Travail's undoubted beauty to blind her. There was something about him that set off her internal alarms.

"I did not have much choice," she said in stiff tones. "Lord Batton's soldiers arrived this morning and captured most of my coven. They are awaiting death in the castle."

He lifted a hand to press it to the center of his chest. "So I heard." He clicked his tongue. "Truly a shame."

Lilah wasn't fooled for a moment. This man was somehow involved with the capture of her coven. In fact, after she'd received his message, she suspected he'd been the driving force behind the sudden arrests.

He wanted something from her.

"Your note promised you had a way for us to escape from this land."

His brows arched at her sharp tone, a hint of humor in his eyes. He obviously enjoyed the knowledge she was uneasy in his presence. "Yes." He gave a small shrug. "There is a price, of course."

She squared her shoulders, allowing her innate magic to flow through her blood. She would not be intimidated. Not by this man or any other. "I assumed there would be. I will warn you, we have little money to offer."

He gave a wave of his hand. "I have no need for gold or riches."

That was no surprise. The house alone was worth a fortune.

"Then it is magic you desire," she said.

"Yes."

"A love spell?"

"No."

Ah. She squashed her sudden urge to smile. No doubt she should have guessed why he had sought her out. And why he'd been so secretive when he'd asked her to join him tonight.

"I do have a spell that is guaranteed to improve your stamina," she assured him. "If you will wait here, I can fetch it and return—"

"Do I appear to need extra stamina?" he interrupted, his voice mocking.

Lilah met his unwavering gaze, refusing to be embarrassed. "No, but it is the reason most gentlemen seek me out."

"Not me." With the elegance of a trained swordsman, he moved toward her. The scent of salt suddenly filled the air. Strange. Was it coming from Sir Travail? "I have a different need."

Lilah shook her head, forcing herself to concentrate on his words. "What is it?"

He paused, studying her with an unnerving intensity. It felt as if he was trying to peer into her mind. Or her soul.

"I have captured a vampire," he abruptly announced.

Her eyes widened, her brain struggling to accept what he'd just said. "Are…" She was forced to halt and clear her throat. "Are you jesting?"

His lips pinched together. "I do not jest about vampires."

Neither did Lilah. She'd done her best to avoid the demons who roamed the world. What little magic she possessed couldn't protect her from such evil.

"I have heard rumors of the lethal beasts, but I have never encountered one," she breathed.

His lips twisted with a mysterious smile. "You are fortunate," he told her. "It is rare one crosses paths with a demon and survives to tell the tale."

Lilah cast a nervous glance around, afraid the beast might be hidden in a shadowy corner. "Where is he?"

"I have him shackled in a nearby cave, although the chains will not hold him for long."

She was shaking her head before he finished speaking. She was willing to sacrifice for her coven, but she had no intention of battling against a demon. "I have no power over vampires."

"Not alone," he agreed. "But with your coven and my own magic user, we can bind him in a prison that will contain him for an eternity."

"Another witch?" Lilah demanded, realizing that would explain the scent of salt. Most witches used it to cast spells. Even minor ones.

He gave a dismissive wave of his hand. "She is much more than a witch, but you have no need to worry about her."

Lilah frowned. Typical male. Always minimizing the contributions of the women who served him.

"Why not just kill the vampire?" she bluntly demanded.

The charming mask slipped to reveal the cold, calculating man she'd always sensed lurked just below the surface.

"Do you wish to crawl into his cell and place a stake through his heart?"

She took an instinctive step backward. "No."

With a visible effort, he regained command of his composure. "Are you willing to assist me or not?"

Lilah hesitated. She didn't want to be involved with demons. They were not only deadly to humans, but they had powers that could do more than just kill her. They could enslave her soul for an eternity.

Unfortunately, without this man's assistance, she had no means to rescue her coven. And a witch alone in this day and age was as good as dead.

"If I promise to cast a spell of ensnarement, you will ensure my coven is released and taken to a home where we will be safe?" she demanded.

"There is a little more." He lifted his hand to stroke his goatee. With the firelight dancing behind him, and his eyes glowing, he looked like the devil himself.

And maybe he was.

She shivered, but with an effort she managed to force the question past her lips. "How little?"

"I will need a key."

"A key?" She blinked in confusion. "To what?"

"The vampire's prison."

Her mouth dropped open. Had this man not heard the horror stories? Vampires fed on blood. They stole virgins from their beds. They could raise the dead from their graves. "Why would you want a way to let the creature out?"

A dangerous expression rippled over the too-handsome face. "My reasons are not your concern."

Lilah bit back her protests. What did it matter what nefarious connection he had to the vampire? She couldn't offer him what he wanted. "I have no magic that would create an opening once I have cast the spell."

He shrugged. "Thankfully, I do."

Lilah clenched her hands into tight fists. She'd spent the day attempting to plead for the release of her coven, followed by a tedious walk through the rain to reach this house. Her feet were soaked and her hip ached. She was in no mood for games.

"Then why do you need my help?" she demanded.

"The key must be kept secure."

"You want me to keep it hidden?"

"I do."

His smooth answers did nothing to ease her frustration. Indeed, it only added to her certainty he was luring her into a wicked bargain. Decent gentlemen didn't imprison vampires and then demand a key. They killed them.

"Why do I sense there is something you are not telling me?"

His eyes narrowed even as he forced a smile to his lips. "You are very perceptive, Lilah," he murmured in a soft voice. "That is what attracted me to you in the first place."

Lilah was flattered despite herself. Her conceit was always her weakness. "Tell me what you want from me."

"First a gift." He held out his slender hand. "Come with me."

Lilah frowned. She didn't trust this man. And she certainly had no intention of being led away from the public area of the house. "It is late."

His lips twitched, as he was once again amused by her apprehension. "Do not fear. We are merely crossing the room."

Reluctantly, she laid her fingers against his palm, startled by the coolness of his skin. If she hadn't seen him during the day, she would have suspected he was one of the vampires himself.

In silence, he led her down the long room, turning her so she faced the wall.

"Stand here."

She sent him a startled glance. "What am I supposed to do?"

He spoke a soft word, and suddenly there was a full-length mirror in front of her.

"Look."

The breath hissed between her teeth. Not at the sudden appearance of the mirror, but at the reflection staring back at her.

Suddenly, she wasn't the old, faded woman who rarely bothered to brush her hair or change her clothing. Instead, she was the beautiful maiden who'd been pursued by endless men. Her hair was a riotous mass of silken curls, her skin smooth and kissed by honey. Her eyes were mysterious pools of green with the shimmer of gold.

She lifted a shaky hand to touch her face. It felt as soft as satin.

"A trick," she croaked.

"A promise," he whispered in her ear. Just like the serpent in the Garden of Eden.

"Sorcery," she accused.

"Perhaps," he agreed. "But does it matter if I can give you this?"

Temptation pulsed through her like a living force. She wanted her youth. With a desperation she'd never realized until it was being offered.

"Impossible," she breathed, fiercely reminding herself that nothing came without a cost.

His breath brushed over her cheek, sending a chill down her spine. "Not only is it possible, but I can offer it to you for an eternity."

Lilah's lips parted, but she couldn't hear the words she was speaking. Instead, the world around her began to fill with a swirling mist, as if she was standing in the middle of a snow globe that had been suddenly shaken. She blinked, feeling a tug in the center of her chest. Then the mist became darkness, flooding her mind and sending her whirling back through the maelstrom.

Chapter 17

Lilah slowly came to her senses. It took a minute to realize she was back in the hidden studio, and that Chiron was bending over her with a fierce concern etched on his face.

She released a shaky breath, a queasy sensation rolling through her stomach. Not just from memories that had burst through the barrier in her mind, but the effort to accept what she'd seen.

Once, she'd heard the saying *Don't ask if you don't want the answer.* Suddenly, she understood the exact meaning of that phrase.

"Lilah." Chiron bent down until they were nose to nose. "Can you hear me?"

Belatedly, she realized he'd been saying her name over and over. Raising her hand, she intended to press it against his cheek. Instead, there was a low roar, followed by the sound of thunderous footsteps.

Lilah knew exactly what was coming even before a huge hand grabbed Chiron by the shoulder and tossed him across the room.

"What have you done to her?" Inga screeched.

"Inga. No."

Lilah struggled to her feet, stepping toward the enraged ogress. But her balance was on the fritz, causing her to sway forward. She would have fallen on her face if Inga hadn't reached out to grasp her upper arms.

"I have you," she said gently.

Ice formed on the walls as Chiron prepared to attack. Carefully, Lilah turned her head and sent him a warning glance.

"No. Please, Chiron," she pleaded. "I'm okay."

The ice continued to crawl around the room, but Chiron halted a few feet away, his fangs fully exposed. As if they needed the warning he was ready and eager to kill.

Inga at last broke into the explosive silence. "What are you doing in here?"

Lilah returned her attention to the female who'd been lying to her for centuries. "I'm looking for answers."

Inga dropped her hands, her expression guarded. "Perhaps you should search for some manners as well. These are my private rooms."

Lilah held her gaze. "I remember."

Inga stiffened. "What are you talking about?"

Chiron swiftly moved to her side, keeping his fangs fully exposed. "You have your memories back?" he asked.

"They're starting to return." She wrinkled her nose. "Most of them are still fragmented."

He cupped her face in his hands. "Are you all right?"

Inga released a low growl. "Of course she isn't. What have you done to her?"

His gaze never strayed from her upturned face. "Lilah?"

"I'm fine." She paused to clear the sudden lump from her throat. "But there's something you need to know."

"Whatever it is, it can wait. You're too weak." Chiron pressed his thumb to her lips. His dark eyes smoldered with emotion, revealing that he was still upset.

Just how long had she been lying on the floor while she was lost in the past?

A stab of guilt mingled with her bitter regret. "No, I need to tell you."

His eyes narrowed. Could he sense the emotions churning through her? "Tell me what?"

"I was the witch."

Distantly, Lilah could hear Inga's sharp intake of breath, but her focus remained on Chiron as he studied her in confusion.

"What witch?"

Inga crowded closer, towering over them as she clenched and unclenched her big hands. "Don't listen to her," she rasped. "She's clearly confused."

"Shut up," Chiron snapped, before visibly restraining his burst of annoyance. In a soothing motion, he brushed his fingers down the curve of her throat. "Take your time, Lilah."

A shiver shook her body. She didn't want to take her time. She wanted to spill out the truth, as if she hoped the quicker she released the poison, the less damage it would do.

"There was a man. Sir Travail," she blurted out. "He was pretending to be a human, but I'm certain he was something else."

Chiron blinked. "Was he a guest here?"

Lilah forced herself to take a deep breath. She was babbling. Never a good thing.

"No. But he's the one who arranged for me to come here." She glanced toward the ogress. "Along with Inga."

The large female pressed her lips together, even as Chiron demanded her attention.

"When?"

"The same time your master was taken."

Chiron jerked, as if she'd physically struck him. "You saw Tarak?"

"No, but the man claimed to have captured a vampire. He needed a coven of witches to help create a prison. And to protect the key."

She'd intended to come straight out with the truth. Like ripping off a bandage. Instead, she'd skirted at the edges of a confession. As if she could protect herself from Chiron's inevitable disappointment.

His icy power wrapped around her. "You know how to free my master?"

She lifted her hand to point toward the ogress. "Inga does."

Inga took a sharp step backward, knocking over an easel and sending the empty canvas skittering across the floor. "I don't know anything."

Lilah faced the female who'd been the center of her life. She waited for the pain. Or anger. Instead, all she felt was an aching sadness.

"I've seen the truth."

Inga shook her head, the oversize muumuu floating around her square body. "It was a dream." She waved a hand toward Chiron. "Or a trick from that vampire. He admitted he could mess with your mind."

Lilah took a step forward. Chiron instantly moved to stand at her side, but she concentrated on the female who was clearly distressed by the realization that the barriers in Lilah's mind had been demolished.

"No more lies, Inga. I beg of you."

"I—"

"Please," she interrupted, her expression pleading. "Who is Sir Travail?"

Genuine fear turned Inga's eyes red. "I can't."

Lilah muttered a curse. Enough was enough. She'd been living in the dark too long. "Tell me or I will leave this hotel tonight and never return."

"No, you can't." Inga's voice held an edge of panic, her eyes darting toward the door, as if she was considering the various means of preventing Lilah from escaping.

"Don't test me," Lilah warned.

Inga grimaced before heaving a resigned sigh. "It's only going to cause you pain."

Lilah held her gaze. "Who was Sir Travail?"

"His real name is Riven, Lord of the Merfolk."

"Merfolk." Chiron intruded into the conversation, his voice sharp. "That's why I smell salt."

Lilah's mouth parted in shock. She'd read the stories that surrounded that mysterious species. The theory was that they'd once walked on land, but had long ago returned to their lairs in the deepest part of the oceans. But she'd always assumed they were either a myth or that they'd perished after they'd disappeared.

"You're a mermaid?" she breathed, trying to wrap her mind around the thought.

Inga flushed, easily sensing Lilah's shock. "My mother was. She was captured by a roaming band of orcs. After I was born, she handed me over to a slave trader."

Lilah's heart clenched with pity. This female might have deceived her, but that didn't erase all the years of loving companionship they'd shared. "Oh, Inga."

She shook her head, as if trying to ward off Lilah's sympathy. "It no longer matters," she said in clipped tones. "I was traded a few times, but eventually my owner was killed and I managed to escape."

Lilah frowned. "Did the mermaids capture you?"

"I went to them," Inga admitted, her voice harsh with a remembered pain. "I didn't know what else to do. I had no family. No home. I thought—"

Lilah reached out to place her hand on Inga's forearm. "It's okay. What else could you do?"

"I was greeted by Lord Riven and promptly informed I was a blemish on my family."

Lilah grimaced. Her memory of Lord Riven was of a sophisticated charmer, but even back then, Lilah had glimpsed something darker lurking beneath the surface. If she hadn't been so blinded by her lust for eternal youth, she would have realized what she sensed was pure evil.

"Bastard," she muttered.

"He promised I could wipe away my stain on my mother if I agreed to help him."

"Yeah, he was good at promising things," Lilah muttered.

Inga nodded. "He took me with him to meet a group of mongrel trolls who were holding the vampire captive."

Chiron stepped forward, making both women shiver at the blast of icy air that swirled around him. "Tarak?"

"I didn't hear his name," Inga said. "He was shackled with silver manacles and his head was covered. All I know is that he was payment for a debt."

Chiron hissed in fury. "What did you do to him?"

Inga met the vampire glare for glare. She wasn't a female who backed down. Not ever. "Once Riven convinced Lilah and her coven to join us, we traveled to this place."

Lilah dropped her hand and stepped away. She'd just learned she was human. Which meant she didn't have the ability of demons or fey to withstand physical damage. She wanted to be out of the path of the two large and potentially violent predators.

At the same time, she determinedly steered Inga's attention back to her explanation.

"Why here?"

Thankfully, the distraction worked. Inga slowly turned her head to meet Lilah's questioning gaze. "This building belonged to the mermaids from the beginning of time." She glanced around the studio. "Until the humans arrived, and they retreated into the ocean."

Lilah nodded, a fuzzy memory starting to return. She was standing in the swamp with her hands lifted toward the sky. She was chanting words that no longer made sense to her.

"I created the barrier around the hotel."

"Along with your coven and me," Inga said.

She pressed a hand to her aching temple. Her coven. Women she'd gathered together for their mutual protection. She hadn't liked them all. In fact, there'd been a few she'd detested. But they'd been a family.

Now…they were gone.

"What happened to the others?" she forced herself to ask.

Inga waved a hand, clearly indifferent to the fate of the other witches who had once lived here. "A few died during a plague that swept through the area."

Lilah felt a stab of surprise. "So there *was* a plague?"

"Yes, but it only affected humans."

"What about the others?"

"They grew jealous of your eternal youth," Inga admitted. "Eventually, they decided you must have made a pact with the devil and fled into the swamps. I don't know what happened to them after that."

Lilah shivered, the queasiness returning. "I *did* make a pact with the devil."

Easily sensing her distress, Chiron moved to wrap his arm around her shoulders. His gaze, however, was focused on Inga. "Do you have the magic that keeps her from aging?" he questioned.

"It's not my magic," Inga corrected. "It comes from the grotto."

Lilah resisted a hysterical urge to laugh. It was all so insanely awful. "A magical grotto?" she choked out.

Inga shook her head. "The grotto is just an illusion. The magic is in the water."

"Oh." Lilah's eyes widened. "There really is a fountain of youth."

"It was a source of power for the mermaids," Inga continued. "That's why they chose this location for a lair."

Mermaids and fountains of youth. Lilah gave a shake of her head, as if it would help her to accept the bizarre tale. "Is that why you insisted I bathe in it each night?"

Inga nodded. "It's not truly necessary. You could submerge yourself in the waters every year or so and maintain your youth, but it always seemed to give you pleasure."

She was right. The water had offered a sense of peace that had been addictive. She'd had no idea it was also extending her life.

"Why only me?"

Inga looked confused. "What?"

"Why was I the only witch offered the waters?"

"That was Riven's decision."

"And I agreed." Lilah pressed a hand to her churning stomach.

She suddenly wasn't sure she wanted the rest of her memories to return. Not when she was going to be forced to recall the nights she was swimming through the magical waters while she knew her coven was relentlessly aging.

How could she have been so selfish?

She must have made a sound of distress, causing Chiron to tighten his arm as he dropped a kiss on the top of her head.

"Shh. It's all right."

She shook her head. It wasn't all right. And it was time she revealed the truth. Turning, she met his searching gaze. "I'm not a very good person," she told him.

He scowled. "Don't say that."

"Why not? I sacrificed my coven. Women who depended on me to keep them safe," she said. "And just as awful, I agreed to help imprison your master. I didn't care if he'd committed some crime or if he was a helpless victim. I thought of nothing but the promise of a pretty face and eternal life." She stopped, giving a sad shake of her head. "Who would do that?"

She expected disappointment. Or even anger. Instead, Chiron pushed her curls from her face, his touch so gentle it brought tears to her eyes.

"The woman who came to this place is not the woman who is standing here now," he said roughly.

"He's right," Inga chimed in. "I've watched you change from a cynical, selfish creature into a tenderhearted woman who is kind to everyone."

Lilah allowed a sad smile to curve her lips. She wanted to accept their assurances. She needed to believe she'd become a better person. That didn't, however, erase the sins of her past.

Swallowing a sigh, she glanced toward the female who'd pretended to be her nanny. "Why did you steal my memories?"

"I didn't," she protested, as if she'd been lying for so long she found it impossible to admit the truth.

"Inga," Lilah chided.

"Well, not at first," the older female grudgingly qualified. "It wasn't until after your coven was gone that you began to regret your decisions. With each passing year, you became more and more restless."

Lilah gave a slow nod. In the back of her mind, a series of images was sparking from one neuron to another, like the flickering frames of an old-time movie. The memories were returning, but they were still random and disjointed, making it impossible to sort through them.

"What did I do?" Lilah asked.

Inga glanced around the room, as if ensuring no one had managed to sneak in while they were talking. "You eventually threatened to open the prison and release the vampire," she said, her voice pitched low.

Was she afraid Lord Riven was lurking in a corner? Lilah shrugged. The mermaid—or was it merman—was the least of her worries. "So you wiped my mind?"

"What else could I do?" Inga hunched her shoulders. "Riven intended to replace you with a new witch."

"Replace?" Lilah flinched. That didn't sound good. "How would he do that?"

"First, he would kill you." Inga's blunt words seemed to echo through the room. "Then a new witch would be chosen to protect the key."

Lilah shivered. "A simple solution."

"I convinced him that I could erase your memories instead," Inga said.

Gratitude flowed through Lilah, helping to ease the sense of betrayal that had been searing through her like acid. Inga had obviously been as much a victim of Lord Riven as she was.

"He agreed?" Lilah asked.

Inga shrugged. "As long as I could ensure you didn't do anything to risk your duty here. That's why I decided to turn the building into a hotel."

Lilah blinked. The ogress's explanation had just jumped from A to Z with nothing in between. "I don't understand. Why would a hotel help?"

"It allowed you to mingle with the guests so you didn't feel so lonely," Inga said. "You have the companionship you desire, plus it gives you a connection to the outside world." Without warning, Inga sent a glare toward Chiron. "You weren't supposed to form any intimate connections. And certainly not with a leech."

Hmm. Lilah realized it did make an odd sense. She truly had enjoyed spending time with the guests and listening to their stories. It had given her the illusion that she was a successful businesswoman, instead of a screwed-up witch trapped in the swamps.

Not that she was ready to admit her gratitude. Not when Inga had lied to her for so long.

"Why were you opposed to vampires?" she instead asked.

Inga's expression hardened. "I was warned the leeches might come in search of their missing clansman. I suspect that's why Riven insisted the barrier be created by the witches instead of using his own magic. He didn't want the vampires tracking him down to seek revenge."

Lilah shook her head. Riven was a piece of work.

She was suddenly distracted by the low growl that rumbled in Chiron's chest.

"You held her prisoner for centuries," he accused.

Inga flushed, her brows snapping together at the accusation. "No, I was protecting her."

"How many times did you wipe her mind?" he snapped.

"Chiron." Lilah leaned her head against his chest, trying to prevent the brewing battle. "I don't believe Inga intended to hurt me."

"Of course I would never hurt you," Inga insisted. "You're like my own child."

Chiron made a sound of disgust. "Are you also going to claim you didn't try to kill me?"

"Why would I? I wanted you dead." Inga tilted her chin to an aggressive angle. "I still do."

Chapter 18

Chiron narrowed his gaze, ready for a fight.

He'd been terrified when Lilah had collapsed after he'd touched her mind. He had no idea if he'd done something that had caused her injury, or if there was some unseen magic attacking her.

She'd passed out for less than ten minutes, but it'd felt like an eternity before her lashes had at last lifted. Then, before he could even take a metaphorical breath of relief, he'd been grabbed by the neck and tossed across the room by the oversize ogress.

It was enough to make any vampire a little crabby.

"That's the first honest thing you've said," he growled, glaring at the towering female.

Lilah shook her head, her fingers lifting to press against her lips. "Why would you try to kill him?"

"Because I overheard him talking to that stupid gargoyle," Inga muttered. "I knew he was here to search for the key."

Chiron frowned. Had the ogress done something to Levet? Dammit, he shouldn't have been so easily convinced the gargoyle had simply scampered into the swamp.

"Why not give it to him to release his master?" Lilah broke into his frustrated thoughts. "You can't have loyalty to a family who considers you a blemish."

Inga scowled, then folded her arms over her imposing bosom. "This has nothing to do with the mermaids."

"No," Chiron swiftly agreed. He'd been shocked by the revelation that Inga had mermaid blood flowing through her veins. And that Lilah was the witch who'd assisted in creating the prison that held Tarak. But he'd suspected from the beginning that Inga would never willingly let go of Lilah. "It has to do with her fear that she will lose you."

A petulant expression settled on her broad face. "You know nothing." "I know Lilah is my mate. And that when I leave this hotel she's coming with me."

The air sizzled with the scent of scorched salt as Inga glared at Lilah. "Is that true?"

Lilah pressed against Chiron's side. "Yes."

Inga returned her gaze to Chiron. "Then you sentence her to death."

A strange premonition slithered down Chiron's spine even as he squared his shoulders. He wouldn't be intimidated by the ogress. She had kept Lilah captive for far too long.

"Do you think I'm afraid of you? Or a mermaid?"

Inga's eyes flashed red. "He's a merman, and you should be afraid of him. Do you even understand his powers?"

He didn't. As far as he knew, he'd never encountered one. But he never doubted for a second that he could defeat any demon or fey stupid enough to try to harm Lilah. "I can protect my mate."

Inga clicked her tongue in annoyance. "You are too rash and arrogant."

"She's not wrong," Lilah murmured.

"Thanks." He sent his soon-to-be mate a wry smile before he pointed a warning finger toward the ogress. "Lilah's future is no longer your concern."

"She will always be my concern," the female stubbornly argued.

Without warning, Lilah stepped away from Chiron, grasping the ogress's hand. "Inga, I realize you've always tried to do your best for us."

Chiron clenched his teeth, his fangs aching. He wanted to yank Lilah back to his side. He didn't trust Inga. Not as far as he could throw her, which wasn't very damned far.

Inga's features softened. "I have. All I've ever wanted was your happiness."

"And I appreciate your loyalty," Lilah continued in a soft voice. "But my place is with Chiron."

"No, you can't leave," Inga rasped.

Chiron's strained patience snapped. "Enough. Just give me the key."

Inga narrowed her crimson gaze. "What do you think it is, leech?"

Chiron stiffened, sensing it was a trick question. "The key?"

"Yes. Are you imagining a lump of iron that fits neatly into a lock?"

Chiron bared his fangs. "Careful, female. I'm done playing games. You will give me the key." He extended his arm, holding his palm up. "Now."

Inga displayed her own teeth, which were razor sharp. "Or?"

Lilah muttered something about pigheaded idiots before she gave the ogress's shoulder a gentle pat. "Inga, please. Where is it?"

The ogress paused, her expression suddenly guarded. Chiron could almost sense the wheels in her brain churning. She was plotting something. He would bet his favorite Jag it had to do with convincing Lilah to stay at the hotel.

"It's inside you," the ogress abruptly said.

Chiron charged forward, the air filled with ice crystals as his power swirled around him.

"I knew it," he hissed. "You'll make up any lie to force Lilah to stay with you."

"Chiron, wait." Lilah reached out to slam her hand into Chiron's chest, her face pale. Grudgingly, Chiron halted. As desperately as he wanted to force the ogress to admit she was lying, there was something in Lilah's expression that warned she wasn't so ready to dismiss the wild claim. "What are you talking about?" she demanded of her friend.

Inga sent Chiron a death glare before glancing back at Lilah. "Riven insisted the key be bound in a way that it couldn't be lost or stolen."

"Bound to what?" Chiron demanded.

Lilah sucked in a sudden breath, her mouth dropping open. "To me," she breathed.

Chiron shook his head, fear blasting through him. "That's impossible."

"It's the truth," Inga insisted. "Lilah is the key."

Chiron continued to shake his head. As if he could alter the truth. "No."

Lilah took a step backward, a stricken expression tightening her features. "She's right. I'm starting to remember."

Chiron forced himself to take a minute to regain command of his emotions. The room was bubbling with a toxic brew of anger, fear, and jealousy. It was clearly adding to Lilah's stress.

Then, grabbing her hands, he turned her so they were face-to-face. "Tell me."

Her eyes were unfocused, as if she was lost in her emerging memories.

"When we arrived here, Riven insisted Inga create the key, but I was the one who spoke the spell that fused it to me." She blinked back tears. "It was the price of immortality, and I did it without caring what it might mean to me, or your master."

Chiron didn't try to ease her guilt. Not now. He knew from painful experience it was something that would take time.

"If the key's inside you, how do you unlock the prison?"

Her brow furrowed. "It's not actually inside me; it's a part of my magic," she said slowly. As if she was struggling to make sense of what she was remembering. "Like the barrier."

Chiron nodded, although she might as well have been speaking gibberish. He would never understand magic. "Can you release Tarak?"

"I'm not sure." She paused before giving a frustrated shake of her head. "It's all still fuzzy, but I have a strange image of standing in a large underground chamber." Another pause. "And there's a woman lying on the slab in front of me," she abruptly continued. "I think she's there to enter the prison."

Chiron carefully studied Lilah's tense features. A woman lying on a slab to enter the prison? That sounded...improbable. "Is she a guest from the hotel?"

Lilah gave a sharp shake of her head. "No, she has the same beauty as Riven. I think she was sent by him."

"A mermaid?" he demanded.

"Yes." She released a small sigh. "That's all I can remember."

Chiron turned his head in a motion that was quick enough to catch Inga's worried expression. The ogress knew exactly who Lilah had seen in her memories.

"What does she have to do with Tarak?" he demanded.

The ogress jutted out her lower jaw. "Nothing."

Lilah lifted her hand to her head, as if it was hurting her. "Inga, please."

The large female's belligerence faded as she studied Lilah's pallor, her eyes darkening with concern. Whatever her sins, Inga loved Lilah as fiercely as any mother loved their child.

"She arrives once or twice a century and demands that the prison be opened," she reluctantly admitted. "I think she feeds him."

Chiron lifted his brows in shock. Was Inga mistaken? A vampire would weaken, and eventually go mad, without food. But he wouldn't actually perish.

"Why would the mermaids feed a prisoner?" he asked. "It would make more sense to leave him weakened."

"I don't know." Inga lifted a hand as Chiron's lips parted to demand the truth. "I truly don't. Riven doesn't explain; he simply commands me to obey." She sent him a pointed glare. "Like someone else I know."

Chiron was distracted by a low sob. Jerking his head back toward his mate, he realized there were tears streaming down her face.

On full alert, he wrapped his arms around her shivering body. "Lilah, what's wrong?"

"This is my fault."

"No. The blame belongs to Riven. As well as the previous Anasso." He held her gaze, willing her to listen to his words. "They were the ones who betrayed Tarak."

"If I hadn't been so selfish—"

"Shh." He pressed his finger against her lips. "It doesn't matter now."

"It does." Her eyes glittered with unshed tears, emphasizing the shimmer of gold. Chiron's unbeating heart twisted with an emotion that felt too big to be contained in his chest. "Your master is still trapped."

"If you created the spell, there must be some way you can undo it, right?"

"Perhaps."

"No." The ogress stepped forward, the floor shaking beneath the impact of her heavy feet. "You can't."

Lilah made a sound of impatience. "Inga."

"Listen to me," the female insisted. "If you try to open the prison without Riven's permission, you will die." She sent Chiron a crimson glare. "Is that what you want?"

He scowled at her ridiculous question. "Of course not."

Chiron felt Lilah shiver. "Why would I die?" she rasped.

"Lord Riven feared that one of us might decide to double-cross him by releasing the vampire and revealing who was responsible for holding him captive," Inga explained. "He placed a curse on you."

Lilah gasped, wiggling out of Chiron's arms to stare at Inga in disbelief. "A curse?"

"If the vampire escapes, you die," Inga said.

She bit her lower lip. "There has to be a way."

Chiron released a low growl. His burning need to rescue Tarak was smothered beneath his need to keep his mate safe. He wasn't screwing around with a curse he knew nothing about. Not when Lilah's very life was hanging in the balance.

"Perhaps, but we're not going to take any chances," he said, his voice edged with a warning that his decision was nonnegotiable. "We'll wait until we can discover more about this curse before we decide what steps to take next."

"But we can't leave Tarak imprisoned," she protested.

Inga took another floor-creaking step forward. "I hate to agree with the leech, but he's right. You can't take any risks."

Chiron turned toward the ogress. Soon, he was going to teach her what happened to demons who shot arrows at him. For now, unfortunately, he needed her help.

"The only certain way to get rid of the curse is to find Riven and destroy him," he said. "I need you to take me to him."

Inga released a sharp breath of disbelief. "That's impossible."

"Nothing is impossible." Chiron stepped toward the female. The last thing he wanted was to be separated from Lilah, but the sooner he killed Riven, the sooner they could start their lives together. And, of course, the sooner he could release Tarak. "You have to have a means to contact him."

"No, Chiron," Lilah protested. "It's too dangerous."

He reached out to brush a soothing hand down her damp cheek. "It's the only way."

A strange expression settled on Inga's harshly carved features. Then, her shoulders abruptly drooped, as if she was conceding defeat.

"Fine," she muttered. "I might be able to reach the mermaids."

"Do it," Chiron commanded.

If he hadn't been so distracted by his fear for Lilah, he would have sensed the shit was about to hit the fan. But he was caught embarrassingly off guard when Inga reached out and grabbed him by the front of his shirt. He glanced down, inanely thinking that it was his last shirt that hadn't been destroyed, when he was lifted off his feet.

Disbelief jolted through him. *What the hell?* The ogress was large and powerful, but she was no match for a vampire. Not even with mermaid blood running through her veins.

He lifted his hand, but before he could strike, he found himself flying through the air. He braced himself for the impact against the wall, already imagining the pleasure of ripping out the female's heart and feeding it to a gator.

As expected, he slammed into the paneled wall with painful force. What he didn't expect was that behind the paneling wasn't stone. Instead, the thin wood splintered, and he hit a hidden window with enough force to burst through the glass.

He roared in fury, trying to grab the frame as he sailed through the opening. This was the last time he underestimated the bitch, he told himself, releasing a second roar as his hands grasped nothing but air. He was hurtling toward the ground and there wasn't a damned thing he could do about it.

He heard Lilah call his name, but before he could answer, he suddenly realized the impending impact wasn't the worst of his problems.

Not even close.

Agony seared over his skin as the first blush of dawn spread across the sky above him. Within minutes, perhaps seconds, he was going to be charred into a pile of ash.

He closed his eyes, filling his mind with the image of Lilah. If he was going to die, he wanted her to be his last thought.

* * * *

With a last smash of Ulric's fist, the steel door flew off its hinges. Pain radiated up his arm from the violent impact, but he barely noticed. He was intent on escaping the dungeon and warning Chiron that the ogress was working with the enemy. Then he personally intended to repay her for breaking his jaw.

Absently wiping his bloody knuckles on his jeans, Ulric stepped into the narrow tunnel and sniffed the air. He'd been sloppy when he'd allowed Inga to blindside him. It wasn't going to happen again.

"Finally," a voice grumbled behind him. "With such large paws you should have been able to dig your way through a dozen steel doors by now."

With a blur of motion, Ulric whirled around and grabbed the gargoyle by one stunted horn. Over the course of his long life, he'd endured the loss of his family, being enslaved and tortured by a demented vampire, and shot by more than one human. But nothing had ever been so painful as being trapped with Levet.

The aggravating creature had never stopped yammering. He complained he was hungry, that he was bored, that he possessed magic that could get them out faster than Ulric's steady blows. Then he'd nearly burned them both to a crisp when he'd conjured a fireball and lobbed it at the door. The stupid ball had bounced around the dungeon, setting things on fire for fifteen minutes before Levet had managed to destroy it.

"One more word and I'll rip out your tongue," he growled.

Levet gave a flap of his wings, managing to escape Ulric's loose hold.

"I am just saying if you would have allowed me to use my magic we would have been out a lot sooner," the gargoyle said.

Ulric glared at him in disbelief. Was he serious?

"You did try your magic." Ulric pointed to the burn on his shoulder, which hadn't yet healed. "You nearly killed both of us."

Levet stuck out his lower lip. "That was a first attempt. I was merely getting steamed up."

"Warmed up," Ulric instinctively corrected, then threw up his hands in frustration. Why was he arguing with the creature? "Never mind."

He stepped over the mangled door before moving through the dark tunnel.

"Wait for me," Levet called as Ulric jogged up the steep flight of stairs.

"Go away," Ulric snapped, pausing to once again sniff the air to make sure no one was lurking in the large central cavern.

Levet appeared at Ulric's side. The gargoyle could move with startling speed considering his legs were a fraction the length of most demons.

"I thought we were partners."

"Partners?" Ulric sent him a horrified glare before following the faded scent of the ogress. She had to have a way to enter the caves that didn't include falling through the ceiling. "I'd rather swallow poison."

"Why would you want to swallow poison?" Levet demanded, staying just inches behind Ulric as they entered the opening on the far side of the cavern. "Of course, I once knew a gargoyle who ate rocks. He thought it would make him grow faster."

Ulric snorted. "Let me guess, it was you."

"*Moi?*" Levet sounded shocked at the accusation. "Certainly not. I may be small, but I am not stupid."

"That's a matter of opinion."

Ulric picked up his pace as the ground beneath his feet angled upward. He could feel a faint breeze stirring the air. This had to be the way out.

Levet thankfully fell silent as they hurried through the darkness. At least until the distant sound of glass shattering echoed through the tunnel, followed by a harsh cry.

"Did you hear that?" Levet demanded.

Ulric didn't bother to answer as he surged forward at top speed. He was no longer concerned with someone lurking in the shadows.

He recognized that voice. Chiron.

Reaching the narrow opening of the cave that was covered by a thick barrier of bushes, Ulric pushed the branches aside.

"Shit," he breathed, his gaze locked on the body sprawled on the terrace.

He frowned, his gaze lifting to take in the broken window before returning to Chiron, who remained unnaturally still. The fall might have hurt, but it shouldn't have knocked him out.

"It's the dawn," Levet said, as if able to read his mind. "You'll have to get him."

Ulric released a low growl. His brain must still be woolly from the blow he'd taken. Otherwise, he'd have realized at once what was wrong.

His muscles coiled as he prepared to rush across the garden. But before he could move, Levet reached up to tug at his arm.

"Ulric."

Jerking free of Levet's surprisingly firm grip, Ulric glared down at the annoying pest. Chiron was frying in the cresting sunlight and he wanted to chat? "What?"

"Bring him back here." The gargoyle's voice held a surprising edge of authority.

"Why? The hotel is closer to him."

Levet shook his head. "We do not know who or what threw him out the window, but it is obvious they intended to kill him. And whoever it was is presumably still inside."

Ulric grunted. As much as he hated to admit it, the gargoyle was right. Until they knew what had happened, he wasn't going to take any risks.

Refusing to be delayed again, Ulric shoved his way through the bushes. Then, crouching low, he ran in a zigzag pattern across the garden. He had no idea if someone was watching from the hotel, but he preferred not to be hit by some nasty magic. Or shot by a gun.

In less than a blink of an eye, he was leaping onto the terrace and scooping Chiron in his arms. Without breaking stride, he was whirling around and heading back to the caves. Still, it wasn't until he was through the bushes and headed down the tunnel that he glanced down at the male he considered a brother.

The sun hadn't turned the pale skin red; instead, it was a sickly shade of gray and stretched tight over his bones. As if he was already starting to turn to ash. Ulric cursed, heading deeper into the caves. He couldn't be sure how far the sun might penetrate.

It wasn't until he was in the central chamber that he at last halted and carefully bent down to lay Chiron on the dirt floor.

He knelt beside his master, fiercely willing him to heal. "Don't leave me, amigo."

Chapter 19

Horror froze Lilah in place. Her brain was still reeling from the deluge of memories. Now she struggled to process the fact that Inga had just thrown Chiron through a hidden window.

It wasn't until a stray shaft of sunlight peeked through the broken glass that the full extent of Inga's treachery hit her like a sledgehammer.

"No," she screamed, making a dash toward the window. With startling speed, Inga had moved to block her path.

"I'm sorry, Lilah, but it's for your own good," the larger female said.

Lilah barely heard the words. Instead, her attention was captured by the sight of a strange male darting across the garden. Who was it? Not a guest. But he moved with the powerful grace of the Weres who'd stayed at the hotel. The mysterious male disappeared from view, but a second later, he was running back across the garden. This time, however, he had a body in his arms.

Chiron.

Hope blasted through Lilah. Could it be Ulric? Chiron had implied his friend was still in Vegas, but it was possible he'd decided to check on his master. Or maybe he'd been lurking in the swamps just in case he was needed.

Whoever it was, he was holding Chiron with obvious care as he abruptly disappeared through a clump of bushes. She had to trust he intended to help him.

In the meantime, she had to keep Inga distracted. If the ogress knew Chiron hadn't been turned into ash, she might very well hunt him down and finish the job.

Taking a deliberate step backward, she allowed Inga to see the betrayal that burned through her like poison. "Killing my mate is for my own good?"

Inga held out a pleading hand. "He would never have been content to remain here. He would have tried to take you away."

Lilah took another step back. "Not until he discovered a way to break the curse."

"There is no way. And I couldn't risk…"

"Risk what?"

Inga's hand dropped, her shoulders hunching. As if she'd just taken a blow. "Losing you."

Lilah made a sound of regret. This female had tried to hurt Chiron. That was unforgivable. But there was a part of her that couldn't forget the endless years they'd spent together.

"Inga, you have never been in danger of losing me," she told the older female. "Chiron is my mate, but you've been my most devoted companion for centuries. All you had to do was tell me the truth and we could have figured this out."

Inga's expression hardened. "There was nothing to figure out. The merfolk will never release you."

"Chiron would have made sure they had no choice," Lilah said, careful not to give away her fierce hope that Chiron was still alive.

"No." Inga gave a sharp shake of her head. "Even if he managed to destroy Riven, which is highly doubtful, the others wouldn't let the death of their leader go without a thirst for revenge. They would hunt you down and kill you. Along with anyone you care about."

Lilah's mouth went dry, a slow, dogged fear curling through the pit of her stomach. When Chiron had been standing at her side, it had been easy to convince herself they would find a way to break the curse. He was a vampire. There wasn't a creature who'd dare try to stand against him.

But as the memories swirled through her brain, her confidence started to crumble and fade.

Riven was an arrogant, ruthless enemy. She didn't doubt for a second that the other merfolk were just as vindictive. If they discovered Chiron had killed their leader, they would hunt him down and destroy him. Along with Inga and herself.

They would never stop. Not until they were dead. And all because of her infinite vanity.

There was only one way to protect the people she loved.

"You're right." She squared her shoulders. "I'm kidding myself if I think I can change my future."

Inga looked wary. As if she sensed Lilah's sudden resignation.

"It's going to be okay, Lilah," the ogress said in soothing tones. "I can make it all better."

Lilah's lips twisted into a bitter smile. "By wiping my mind?"

Inga held out her hand, as if she was preparing to touch Lilah's face. "You'll awaken and all of this will be forgotten," she assured her in a soft tone. "We can start over. You just have to trust me."

Lilah heaved a small sigh. "I do trust you, but this has to end."

"What do you mean?"

"I'm sorry, Inga."

Lilah jumped backward, even as she spoke a spell she hadn't used for centuries.

Sensations thundered through her, rasping against her raw nerves. She clenched her teeth. How had she forgotten the addictive elation of using her powers?

Lifting her hand, she released the spell and watched the shimmering webs of magic wrap around the female standing in front of her.

Inga glared down in shock at the translucent bands that encircled her from neck to toes. The ogress tried to move, gasping in outrage when the bands pulsed and tightened in response.

"What have you done?"

"When my memories returned, so did my magic." Lilah glanced around the studio, taking in the portraits that had marked her long life. No, she silently corrected. It hadn't been a life. Not a real one. She'd been an unwitting prisoner, spinning in a wheel like a hamster. And now she'd put Chiron in danger. "This has to end," she muttered. "Today."

Inga's eyes widened, the scent of salt spicing the air. "Lilah, what are you going to do?"

Lilah offered a sad smile. "What I should have done five centuries ago."

"No." Inga's face flushed, the veins in her neck sticking out as she struggled against the magic that held her captive. "Lilah."

With a last, lingering glance toward the female she would never see again, Lilah turned and walked out of the ogress's private rooms. Once she reached the corridor, she didn't hesitate as she moved toward the nearest staircase that led down to the lower floor. First, she had to make sure Chiron was okay.

Then she would do her duty.

* * * *

The pain was shattering.

It touched every part of Chiron, from his skin, which was on fire, to his bones, which felt as if they'd been crushed to powder. He knew he teetered on the edge of death. Even after he'd sensed Ulric scooping up his body and taking him to a place of blessed darkness.

The sun had drained his ability to heal himself.

Now he could only struggle to survive from one second to the next.

Lost in his agony, Chiron was vaguely aware of the sound of raised voices. *Shit.* Had Inga followed them? The bitch was determined to keep Lilah trapped in the hotel. Which meant she knew she had to get rid of Chiron. Permanently.

Then the sweet scent of ambrosia filtered through the air, and Chiron forgot all about his pain.

Lilah...

Despite his weakness, Chiron struggled to open his eyes. He could hear Ulric's raised voice, as if he was trying to get rid of Lilah. Why? Did his friend think the young female was responsible for tossing Chiron through a window?

Or was he just being his usual overprotective self?

Whatever the cause, he might actually hurt Lilah in his effort to keep her away.

Panic thundered through Chiron, and he forced his parched lips to part. "Lilah," he rasped. "Please...come..."

There was a startled silence; then the soft patter of feet echoed through the air. His panic eased, a sense of peace flowing through him as he felt the light touch of Lilah's hand on his face. He could die a happy vampire, knowing Lilah was safe. Ulric would protect her...

The thought was still forming when he felt Lilah's arm press against his parted lips. What was she doing?

Then she leaned down and whispered in his ear.

"Feed."

Chiron shuddered. He desperately ached to drink her blood. Just a taste. It would fulfill one of his deepest fantasies. But despite the urgency of his hunger, he was too weak. He couldn't extend his fangs, let alone suck the nectar from her veins.

But even as a darkness started to crawl through his mind, he felt a warm drop of blood hit his tongue. The rich liquid slid down his throat, sending an explosion of heat through his damaged body.

Chiron moaned as more blood flooded his mouth. She tasted just as he'd anticipated. Delicate. Feminine. Magical.

Ambrosia.

Intent on savoring the unexpected treat, Chiron didn't immediately realize the heat spreading through his body was more than mere pleasure. Not until the grinding pain started to ease and his skin no longer felt like it was going to peel off like a molting snake.

Slowly, he opened his eyes, his heart swelling with pride. His clever, beautiful Lilah. She'd known exactly what was needed to heal him. Nothing was more potent than the blood of a mate.

It had accomplished what nothing else could.

His hand lifted to touch her cheek. Damn, he'd been so certain he was about to die. Now his body was healing, and the female he intended to share eternity with was kneeling at his side.

Intending to tug her head down for a kiss, Chiron frowned when she slowly rose to her feet. She stared down at him for a long second, her expression impossible to decipher. Then, turning, she walked away.

Chiron struggled to sit up. Was she looking for something? Or did she fear an enemy was approaching?

"Where are you going?" he called, his voice frail.

She continued forward, not halting until she reached the altar set in the center of the chamber. Reaching out, she touched the smooth stone, her hands tracing the carved runes.

A terrible fear began to grow inside Chiron. "Lilah?"

She glanced back, a wistful smile touching her lips. "It's the only way."

He tried to struggle to his feet, nearly falling on his face. Quickly, Ulric was at his side, wrapping an arm around his waist to keep him upright.

"Easy, amigo," the Were murmured.

Chiron dug his fingers in his friend's arm, his horrified gaze on Lilah. "Stop her," he rasped.

"She's not leaving," Ulric tried to soothe, as if afraid Chiron's mind had been compromised by his sunbathing session.

"She's going to break the spell," he croaked.

There was a flutter of wings as Levet abruptly appeared from one of the tunnels.

"What spell?" the gargoyle demanded.

Chiron ignored him, cursing his weakness. There was no way he was going to be able to reach Lilah before she did something stupid. "The one that's going to kill her."

The words had barely left his lips when there was the faint sound of a *pop.* Everyone froze as the air in the cavern grew heavy. Like the ominous pressure right before a thunderstorm.

Lilah made a strangled sound, her head tilted back as if she was capable of seeing something that was hidden from the rest of them. Then her hair suddenly stirred, although Chiron couldn't detect a breeze.

"*Mon Dieu.*" Levet shuffled forward, his own gaze locked on the ceiling.

"What is it?" Ulric demanded, his voice thick with the power of his wolf.

The danger prickling in the air had them all on edge.

Levet's tail twitched. "Something's coming. Something...powerful."

Chiron grimly tried to take a step forward. If Riven thought he could harm Lilah, the merman was going to have to go through him.

Refusing to acknowledge he could barely stand, let alone fight a mysterious fey creature, Chiron took another step. Nothing was going to stop him.

A brave goal, but it turned out to be a waste of effort as a blast of frigid power rocked through the cavern. Chiron flew backward, landing against the wall with enough force to break a couple of ribs.

Shit. They'd just healed.

He groaned, lifting his groggy head to peer around. Ulric was next to him, clearly knocked out. On the other side, Levet was already on his feet, wiping dust from stubby horns.

"Stupid vampires," the tiny creature groused.

Chiron jerked in shock. The gargoyle was right. That blast of power hadn't been from a merman. It had been a vampire.

And he knew which vampire.

Tarak.

Lilah had released him from his prison.

His gaze made a quick survey of the cavern. He didn't know if his master had actually entered the caves, or if he was somewhere else. Wherever he was, Chiron couldn't sense him.

And right now, he wasn't concerned about Tarak.

Instead, he was focused completely on Lilah, who was collapsed on the floor next to the altar.

"Shit." Not bothering to risk standing, Chiron crawled on his hands and knees across the hard ground. It felt as if it took an eternity before he was at last able to gather her soft body in his arms. "Lilah."

He cradled her head in the crook of his elbow, her curls tumbling over his arm. His heart clenched as he recalled the first time he'd caught sight of her.

She'd been so vibrant. So full of lush, glorious life.

Now her exquisite face was pale, and ghastly still. A sound of unbearable pain was wrenched from his lips. No fate could be so cruel as to give him a taste of paradise and snatch it away.

There was the sound of claws scratching against the floor before Levet was standing next to Chiron.

"What is wrong with her?"

Chiron instinctively tightened his hold on Lilah, his fingers threading through her silken curls. He didn't want the creature near his mate. Not when she was weak and vulnerable.

"A curse," he rasped.

Levet gasped in surprise. "Why would you curse her?"

"Not me, you idiot." He lifted his head to glare at the aggravating demon. "A merman cursed her."

"Ah." Levet wrinkled his tiny snout. "Merfolk are tricky creatures. And that Inga is the worst." He planted his fists on his hips, his tail twitching. "Did you know she locked me in the dungeon? And then—"

"Not now," Chiron snapped.

Levet sniffed. "You are a crabby pants after a morning in the sun."

Chiron released a furious roar. If he hadn't had Lilah in his arms, he would have reached out and ripped off the gargoyle's head. "My mate is dying."

Seemingly unaware that he was stomping on Chiron's last nerve, Levet leaned forward to sniff Lilah. "She is your mate?"

Chiron bared his fangs. Yep. He was definitely killing the gargoyle.

"We didn't complete the ceremony. But yes, she belongs to me," he warned in a harsh voice.

Levet furrowed his brow. "Then why don't you just finish it?"

Chiron glared at the gargoyle in confusion. "What are you babbling about?"

Levet spoke slowly and concisely, as if Chiron was too thick-skulled to understand simple words. "Complete. The. Mating. Ceremony."

Chiron stared at the gargoyle in amazement. How the hell had he survived for so long?

"I swear, I am going to rip you apart limb by limb," he finally managed to choke out.

Levet spread his arms, the flap of his wings stirring the loose dirt that covered the floor. "Are all vampires so ignorant of curses?"

Chiron swallowed his infuriated words, studying his companion with a sudden sense of urgency. There was something in Levet's voice that suggested he knew something Chiron didn't. Something that might save Lilah. "What do you know about them?"

Levet pointed toward Lilah, who was no longer breathing because her life was being sucked away by the dark magic.

"The curse bound her to Riven."

Panic thundered through Chiron. They were running out of time. He had to find some way to break the curse in the next few seconds or she was going to die.

"I know that," he rasped.

Perhaps sensing Chiron's pounding fear, Levet's expression softened with compassion.

"Once you complete your mating, it will break the curse," he said, managing to avoid his usual snide comment. "She can't be bound to two different creatures."

A faint hope stirred in Chiron's heart. It made sense. A mating created a bond that was soul deep. It overrode any loyalty to clan or family. And it was unbreakable.

Still, Levet was right when he claimed Chiron didn't know a damn thing about curses.

"You're sure?" he demanded.

Levet waved his hands in a dramatic motion. "Love triumphs hate. Everyone knows that."

Chiron hesitated. He didn't fully trust the idiotic gargoyle, but what did he have to lose? Bending down, he gently brushed Lilah's curls away from her face. Her skin was already growing cool to the touch. *Shit.* His terror charged through him with enough force to make it difficult to think. Thankfully, his most primitive instincts knew exactly what to do.

His fangs lengthened, and with lightning speed, he slashed his teeth across his wrist. Blood spurted and ran down his fingers. Quickly, he used his thumb to part Lilah's lips before he allowed the thick liquid to drip into her mouth.

The exchange of blood was all that was needed to complete the mating ceremony.

For what seemed like an eternity, she remained motionless in his arms, her body limp. Refusing to dwell on her fading heartbeat, Chiron instead allowed the blood to continue to fill her mouth. It was the sudden heat that burned a path up his inner forearm that made his unbeating heart leap with hope. He didn't need to look to know there was a crimson tattoo appearing on his skin. It was the mating mark. A visible symbol that he was claimed by Lilah.

At the same time, he heard her draw in a shallow breath. She was returning to him. Bless the goddess.

Releasing a choked sound of joy, Chiron bent his head to place his lips against her forehead. Her skin was still cool, but he could already feel it starting to warm.

Minutes passed before Lilah finally gave a small cough, then reached up to touch his face. "Chiron?"

Lifting his head, he stared down at her with a sense of massive relief. Nothing had ever been more beautiful than the sight of her bright, fully focused eyes.

"Don't ever do that again," he chided in a harsh voice.

She blinked, her brow furrowed with confusion. "The curse…"

"It is broken." Levet intruded into their tender moment, bending over Lilah with a wide smile. "You may thank me later."

"You?" Chiron growled.

"You would have sat here and watched her die if it was not for me," Levet insisted. "I am once again the hero."

As if trying to avoid the inevitable battle, Lilah smoothed her fingers down Chiron's throat.

"What about your master?" she questioned. "The barrier is down. He should be free."

Chiron shrugged. "I felt his power, but I'm not sure where he is."

"You should go look for him."

"Later," Chiron said. As much as he wanted to ensure that Tarak was free and hopefully sane, he was far more concerned with taking care of his mate. "I'm not leaving your side until I'm certain you're fully recovered."

"Okay," she agreed, then, with a small frown, she studied her arm. The sleeve of her robe had fallen down to reveal the crimson tattoo that scrolled from her inner wrist to her elbow. "What's this?"

The joy that had been muted when he feared for Lilah's life exploded through him. He had his mate. And she was the most glorious creature he could ever have imagined.

"I'll explain when we're someplace private." Keeping her wrapped tightly in his arms, Chiron rose to his feet. He was going to find a dark, quiet spot where they could spend the day in peace. Pausing, he glanced over his shoulder at Ulric, who was loudly snoring. Thankfully, the Were's skull was thick enough to withstand a few knocks. He would no doubt wake with a headache, but he would be fine. "You stay here and watch over Ulric."

Levet scowled. "Why *moi*?"

Chiron ignored the question, heading toward a nearby tunnel with Lilah cradled against his chest.

There'd been one barrier after another separating him from his mate. For the foreseeable future, he intended to savor the knowledge that nothing would ever stand between them again.

Chapter 20

Lilah sensed that darkness was spreading over the swamp despite the fact that they were in a small cave that was far enough belowground to block out any stray bits of sunlight. It was in the stillness of the air, and the enthusiasm with which Chiron had just made love to her. He was a nocturnal creature, which meant he did his best work at night.

And his best was fabulous.

Releasing a sigh of utter satisfaction, Lilah rubbed her hand over the crimson tattoo that ran the length of his inner arm. Currently, they were snuggled in the corner of the cave, where they'd spent the day sleeping and recovering from their mutual brushes with death.

When she'd awakened, Chiron had explained that it had been the completion of their mating that had destroyed Riven's curse. He claimed that love conquered all. Right now, Lilah believed him.

"Yep, they're still there," she breathed.

Chiron brushed his lips over her damp forehead. Because she wasn't a vampire, their energetic sex had left her hot and flushed and dripping with sweat. Chiron, on the other hand, looked like he was ready for a *GQ* photo shoot.

"What's still there?" he asked.

"Fireworks."

He lifted his head, studying her with a searching gaze. "I'm afraid to ask."

"The first time you kissed me, I felt fireworks," Lilah told him, her voice soft at the memory.

It seemed a lifetime ago, and in some ways, it was. They'd both changed. Chiron had found…and lost…his master. Finally, he could purge the guilt that had festered inside him like poison. And she was slowly regaining the memories that had been stolen from her.

And, of course, the biggest change of all. Her fingers continued to stroke his tattoo.

"Did you think the fireworks were a fluke?" he demanded.

"Well, we're an old mated pair now," she teased. "I was afraid the magic might be gone."

He pretended to be outraged by her words, his hands skimming over her naked body.

"The magic will never be gone."

She shivered. His touch was cool, but it heated her blood until it felt like lava was flowing through her veins.

"Is that a promise?"

"I'm mated to a witch," he rasped, lowering his head to scrape the tip of his fang down the side of her neck. Lilah groaned. She loved the feel of him feeding from her. It was intoxicating. "Fireworks and magic are guaranteed."

"Mmm." She tangled her fingers in the soft silk of his hair. "It still feels like a dream."

He kissed a path over the upper curve of her breast. "Because you can't believe your astonishing luck in having a gorgeous, successful, highly intelligent vampire as your mate?"

She chuckled. There was nothing wrong with this male's ego. "Something like that."

"Why does it feel like a dream?" he demanded, using the tip of his tongue to trace the line of her collarbone.

"I thought I would be alone forever," she whispered, as if she said the words too loud she would wake to find Chiron was gone. "That I would be isolated here until I died."

Easily sensing her lingering fear, Chiron wrapped her tightly in his arms and pressed a kiss on the top of her head.

"You're free now," he assured her. "No barrier, no curse, and no damned ogress wiping away your memories."

She snuggled against him, absorbing the icy power that pulsed around him. It made her feel protected. As if nothing could harm her as long as she was in his arms.

"Thank the goddess, I never want to forget you," she murmured.

He stroked his lips over her forehead. "No danger of that. As soon as you're fully healed, I intend to take you around the world to visit our hotels and casinos. I want the staff to admire my exquisite taste in choosing a mate, plus I want your input on how we can improve the Dreamscape Resorts."

Lilah sucked in a startled breath. "Seriously?"

He lifted his head, his expression puzzled. As if he was confused by her astonishment.

"We're partners now. Right?"

Pleasure exploded through her. It was one thing to accept that this astonishing, wonderful male was now her mate. And that he seemingly adored her beyond all reason. That was biology. Splendid biology. But his eagerness to include her in his business revealed a respect for her talents in running her hotel.

That touched her in a way that made her feel oddly vulnerable.

She flushed, unable to put into words her tumultuous emotions. Instead, she turned her attention to the problems that still lurked outside the small, secluded cave.

"Yes, but—"

He dropped a quick kiss on her lips, interrupting her protest. "No buts."

"Bossy," she chided, refusing to be silenced. "But what about Tarak?"

"Ulric is on his trail," he reminded her. "No one, not even a vampire, can stay hidden from a pureblooded Were. He'll have Tarak safely brought back here before we leave."

Lilah could only trust that Chiron was right. Poor Tarak had endured enough suffering. She hated the thought he might be out there, lost and confused.

"And Inga?" she demanded. "We can't leave her trapped forever."

He scowled. "Why not?"

Pain sliced through her heart at the thought of her devoted companion. She hadn't wanted to hurt the older female but had to protect her mate.

"Chiron, she's no guiltier than I am. We both were responsible for imprisoning your master," she reminded him. "In fact, I'm worse. Inga was manipulated into agreeing to help Riven. I did it out of pure vanity."

His scowl deepened, but staring down at her stubborn expression, he clearly realized she wasn't going to budge.

"Fine, we'll decide what to do with your nanny." His head started to lower. "Later."

Well aware that once he started kissing her, she would become lost in a world of sensual pleasure, she placed a hand in the center of his chest.

"But—"

He made a sound of frustration. "Another but?"

"I haven't used my magic in a very long time," she reminded him. "I can't guarantee the spell will hold for the entire night."

It took a full minute for Chiron to leash the desire that Lilah could see smoldering in his eyes. Then, with one fluid movement, he was on his feet.

"I'll find someone to keep an eye on her," he told her, a wicked expression on his face. "And I know the perfect demon."

Lilah sat up, watching as he headed toward the entrance. "Chiron?"

"Don't move from that spot," he commanded. "I'll be right back."

"Where are you going?"

He flashed a smile filled with lots of fang. "To kill two birds with one stone."

* * * *

"Why *moi*?" Levet groused, glaring at the vampire who was regarding him with an arrogant expression.

Night had fallen, but even as Levet had prepared to head into the swamps to enjoy a few hours with a lovely water sprite, Chiron had grabbed him by the horn and carried him back to the hotel. They hadn't halted until they were in a strange room filled with paintings. As well as a large ogress who was standing as still as a statue next to the window. It had taken a few minutes to realize Inga was being held by a web of magic.

Then, Chiron had commanded that Levet stand guard, as if he had nothing better to do.

"What's your problem?" the vampire demanded.

"I do not want to guard the ogress," Levet protested, pointing a claw toward Inga. "I do not even like her."

"Tough," Chiron said with a rude lack of sympathy. "Ulric is busy hunting for Tarak."

Levet wasn't impressed by his explanation. "And why can you not stand as a guard?"

A slow, smugly satisfied smile curved Chiron's lips. "I have more important matters demanding my attention."

Levet snorted. "I suppose those things include your new mate?"

"They do."

Levet released his breath in a loud huff. He was a romantic at heart, so he could hardly quibble at Chiron's desire to be with Lilah. What newly mated couple were not desperate to spend time alone?

Still, he did not want to be stuck in the smelly room with the smelly ogress.

"This is *très* unfair." He stuck out his lower lip. "Why do we not just lock the creature in the dungeon? That is what she did to me."

Chiron glanced toward Inga, his features hardening. "We will need her to locate Riven."

Levet widened his eyes. "You intend to go after the merman?"

"Did you doubt it?"

Levet shivered as an icy blast swirled through the air. The Lord of the Merfolk had not only imprisoned Chiron's master, he'd nearly killed Lilah. Chiron wasn't going to be happy until the creature was destroyed.

"I suppose not," Levet admitted, his wings drooping. He was never going to get to the water sprites.

"Until then, I want to make sure Inga remains where I can find her when the time comes."

"Fine," he muttered, glaring at the vampire. "But you are in my debt."

Chiron had the nerve to look confused. "Debt?"

Levet clicked his tongue. The male was being deliberately tushy. No wait. *Obtuse. Oui*, obtuse.

He extended one claw. "First, I led you to this hotel." He extended a second claw. "Then I searched for the key."

"Which you didn't find," Chiron interrupted.

"Because I was being held captive."

Chiron shrugged. "Not my fault."

Provoking leech. Levet held up a third claw. "And then I helped to break the curse that would have killed your mate."

Chiron flattened his lips. He couldn't argue with Levet's spectacular logic. Finally, he gave a resigned shake of his head. "What do you want?"

Levet considered before giving a wave of his hand. He wasn't going to waste such a powerful favor on a whim.

"I am not yet certain. But trust me, when I decide, you will be the first to know."

"I can't wait." Chiron rolled his eyes, heading for the door. He paused long enough to send Levet a warning glare. "Don't leave this room."

Levet waited until he was gone before sending a raspberry toward the empty doorway. "Levet, stay here," he muttered. "Levet, do not move. Levet—"

"Levet," Inga suddenly intruded into Levet's conversation with himself. "Release me."

Turning, Levet sent her a sour frown. "No way. You locked me in a dungeon."

The ogress licked her lips, a film of sweat on her broad face. It looked as if she'd endured a long, terrible day locked in the magical bands.

"It wasn't personal. I had no choice," she said.

Levet heaved a disappointed sigh. He'd had a brief sense of fellowship with this female. They'd both been abandoned by their families. They'd both been slaves. And they were both judged by their unique beauty.

Now it was obvious she was the villain.

"I always say I have no choice, and it is never true," he told her.

"It was true. I had to protect Lilah."

Levet waved a hand. "You did your duty. Lilah is safe, and now it is Chiron's duty to keep her safe. Your work is done."

"No." There was a harsh edge of fear in the woman's voice. "The curse might have been broken, but that won't stop Riven from hunting us down and killing us. *All* of us."

Levet studied the ogress's lumpy face. She was truly terrified.

"The vampires are powerful creatures," he assured the female. He did not know much about the merfolk, but he refused to believe they would be stupid enough to start a war. "Once Chiron has killed Riven, this will all be over. You can go free and I can return to my lava bath. Or perhaps I will remain in the swamp and enjoy a few days with the local sprites."

There was a silence, as if Inga was trying to decide whether to continue her arguments or concede defeat. Then her features smoothed into an unreadable expression and she was speaking in a soft, oddly mesmerizing voice. "Look at me."

Levet didn't want to. He had a sudden fear at the salty scent of power that was floating in the room. But even as his mind screamed to turn and flee, his gaze was locking with the crimson eyes.

A bright light exploded behind his eyes. It seared through his brain, erasing everything in its path. Eventually, he blinked in pain, giving a slow shake of his head.

He didn't know what happened, but he didn't like it.

Glancing around the strange room, his gaze landed on a large female who was wearing a dress in a shocking shade of purple and watching him with a guarded expression.

"Where am I?" he demanded, his snout abruptly wrinkling in confusion. "Wait...who am I?"

A slow, sad smile touched her lips. "You are Levet, a famous gargoyle hero. And you are here to rescue me."

Printed in the United States
by Baker & Taylor Publisher Services